To Christy,
Always Pu
Gold,
Jsa 51:1
Cynthia L. Simmons

Pursuing Gold

A Novel of the Civil War

Endorsements

Combining a Civil War setting with dynamic characters, author Cynthia L. Simmons has produced a story of romance, friendship, adventure, historical authenticity, and suspense in *Pursuing Gold*. A page-turner that will hold you from the first page to the last, *Pursuing Gold* will leave you anxiously awaiting the next release from this talented author.

—**Kathi Macias** (www.kathimacias.com)
multiple award-winning author of more than fifty books,
including *Red Ink*, a 2011 Christy finalist,
and Golden Scrolls 2011 Novel of the Year.

Cynthia L. Simmons' novel is fabulous. I was unconsciously drawn into the story through vividly written scenes. I felt I was in the midst of the characters while reading this extremely well-crafted novel. I found myself rooting for the characters as if they were personal friends.

—**G.E. Hamlin**, Author, *Marriage Takes Three*

In her breakout novel, *Pursuing Gold,* Cynthia L. Simmons richly weaves romance and intrigue with history and Scripture. When relationships are lost, or betrayed, the economy is tenuous, and every venue of security is threatened, is belief in a Savior possible? With the Civil War as her backdrop, Simmons keeps readers turning pages in this fast-paced and character-driven story that explores the timeless tension of living out faith in a world opposed to trusting in God.

—**Peggy Sue Wells**, bestselling author of
Slavery in the Land of the Free, The Slave Across the Street,
and *Bonding with Your Child Through Boundaries*

Cynthia Simmons' historical novel, *Confederate Gold,* is set in the Deep South during the early years of the American Civil War. With the elements of family drama, mystery, romance, and intrigue, Simmons weaves a story that puts the reader in the midst of the action. Many books have been written about the battles between North and South, but this story focuses on the behind-the-scenes activity of those who attempt to use counterfeit money to destroy a Confederate bank in Chattanooga, Tennessee. The plot moves forward with many twists and turns and keeps the reader turning the page. This book focuses on the lives of ordinary people whose fate is being decided on the battlefield and by their political leaders.

—**Frieda Dixon,** author, blogger, speaker

If you are looking for a compelling Historical Romance, read Cynthia Simmons' *Pursuing Gold.* In it, you will see life prior to the fall of Chattanooga under General Sherman's drive to the sea. Her characters not only faced the dangers of war, but life with all its complexity. Overall, you will experience God at work in the lives of her three-dimensional characters and see how He brings them together amidst false accusations, danger, and even murder.

—**Bryan Powell**, President-Christian Authors Guild,
teacher, speaker, and author of
The Stranger series, the *Jared Russell* series

Pursuing Gold

A Novel of the Civil War

Cynthia L. Simmons

Elk Lake
Publishing, Inc.
Plymouth, Massachusetts

Library Cataloging Data
Names: Simmons, Cynthia L (Cynthia L Simmons)
Title: Pursuing Gold; A Novel of the Civil War / Cynthia L Simmons
308 p. 23cm × 15cm (9in × 6 in.)
Description: Elk Lake Publishing digital eBook edition | Elk Lake Publishing Trade paperback edition |Elk Lake Publishing POD edition | Massachusetts: Elk Lake Publishing, 2016.
Summary: With his father dead and his business partner incapacitated, Peter Chandler inherits the leadership of a bank in economic crisis. With only a newly-minted college degree and little experience, Peter joins his partner's daughter, Mary Beth Roper, in a struggle to keep C&R Bank afloat while the Civil War rages around Chattanooga. Political pressure for unsecured loans of gold to the government stirs up trouble as tempers and prices rise. Their problems multiply when Mary Beth discovers counterfeit money with Peter's forged signature. Can they find the forger before the bank fails? The two friends must pursue gold on behalf of their business, as they learn to pursue their heavenly Father to find hope and peace.
Identifiers: ISBN-13: 978-1-944430-43-6 (trade) | 978-1-944430-76-4 (POD) | 978-1-944430-75-7 (ebk.)
1. Civil War 2. Confederacy 3. Chattanooga 4. Rebels 5. Gold 6. Banking 7. Customs of the 1860s

Dedication

To my late father, C.L. "Buddy" Thomas, who sat with me in the
Chattanooga library for hours while I researched.

Acknowledgements

Abundant thanks go to my husband, Ray. His financial mind gave me an understanding of money and bookkeeping. And, he believes I can do anything.

I must also thank Christian Authors Guild for all their encouragement and support.

My AWSA sisters have blessed me beyond measure with their love and kindness.

Thanks also go to Jennifer Slattery, Fay Lamb, Christina Miller, Deb Haggerty, and Sandra Byrd. They deserve millions of hugs for their patient editing.

Chapter One

What a dilemma! Peter Chandler glared at Mr. Shaw, the burly Confederate bureaucrat lecturing him. Shaw could easily snap someone's neck and in his role, the man posed a real danger. After Peter had seen the Confederate government sell Negroes like cattle, he had to turn them down. Somehow, he must appease Shaw and convince him to leave. More important chores demanded Peter's time. His black leather chair groaned as he leaned forward, taking advantage of a pause in Shaw's diatribe. "I'm sorry. C&R Bank will not loan money to the Confederacy."

Lifting one massive eyebrow, seemingly reflecting his opinion of Peter's idiocy, Shaw slapped a sheaf of letters on the desk, and growled, "These refusals you sent me place you in danger. We want to know where your loyalties lie. When the war is over, you will be glad you sided with us."

Peter had to think fast. "We are a small bank fully invested in the community, so we cannot shoulder the risk of another loan."

The man's dark eyes flared. "You are far too hasty. I might have to speak to my Nashville friends about your bank charter."

"Nashville? The Union holds the city now. You won't get anywhere talking to them."

"My friends still have the reins of power. Let me enlighten you—"

Peter tuned out the rest of the speech. If Shaw knew the right people, he could attempt to get the bank charter revoked. Assuming he succeeded, Peter would lose the bank.

"Our employees are busy helping farmers and businesses provide for our citizens."

"Surely you can spare a few hundred dollars for your country."

Peter shoved his chair back and rose. "Those dollars have been invested in blockade runners. We all know our dependence on those valiant men who slip goods past the Union barriers."

"I recommend austerity measures—after providing for your country."

Peter had poured over his law books for hours. Every decision he made would be legal and fair. No government official had the right to dictate how he handled the bank's money. "As I said, we are invested in local businesses and local citizens."

"I shall tell you what I suspect." Shaw's face reddened. "You are not brave enough to stand up to the Union sympathizers in Chattanooga. But the people in power after the war might make sure you don't have a bank or any other job."

Peter itched to get his loaded rifle out of the cabinet behind him, but his father had taught him to be a gentleman, even under pressure. "The government does not require this loan you request."

Shaw stood and pounded Peter's desk. "They should. I could throw you in jail where you belong. I cannot respect someone who refuses to support his country."

No one would abuse bank property. Peter slid open the drawer and pulled out his father's ancient pistol to tuck under his belt. "It's time for you to go, sir."

Shaw spread his legs and folded his arms. "If you shoot me, the sheriff will incarcerate you."

Peter pointed the man toward the exit. "This way out."

"Traitor."

Opening the door, Peter swallowed the fiery words on his tongue. "Mr. Riddle, will you help Mr. Shaw outside?"

"I shall return in a few weeks to collect your loan."

"Don't waste your time."

Once Shaw was gone, Peter threw a sharp right punch, smacking his left palm. The clock proclaimed the time as seven—past closing—yet he still had unfinished paperwork. He was, however, too riled to work now.

"Sir?" Mr. Riddle opened the door. "There are a couple of things you need to know."

Peter braced himself for more. Real men accepted such burdens. "Go on."

"Today I heard rumors … Northern spies approach us."

He'd grown weary of the gossip, but sometimes small talk rang true. "Do you have confirmation from city officials?"

"No, sir. But two families withdrew their funds so they could leave."

Peter maintained outward calm while gritting his teeth. Notwithstanding inflation and the Confederate policies, clients who moved away could ruin his bank. "Thanks for the update."

"You also received this missive from Miss Roper."

An image of Mary Beth flashed in his mind. He pushed down the pang of longing and tenderness so he could focus. His fingers eagerly broke the seal.

"I hope the news is good."

"Indeed. Roper is improved." Talking to his partner outranked all his other work. "I shall stop by the Roper home tonight."

He stalked across the room to retrieve his leather portfolio and stuffed in a pile of prospectuses from potential clients. Briefcase in hand, he paused at the painting of his late father. Papa's eyes exuded a confidence Peter lacked, yet longed for.

You abandoned me, Papa. God help me.

Peter stepped outside and locked the door, the weight of C&R Bank, indeed, the future of the Confederacy, burdening his shoulders.

Mary Beth Roper arched her back to relieve muscles stiff from nursing and paced across the woolen rug. The sitting room, all the mahogany furniture gleaming with a new coat of wax, was ready for visitors. But none had arrived.

Maud entered holding folded papers. "You must be mightily important, ma'am. These here jus' came for ya."

"Thanks." How she longed for companionship tonight. She broke the first seal and read silently:

Mary Beth,

Have you heard the rumor about spies approaching the city? My mother is beside herself and has decided to leave for my grandparent's home. Since my father is gone to fight, I may not return until the war ends.

Best Wishes,

Emily

With a groan, Mary Beth opened the next one:

Dearest Mary Beth,

I hate to cause you distress right now, but I must beg your forgiveness tonight as I will not attend your tea party. My father was at the telegraph office when news of the stolen train reached the city. He believes the spies are coming here. Further, he convinced Ida's father of the danger so she will be absent also.

I offer my deepest apology. You and your father remain in my prayers.

Jane

Maud turned to leave. "I be getting that tea."

"There's no need. I shall have no guests. Papa is so much improved I felt I could spend a few hours with friends, but this horrid war interfered."

"There be no fightin' here abouts, ma'am."

Mary Beth held up the pages she'd just read to herself. "These came from my friends. Rumors of approaching spies frightened everyone No one wants to be on the streets for fear they'll be in danger."

"I wished I'm a never. I be hearing nothing today, not even a word of such."

"I should be thinking of marriage and children at my age instead of all this worry. Once Papa gets well, I want to marry and have a houseful of children. But this war frightens me."

"You be gettin' upset. I can see that. I'd best be gettin' that tea. Nothin' like a warm drink ta calm ya nerves." Maud darted out.

Mary Beth jumped as something brushed her leg. Mr. King! Her cat rubbed against her skirt with a loud purr.

Her heart pounded hard as she glared at him. "I prefer someone who talks, Mr. K."

He tossed her a superior look and jumped onto the brocade sofa.

"I see you are more concerned about your comfort than the rumors. Maybe you are wise." She edged onto the plush cushions beside her cat. "Perhaps we all must take comfort where we may."

Mr. King closed his eyes as she caressed his soft fur. "You are so elegantly clothed. My dresses are threadbare—I cannot find even a small bolt of new fabric."

"Miss Mary Beth?" Elsie, her former nanny, stepped into the room. Her plump form filled the doorway. "Mr. Peter is comin' up the sidewalk. I thought you be wantin' to know."

"I appreciate the warning." Peter. Like his father, an air of confidence surrounded him.

Elsie stepped out. Mary Beth's pulse tapped a happier rhythm. She'd hoped her message would bring Peter right away. One could depend on him.

She stood and turned to the gilded mirror over the sofa and arranged her blonde curls. At least, she hadn't pinned up her hair. Peter preferred the waves about her shoulders.

Elsie opened the door and gave her a covert nod. "Mr. Chandler is here."

Peter came toward her offering a smile. "Good evening."

She'd always thought him as handsome as his late father. Right now, she'd welcome a gentle hug like her father gave her when she was young. But she shouldn't think such. "It's so good to see you."

"You look so tired. I've been concerned about you."

"I despise this war, but father's illness truly wears on my soul. Should something happen, I would be alone."

"Not quite." He took her hand and squeezed. "You have me. If the worst happens, we would be business partners. But I understand your father has improved."

Did she see wistfulness in his eyes? She hoped so. What a mistake she'd made with Eddie.

She sighed deeply as she searched Peter's face. "He is not out of danger, but much improved. I vowed to do anything and everything for him. Dr. Smith recommended several herbal preparations. I now grow the herbs and mix them myself."

Peter's face brightened. "I admire your persistence, and I know the strong ties you have with your father."

She nodded and then waved him to a chair before sitting on the sofa. "Have you heard the rumors today?"

He sat in the wing chair beside the sofa. "Mr. Riddle said something about spies."

"A band of Union soldiers stole a train somewhere north of Atlanta, and everyone says they are coming—here."

"Where did you hear of this?"

"Jane said her father believed the news and convinced Ida's father."

"Ah, Jane's father is quite reliable. However, I should have heard from the local militia." He leaned back as he drew down his brows. "Did you talk with either of them in person?"

She shook her head. "Each sent a written message. Jane said the news came from the telegraph office and set the city abuzz. Spies stole a train called 'The General.'"

"The news sounds authentic."

"Northern spies have been burning bridges nearby, but these men are supposed to be coming toward us. Do you think it safe to stay here?"

He rubbed his chin. "At this point, I cannot say for sure. This story could be another wild rumor like the ones we heard when Nashville fell. But maybe not. We need more information."

"I long to feel safe—like the days when we played together as children. First, they draft all the young men in the city, and then we experience shortages. I'm so weary of baseless rumors about an attack."

He gestured toward the window. "Sooner or later Union forces will target Chattanooga."

She shut her eyes and moaned silently. They could not fight here. Must not fight here, ever. "But when the war began, the newspaper said the mountains around Chattanooga would protect us from advancing armies."

"Whoever wrote that did not consider the steam engine. The railroad will bring the battle right to our doorstep. I feel sure the Union wants our city."

She cringed as she pictured soldiers marching into Chattanooga. "How dreadful. Papa will not be able to travel for quite some time, and I cannot leave him alone."

The muscles in his face tensed, but he offered no resolution.

She inhaled, trying to keep her dinner in place. Peter always told the truth, and sometimes he dumped it by the bucketful.

"I fear I alarmed you. That was not my intention, I assure you. Considering the war, we must keep praying for your father's recovery."

She turned away, trying to focus on her father's improved health. *Breathe. In and out, in and out.*

"The war unsettles everything,"

"Sometimes, especially at night when I sit with my father, I wonder if we truly have a God who is good. Why wouldn't he stop such suffering?"

"He's our only hope." Peter's voice was soft.

"You have no idea how sick my father has been. Several nights, I feared I would lose him. I watched each tortured breath and hoped it wasn't his last."

"I'm sorry you must suffer like this."

She no longer had the energy to continue this topic. If only she had kept her uneasiness to herself, but her fears slipped out. "I believe you came to see my father."

"Yes, I did." He eased toward the door. With his hand on the doorknob, he turned. "But I should like to talk with you again before I leave."

As he slipped out, she bowed her head, putting her hands to her face. *What will become of me?*

Chapter Two

Moments Later
Mr. Roper's sick room

Peter had never adjusted to seeing his partner lying abed with rumpled clothing and hair. He moved near Mr. Roper's face to be certain of catching everything the man said. The faded green eyes, pasty skin, and trembling hand contrasted with the robust man Peter had admired in his youth.

"Dr. Smith finally shared the prognosis this morning. I'm not going to recover."

The thought made Peter cringe, but he should not be thinking of himself. "What do you want me to do?

"Your job is to earn money with funds your clients entrust to you. Your father and I usually chose to invest in strong businesses that improve the community."

"I have researched businesses while waiting for you to recover."

"You must find ways to earn gold or commodities we can sell for gold." Mr. Roper cleared his throat, initiating a coughing fit.

Peter helped him to a sitting position. "Can I get you anything?"

"Water." Roper clutched his throat.

Peter poured a glass of water from the pitcher at the bedside and slipped his left arm behind Mr. Roper to help him drink.

Mr. Roper took a few sips. "Ah, much better. Thank you."

Peter returned the glass to the bedside table and lowered Mr. Roper back down onto the bed.

"You no longer need me to approve your investment decisions, just choose with care. The economy won't completely recover until after the war, but you can make money if you are wise."

Peter nodded. "A munitions factory opened nearby, and the owner solicited a loan. I planned on refusing."

"I agree with that." Mr. Roper tapped his forefinger on the bedcovers. "Should the Union reclaim Chattanooga, the military may examine your books. A munitions factory would be hard to explain."

"Any thoughts on investing in blockade runners? I believe I can make a case for that since the South needs goods brought in from overseas?"

"Be prepared to defend that decision," Roper said.

Peter worried the man was tiring, but determined to ask one more question. "I have several clients asking for larger loans. In particular, Mr. Allen is not reporting on his farm and is asking for a huge amount."

"Mr. Allen can be difficult. I know how to handle the man. Bring me his file tomorrow, and I'll take a few others you haven't had time to deal with."

"Thanks. I brought his dossier with me." The small knot between Peter's shoulders eased.

"Good. I look forward to doing something useful. Put the file in the library as you leave."

"I planned on a visit to Savannah soon. Should I cancel?"

"No. Check on our investments there and in Atlanta. Also, try to meet with Mr. Field. He will be a great contact for you. I shall ask Mary Beth to assist me with some banking issues here at home."

"Are you sure you are able?"

"Of course. The doctor gave his approval for an hour or so a day." Mr. Roper flexed his hands. "I'm not accustomed to all this rest."

"I'd best go." Peter hopped to his feet. "Dr. Smith will scold me if I stay much longer."

"One more thing. I want to discuss Mary Beth."

Peter was stunned. "Sir?"

"Please take care of her. I shan't be here to look after her. But I will be fine … if you will promise me. You must marry her."

Heat rose from Peter's chest. She had abandoned their long-term relationship for Eddie, and Peter had grieved a long time. He wasn't sure he could make such a promise when he didn't know her feelings.

"Don't worry yourself about romance. She's almost like your family."

Peter's tongue refused to move. *Oh, please don't talk about this!*

"Friendship is a great foundation for marriage. Romance might come later."

Might? What an impossible assignment. "But—she's the one who chose someone else. She might not want me now."

"Please!" Roper extended trembling hands. "Otherwise, I can't feel comfortable about leaving her."

Peter couldn't imagine life without Mary Beth's friendship. Since her flirtation with Eddie, however, he'd kept his distance. "Before I came to see you, I managed to upset her. She's not likely to respond to courtship with me again."

Mr. Roper's features relaxed. "She is ... like her mother. I learned to reassure Helen. Later, I could reason with her. Mary Beth will respond to such an approach."

How can I refuse? Maybe I can promise to do as much as I can.

"Death is not far away for me, but I shall be with the Lord. Just promise me you will marry my girl."

"I ... I agree to take care of her." And as a gentleman, he would make sure she had what she needed, but perhaps not marriage. This promise would haunt him, though.

Mary Beth examined the good-looking soldier who had just entered her sitting room. She intended to learn all she could about this man. "Lieutenant McDonald, when should I expect my boarders?"

He offered a slight bow while keeping his gaze on her. "I am delighted to say they will arrive tomorrow evening."

His manner struck her as too formal and too familiar at the same time. "You are aware of the rumors?"

"Indeed, milady. We are taking special precautions."

He reminds me of Eddie. I must keep my wits about me. "How odd. No one uses the word *milady* here."

"For someone so lovely, the word is more than appropriate."

Her cheeks grew warm, but her heart softened. She caressed her mother's gold chain hanging around her neck. "You are so kind."

Peter entered the sitting room just as she rang the bell to tell Maud about the boarders. He nodded toward the soldier. "I am on my way home, Mary Beth."

"Peter, I do not believe you know Lieutenant McDonald. Lieutenant, this is Peter Chandler, co-owner of C&R Bank."

The soldier raised one eyebrow. "Sir, you must have a significant injury to prevent you from fighting for your country. Am I correct?"

"Some of us have responsibilities elsewhere." Peter wore a pinched expression, seemingly displeased.

Mary Beth held her breath. Would the conversation would become heated? She exhaled as they shook hands. Maybe she overreacted.

Maud came in the door. "Did you ring for me?"

"Maud, the lieutenant said the two Confederate officers arrive tonight."

"I'll be havin' the rooms in fine shape by then," Maud said.

Lieutenant McDonald grinned at Mary Beth. "I'm sure your slave is well-trained, so all should be well."

"Maud is a free woman," Peter said.

"I trust Maud to do as I ask. She's almost like a family member," Mary Beth affirmed.

The lieutenant's eyes widened. "Really?"

Peter stiffened. "We value—"

Mary Beth placed a hand on his arm to restrain him. She'd rather not have this conversation, especially with an outsider in her home. "I have found her quite clever," she said.

McDonald bowed and eased toward the door. "Of course, miss. I shall see you tomorrow night."

Once the door closed behind the soldier, Peter said, "Does your father approve of you having Confederate soldiers live here?"

"I didn't ask him. He's been too ill."

He shook his head. "I doubt he will be pleased."

"I didn't think I had a choice. The lieutenant's insistence frightened me. But I shall speak to Papa. Having officers here will provide extra income and protection."

"You may *feel* safer, but your home could become a target for the Union army."

Chapter Three

Sunday, April 13th
Dinner on the Grounds

Anna Chandler focused on the serving table from across the room and waved for Billy, her butler. He didn't usually attend such events, but she asked him to come. She wanted this dinner to be perfect.

Billy came right away. "You called, Mrs. Chandler?"

"Let's refill the tea, and get me a basket of warm rolls."

"What about cornbread? We be havin' plenty."

"Good idea. Do it."

He nodded and marched off.

She noticed an acquaintance from her Bible study swallowing the last of her tea. "Would you like more, Martha?"

"No. I'm quite satisfied. Did you hear about those spies who stole the train? They dressed as civilians. With all the soldiers in town, they might mingle among us and go unnoticed."

"I heard that, Martha." Anna wished her friends would forget the war today. "I do love your sweater. I assume that's your handi-work?"

"No! What nonsense. I purchased this before the war. These days it's harder to obtain such pretty yarn. And I cringe when I see the cost of sugar."

The grim reminder annoyed Anna, so she eased away. She spotted Sheriff Campbell and his wife "I haven't seen Ida today. Is she here?"

Mrs. Campbell smiled. "She's out back playing with the White's twins to give their mother a break."

"How sweet. Tell her hello for me. There's Mrs. Reverend McCallie waving at me. I'd best see what she wants," Anna said. She patted Mrs. Campbell's shoulder and moved toward the pastor's wife.

Ellen McCallie took Anna's hand as she came to her side. "Thank you for taking over this dinner. My husband hopes Mr. Weston will plan another event on the mountain soon as well. The congregation surely needs the rest."

Anna would never admit how hard she'd worked. "I was delighted, Ellen."

"My husband and I are usually taking soup to the military hospital. The rumors kept us home yesterday," Ellen McCallie said. "Thanks. You freed me up to do this."

Jane Haskell, Mary Beth Roper's best friend, walked up as Mrs. McCallie left. "I came to say thanks too." Jane's new coiffure made her appear quite grown.

"I'm so glad you could stay, Jane. Yesterday I worried your parents would flee the city."

"Your persuasion won them over."

Anna clasped her hands together. "That's good to know. I wrote many notes yesterday. Your mother is the only one I chatted with."

"I was most unhappy about leaving," Jane said. "When the news came, my father was in the telegraph office. He heard a band of men took the train at Big Shanty and destroyed rail lines as they moved North."

"And you notice nothing happened here." She hated the panic following each tidbit of news. "We drafted our boys to defend us, and it's time we trust them and dwell on happier topics."

"Oh, the danger is not over. My father, however, said your idea about waiting for more information was very sound. He believes the Union will take over the city at some point."

"We've been edgy for too long. I felt it was time for some rest. By the way, have you heard from Mary Beth?"

"I did." Jane's brown eyes lit up. "She asked me to tea last night, but Father wanted me to stay home. While her father hasn't recovered, I understand he has improved."

"What good news." She hoped Peter and Mary Beth renewed their courtship. Anna caught sight of a familiar face across the room and walked toward him. "Fred Bell? What a surprise to see you here."

"Hello, cousin." A mischievous smile formed on Fred's round face.

"We aren't related," Anna said.

"I want to go home." Ruth, Anna's youngest child, grabbed her arm and tugged her toward the door. "Come on."

Anna brushed a few crumbs off Ruth's face and dress. "Ruth Inez Chandler, I have told you before, it is quite rude to interrupt conversations. I was speaking to this man." She motioned toward Bell, but he was no longer there.

Ruth rubbed a hand over her eyes. "I'm tired, Mums. There's no one to talk to. Can't we just leave?"

"No. Look. Over there is Alice Long. She has matured a lot this year, and I believe her best friend moved too. I think you should befriend her."

"But, Mummy." She buried her face in the folds of Anna's clothes.

This behavior wasn't normal for a twelve-year-old. "But sweetie, why not make a new friend. I'm sure she's lonely too."

"I don't know. I want a nap."

How Anna wished her husband had not left her to raise this girl alone. "Think about it, then. And perhaps we can have her over for lunch one day." An arm encircled her, and she gazed up at Peter.

"Mama, I'm going home, and I shall be happy to take Ruth with me if she would like to go."

"Must you go so soon? Our little party has hardly started. I hoped people would stay and chat and perhaps play some parlor games. We must get our minds off the war."

Peter shook his head. "Banking requires much more work these days, and this is the only day I can rest."

"But shouldn't you be interacting with customers and making friends? Your father did that as much as he could."

"Father also had a partner. With Mr. Roper ill, work is piling up. Besides, banking during a war creates numerous challenges."

Anna didn't miss the tension in his voice. Peter never exaggerated. How distressing to think the bank might be in trouble.

Sunday Evening
The Roper Home

Mary Beth ignored her trepidation as she gazed at her new boarders. "Lieutenant McDonald, please introduce us."

"We left their bags on the porch. Shall I summon your slave?"

She flinched at the use of the harsh word. Peter's warnings came to mind again. "You must have forgotten we hire our staff."

"As you wish. This is Dr. Bell," McDonald said.

The older, rotund gentleman bowed. "Madam. 'tis a pleasure."

McDonald gestured to the shorter man. "And Sergeant Glass."

Bell frowned.

What an odd reaction. She offered her best hostess smile. One must not give men the wrong impression. "Maud prepared your rooms upstairs. Cook serves breakfast at seven, lunch at noon and dinner at eight. I prefer to know if you will be absent from meals as early as possible."

Glass jutted out his chest seemingly displeased. "That's unreasonable. Any emergency could keep us away."

"I am aware of that. We shall try to accommodate you, but please try." These days managing her budget demanded prudence, even with food.

"Given our long and unpredictable hours, you should bring breakfast to our rooms." Glass flexed his fingers into a fist.

Mary Beth's throat clogged. She didn't feel comfortable with military men. This man, however, looked ready to attack.

"Sergeant," McDonald said. "You frightened her. That's not the way to treat a lady."

Dr. Bell nodded. "Glass, I agree. Miss Roper is our hostess."

The sergeant's face reddened as he stepped back. He stumbled, bumping the sofa where the cat sat.

Mr. King snarled and hissed before running under Mary Beth's skirt.

Not a promising beginning.

Mary Beth tensed as Glass ascended the stairs. After a quick look in her direction, he banged both the walls with his bags, and she believed he was tormenting her on purpose. Acquiring fresh paint and wallpaper in the midst of war would be difficult. She must learn to stand up to men.

"Now they are settled; it's time for a chat."

She glanced up as the lieutenant inched closer. Her face flamed as she fingered the fat roll of bills from the new boarders. "Excuse me?"

"Let's take the air and get better acquainted. Such a lovely lady mustn't stay indoors all the time."

"Oh, I cannot leave. You see, my father is quite ill."

"Such devotion! No one but you can watch him?"

Dr. Smith never told her she must remain by his bed. Nor would she ask the servants to add caring for Papa to their other work. "No."

"Think of yourself. What of your health? Have you been getting exercise and fresh air? A short walk would be refreshing. You must have a break."

How she longed for the freedom she enjoyed before her father's illness. "I could sit with you on the front porch. I shall ask someone to *listen* for Papa."

"Wonderful! You'll feel so much more rested."

"Give me a moment." She scurried upstairs feeling uneasy. The lieutenant reminded her too much of Eddie. But she how could she refuse an officer? She found Elsie in the hallway. "Could you listen for Papa? I'll be on the front porch for a while."

A crease formed on her dark brow. "Your Papa will be objectin' to them there bills."

Mary Beth didn't intend to let him find out. "With growing inflation, I feel I must use some of the new currency."

"The days we are a-livin' in. Are you gonna be out alone?"

"No." She disliked being treated like a school girl again. "The lieutenant will sit with me."

"What? Honey chile, I thought you had more sense than that. He bein' a Confederate."

"We'll be nearby in the rocking chairs." She hated upsetting Elsie, but McDonald awaited her.

"Hmph. Chattin' now and kissin' later."

"I won't be kissing him."

"I be putting this sewing job aside for now." She wagged a finger at Mary Beth. "Be comin' in soon, ya hear?"

She'd seen that look on Elise's face before a severe scold. If only Peter didn't see her with McDonald.

Chapter Four

Monday Morning
April 14th

Peter pushed aside the *Chattanooga Advertiser* and glanced toward the dining room door. "Where is Ruth?"

Shrugging, his mother said, "She told me not to wait on her for breakfast. Would you like gravy?"

"Yes, thanks. I wanted to discuss our upcoming trip."

"There's no need. I have gone over the details with her."

Ruth often dallied, but maybe if he ate slowly, he could still talk to her.

"Your father's sudden accident and death … upset her terribly. She's still grieving, even though it's been a full year."

"We were all shocked, Mother. I had no idea I would never see my father again when I boarded the ship for France."

"At her age, I was difficult, even without such a loss." She met his gaze. "Parenting requires wisdom and prayer."

Mother is getting defensive? "I would like to explain my safety concerns and gain her cooperation."

She motioned for the kitchen maid. "My son will need more jam, please."

What? He'd just spread a thin layer on one biscuit, so maybe she thought he was trying to conserve. "Oh, no. Don't get more on my account. I'd rather have strawberry."

Mrs. Chandler handed the jar to the servant. "Take back the grape jam and bring strawberry, please."

"I appreciate your kindness, Mother. But that was not necessary."

"At home, you shall have whatever you wish. Does anything in the newspaper dispel our recent rumors?"

"No. This newspaper repeats what Mary Beth said about the stolen train."

"Are you worried?"

He paused to consider his answer. His mother didn't need to be unduly alarmed yet. "Frightened people tend to distort the truth. You noticed a smaller crowd attended church. People were probably too worried to leave home."

"Yes, I did. And it annoyed me, but I had the dinner anyhow. I think we needed to enjoy ourselves."

"A small detachment of soldiers now reside here in Chattanooga. I imagine they are on alert."

Hair mussed, Ruth entered and plopped into her chair. "Someone's alert? I am glad about that," Ruth said.

"Good morning." Peter passed serving dishes to her.

"This looks wonderful." Ruth loaded her biscuit with butter.

"Ruth, I am taking you and Mother to Savannah to ensure your safety. We shall encounter military on the train," Peter said. "You must be on your best behavior. It's a dangerous time to travel."

"You have no cause for alarm, dear," Mrs. Chandler said.

Ruth shrugged. "I've seen many soldiers in town, and no one harmed me. Don't we have an outpost here?"

"The railroad brings wounded soldiers to our hospital, and more arrive daily." Mrs. Chandler reached for the coffee pot. "At least, we have no fighting here."

"Not now at least," Peter said. "But having soldiers in town is wise. The railroad makes Chattanooga a Union target."

Peter's mother dropped the coffee pot. Coffee drenched the tablecloth and ran onto the floor. She hopped up, scooted back her chair, and brushed off her clothing. "Ouch!"

"I'm leaving before I get wet." Ruth darted out of the room with her hands full of biscuits.

Dreadful! I have just terrified Mother. He tossed his napkin on the growing puddle. "Mother, are you burned?"

"No. No, I'm fine." She grabbed for the pot but missed. The remaining coffee spilled, drenching her side of the table as it clattered to the floor. "What a mess."

Peter rang the bell for the maid.

Anna blotted her clothing first and then used her napkin to absorb the hot liquid in her plate. "I can't eat this now," she said. "What came over me?"

Peter snatched Ruth's napkin and threw the cloth on the puddle at his feet. He couldn't wait to get his family to a safe place. "It was my fault. I commented the railroad made our city a target."

"Nonsense. You said that in the context of the soldiers who are here to protect us."

He hoped trouble didn't come before they could leave.

Thirty Minutes Later

Briefcase in hand, Peter hurried along the wooden sidewalk down Market Street to the bank. His muscles tensed as he pondered ways to gather details on the recent rumors so he could reassure Mary Beth. He had learned to get the facts behind the hearsay.

His mind still reeled at the promise he'd made to Mr. Roper yesterday. Even though he cared about Mary Beth, he was not sure how she felt about him. Nevertheless, he'd do what he could.

Richard Henderson, his arms full of papers, halted in front of him. "A thousand pardons, Mr. Chandler. I do believe we almost collided."

Peter stopped. "Excuse me?"

"Might I hope no dark clouds precipitated your inattention, sir? Since I know you possess all the cardinal virtues, I assume you entertained thoughts of the lovely Miss Roper."

Peter had never been more embarrassed. He wasn't lovesick, and he detested having his private affairs blasted all over town. "Miss

Roper heard a distressing rumor this weekend about spies approaching us."

Mr. Henderson nodded. "What a happy coincidence. 'tis but a mere moment since I departed the telegraph office, and I possess the latest news. How it pains me to declare the rumors to be true. 'tis simply odious. Northern spies captured the steam engine called The General from Big Shanty, Georgia."

"Is there imminent danger?"

"These dreadful villains attired themselves as civilians, but our valiant military apprehended several without ado. As we speak, they courageously seek the remainder."

"I see," Peter sighed heavily. "What precautions do you recommend?"

"Let me assure you we shall alert you should the city require the local militia. Obviously, be wary of strangers."

"I shall." Peter thought of the rifle in the bank office. He should clean the gun and check to see if he possessed ample ammunition. One must be ready. "Would you send me a message when the remaining spies are captured?"

"Indeed. I would be most delighted. We feel confident the military will apprehend these scoundrels, but in the upcoming months, we could face a clash of arms. Even now we make contingency plans should the worst happen."

Henderson's words wouldn't comfort Mary Beth. What Peter needed was to devise a contingency plan. "I'm grateful for all you do."

Mr. Henderson engulfed Peter's hand and squeezed. "Return to your banking duties. Your work is vital."

Chattanooga could face a battle soon. Peter would be prepared.

Chapter Five

Tuesday Morning
April 15th

Mary Beth groaned as she entered her father's bedroom. She found him sitting in a large overstuffed chair pouring over bank documents as if he'd never been ill. He would endanger his fragile health. Didn't he know how much she needed him?

"How did you get there without help? Are you sure you should be doing this?"

He nodded without glancing up. "We discussed this, honey. Dr. Smith gave me permission."

"I shall ask the doctor."

"Write a couple of letters for me. I'll tell you the content, and I shall sign when you finish."

"The doctor will fuss if you overwork."

He shrugged and shuffled documents. "I won't."

She pulled a sheet of paper from her mother's secretary. "I'm ready."

"The first letter will be to Mr. Allen. I want you to say I plan to come and inspect his property."

"You can't do that right now, Papa."

"Sometimes banking requires us to motivate people."

"And just how do you expect to motivate anybody from that chair?"

"Tell him someone will visit in … ten days. Deadlines work well. If I can't, Peter will.

"Just so you don't intend to make the visit yourself." She scribbled notes to herself. "What's the next letter?"

"Send a message to the grocer and say you will drop in sometime later today or tomorrow."

"Me?" Stunned, she stopped writing. *What is he thinking?*

"I'll tell you what to look for and what to ask. Bankers must know how clients use the loan. I prefer to tell my clients I am their partner, helping them to succeed. It's even more important when a society experiences upheaval."

"Are you saying war makes banking harder?"

"Yes."

The possibility of the bank failing made her skin prickle.

Wednesday Morning
April 16th

As Mary Beth and Elsie hurried down Market Street toward the grocer, the morning sun blazed down, wilting the pansies in front of the town café. Maybe they all dreaded the job she must do today. She paused outside the door of the Nelson General Store.

"Elsie, why did I agree to do this?"

"You are bein' a good girl."

"Do not bring slaves in this here door." Mr. Nelson stood before her, blocking her entrance.

Mary Beth bit her tongue to hold back hot words. She focused on Papa's instructions. She had come to learn how the grocer's income fared, not to end slavery in Tennessee. "No doubt you hurt her feelings, sir."

"It's not proper for us to mix with them." Mr. Nelson's face reddened. "She should go 'round back."

Mary Beth waved Elsie around to the rear of the store, even though she hated the situation. "May I come in, Mr. Nelson?"

"Oh, yes'm. So long's you do not bring slaves."

She stepped inside wondering if Elsie would come in or stay out back. How dreadful to be hated because of your skin color. Her father kept saying the war would end slavery, while Peter worried states would lose the right to disagree with the federal government. However, now she must focus on the job.

Mrs. Nelson nodded a greeting from the counter on the left. Mary Beth gazed at the counters and the shelves behind them trying to devise questions. The dried herbs hanging from the ceiling caught her attention. "Is this something new?"

Mr. Nelson shrugged. "Yes, fer medicine. Ain't nothing you need."

"Oh, but I do. I'm here, in place of my father, to see how you are doing."

"I reckon it's a woman doin' a man's job." Mr. Nelson's face stiffened.

Mary Beth took a deep breath. Should she explain? Not many knew she prepared dried herbs to use for her father, or that she understood banking. "I'm just curious about how well they sell."

The grocer huffed. "Land's sake. We are here to sell things."

Mrs. Nelson hurried over and whacked her husband with her duster. "Husband, just answer her question. The doctors from Newsome Hospital often purchase our herbs for medications."

Mary Beth flashed a smile. "Thank you."

"Remember the letter," Mrs. Nelson said to her husband. "I told you she'd come … the way her father used to."

"Hmph. She'd best be getting home to see about 'im, I think." Mr. Nelson stepped behind the counter, and his wife elbowed him.

"We have our quarterly interest payment ready," Mrs. Nelson said. "Should we give it to you today?"

"Woman, you ain't going to give that girl nothing," Mr. Nelson said.

"I would prefer you pay as usual." Mary Beth didn't want to come between husband and wife. She chose to examine a huge glass jar on the counter filled with colorful candies. Anything to change the subject. "Tell me about this."

"I'm right proud of that—peppermints for the young'uns. Would you care for one? On the house, of course. You've got no young'uns, but these are nice for a lady." He shot a quick glance at his wife.

"I've always loved the flavor, but such treats are rare."

He wrapped a piece in white paper and handed her the candy.

"Thank you, sir. How well do these sell?" She tucked the candy in her drawstring bag to eat later.

He grunted seemingly unwilling to talk. "Not much since Nashville fell."

"I see." Mary Beth kept glancing around. She'd have to get more information than this to satisfy her father. "It appears you have a good selection of baskets."

He puffed out his chest. "We have more 'n any general store I've ever visited."

"What about fabric?"

He frowned. "It's hard now to locate materials for ladies."

"What about fabric for uniforms?"

"Ain't no reason for a woman to wear such."

"Mr. Nelson!" Now his wife scowled.

Nelson seemed determined to make her job hard. "We have soldiers in town who wear uniforms, sir."

"Indeed, ma'am." Mrs. Nelson nodded.

She came to a display of military buckles, and she pictured a balance sheet. Income must exceed expenses, and she hoped to find out if his did. Buckles might add income with soldiers in town. "I'd like to know how many of these you sell monthly."

"Don't bother your mind with all that figuring."

Her temples throbbed. "My father wanted to know. Indeed, as your banker, he has a right to know. He heard a buckle factory started here in town."

Mrs. Nelson moved toward the back wall, pulled out a ledger, and handed it to her. She flipped through several pages pointing out sales. "You can tell him we sold five in the last two weeks."

"What about flour and sugar?" At least, these items fell into a category Nelson might believe she understood.

His expression softened. "Two barrels of flour. Not so much sugar. It's very pricey."

She nodded. The war brought a need for goods the grocer didn't usually carry. Perhaps sales of the other items could make up for the loss of customers since some citizens had moved away. "What about farm implements and seed?"

"Yes 'm."

A glance at the clock told her she'd stayed too long. She would pose one more question, even at the risk of annoying him. "Guns and bullets?"

"Don't worry your pretty head about that. You wouldna' understand them anyhow."

Mrs. Nelson spoke up, "Indeed we do. We carry almost any brand of pistol made. The customer has to ask before we display them."

Mary Beth needed to leave before she lost her temper. "Mr. Nelson, you have a lovely store. I shall report what I've seen to my father. Thank you both."

"Lemme know if you should need anything. Perhaps some trinket or a pretty bracelet. I'm sure I could find one. Or a husband? My youngest son would surely do." He reared back and laughed, slapping his leg.

Mary Beth's face blazed as she scurried toward the door. *Husband?* What right did the man have to tease her about something so embarrassing? She looked back into his unblinking eyes and decided he was not joking. "I'd best be on my way."

Mr. Nelson rubbed his hands together and chuckled.

I hope all such encounters aren't this unpleasant.

Mid-morning Thursday
April 17th

Standing in the empty kitchen, the odor of the cold, uneaten food on her father's breakfast tray made Mary Beth's stomach queasy. She fought to squelch the disturbing thoughts springing up in her mind. Her father's health worried her and so did Peter's revelation of an upcoming clash.

"Whew! We's havin' some warm weather." Carrying a sewing basket on her arm, Elsie came in from the back door. "Honey chile, is there somethin' ailing ya?"

Since she'd attained her majority, Mary Beth seldom aired her feelings, but if anyone could handle them, Elsie could. Frustration made the words rush out. "I'm worried."

"About your pa?"

"Yes. Despite all the medicine, he's not recovering. Plus, thinking of war unsettles me. Surely the Almighty should not allow so many calamities all at once."

"Girlie, be watchin' your mouth."

Mary Beth leaned back against the worktable. She deserved a scolding for doubting, but she didn't know what to do with all the painful thoughts. "I apologize."

"You be havin' no idea about sufferin'. My mama's master sold her before I was even weaned. I knowed I shall never be seeing her on this earth. You best be buckin' up courage and face whatever be comin'."

Mary Beth inhaled sharply, grieving for Elsie. Perhaps everyone had some sorrow or trial. She gave her old nurse a huge hug. "How tragic."

"I be hidin' my tears when you were little. Your pa done ask me not to mention my mama after yours died."

"I'm so sorry, Elsie, and I guess this sounds terribly selfish, but I don't want to be an orphan at twenty-one. Reverend McCallie assures us prayer works. I've been praying and praying for Papa, but he's not better."

Elsie wrapped an arm around Mary Beth's shoulder. "There, there. It don't do to question our Lord's wisdom."

"I hate these thoughts. Despise them! You see God is powerful, and he could have prevented this war. Southern states insisted on their right to have slavery. Why didn't God sink slave ships?"

"He can, but he knowed best."

"And then there's Eddie. He insisted on joining the moment guns went off at Fort Sumter, and he lost his life." She brushed away tears. "Then I discovered he was chasing three or four other women."

"Be giving grace, dear God." Elsie raised her hands. "Oh, Lord!"

"And look at all you've had to live through, Elsie. God could have stopped that man from selling your mother."

Elsie continued to chant prayers with her eyes closed

Mary Beth collapsed in a chair and let the tears flow. The future brought an empty house divorced from all warmth and love. How could she live in isolation?

Chapter Six

Early Friday Morning
April 18th

Mary Beth squinted to see the pewter clock by her bed. Only two a.m. She untwisted her blankets. She'd tossed and turned so much, dawn should be here. Draping her robe over her shoulders, she padded across the cold wooden floor to her father's room. She asked the dark shape by the bed, "Doctor, how is he?"

"Sh-sh."

"Is he improving?"

Dr. Smith pulled her into the hallway toward her room. "Your father weathered this episode. No doubt your excellent nursing has kept him going this long, but I fear the end approaches."

Every nerve went on alert. "Surely you can devise a new medication—"

"Mary Beth, I shall do everything I can, but his time is nearing. His heart was never strong, and grows weaker daily. His workload doubled after Andrew Chandler died, and he lacked the physical stamina to absorb the load."

He must be wrong. She had worked so hard. Wouldn't the Almighty reward her efforts?

"Did you take the preparation I made you?"

How could she explain sleep would never come unless she weren't worried about her papa? She did not want to leave his side. Every moment now was precious.

"No, she be disobeyin' you, doctor. I be tiptoein' into her room and found this on her dressing table," Elsie said.

Dr. Smith took the cup from Elsie and held it to Mary Beth's lips, pouring it into her mouth. "Drink this. You will sleep."

The bitterness made her facial muscles twitch. She retched but managed to swallow.

"There now. Get some rest. Your father no longer needs me tonight, but I shall check back tomorrow."

Rubbing her eyes, Mary Beth returned to her bed. If only she could forget Dr. Smith's words. Before her grief turned to sobs, she grabbed a handful of her blanket to muffle the sound.

Life without Papa would leave a gaping hole in her soul.

Friday Morning
April 18th
C&R Bank

Peter stared at Mrs. Phipps, praying she would find a way to curb her tears. The sound of her weeping filled the tiny storage room, unnerving him. Mr. Riddle had left the door ajar for the sake of propriety, and he hoped customers did not hear.

Peter checked his watch. His new employee had not cried as long as he thought. He moved the glass of water closer to her. "Drinking some water might help. I'd like to know what upset you."

She swiped at her face with the back of her hand. "Mr. ... Sadler."

"Are you saying Mr. Sadler is responsible?"

"Yes, sir ... I make ... mistakes as I ... learn. He hates it," Mrs. Phipps said. She sniffled and released another sob.

Peter sighed and stood, handing her a coin. "Go to the café across the street and purchase some coffee."

"Oh, please don't fire me." Her lips trembled as her face contorted. "I don't know what I shall do without this job."

"We need you." He tried to sound reassuring. She had applied for a job just after her husband died in a duel. This job was her only source of income. "But you must be calm to work."

"Thank you." She stood and rushed out the door.

If only Peter could get his employees to work in harmony so he could keep his job.

Thirty Minutes Later

Peter stood and glanced over his notes again before inserting them in his inner jacket pocket and heading downstairs to confront Mr. Sadler. He'd given himself time to calm down and consider what he must say. Such encounters were his least favorite part of banking. Once in the lobby, he slowed to acknowledge and shake hands with several customers. When he could delay no longer, he strode across the hardwood floor and stepped behind the counter to his right. Peter knocked at Sadler's office, even though the door stood ajar. "Excuse me."

The old man's arthritis-twisted body hovered over a ledger. He raised his head, and his dark eyes glared into Peter's.

Peter glared back. His father hired Sadler not long after he founded the bank. The man preferred to work alone, and his complex personality made him tough to manage. Peter wished he'd paid more attention in diplomacy class. "I need a word, please."

Sadler balanced his pen on the inkstand. "Yes?"

Peter eased the door shut behind him. "I would like to know what happened with Mrs. Phipps this morning."

"The fool woman. She entered accounts in the book incorrectly. How many times must I say debits on the left, credits on the right?"

"Mr. Riddle reported you screamed at her." He pulled a paper from his pocket. "He overheard you use the words *brainless woman* and *impossibly incompetent*."

"I cannot help the woman's ignorance."

Peter waved the note Mr. Riddle had given him. "Did you say these things?"

"I am unable to recall my exact words, and your father would not have asked."

"My father is dead."

"His death will be the end of us," Sadler spat.

"We aren't discussing my father's death." Peter couldn't believe Sadler's response.

Sadler's face hardened into a scowl. "You can't run this bank. I know you are holding onto your Union investments. That's not terribly wise."

Peter moved closer and spoke with firmness. "Let me make this clear. We will not mix politics and banking. At C&R Bank, we correct mistakes without raising our voices or using insults."

Sadler pointed a crooked finger at Peter. "You're supporting the enemy and destroying what your father built."

Peter's heart sped up. The challenge in Sadler's tone caught him off guard. Until now, no one had openly questioned his political stance, and Peter did not intend to advertise where he stood. "Mr. Sadler, you worked for my father for many years. Your excellent work has kept the books in order. I am certain you will prove your loyalty."

The man glowered at him for a moment before turning back to his work.

Peter went back to his office and collapsed into his chair. He massaged the tight muscles in his neck as his pulse slowed. Clever, cutting retorts occurred to him after the fact, but none of them would have accomplished what he needed. Somehow, he had to keep his employees away from politics if he was to keep the bank running successfully.

Friday Afternoon

Peter scanned a balance sheet and checked the math. As of last month, the bank was still solvent. Praise God! Should profits decrease, he would drop or eliminate his salary, but he needn't face austerity measures yet. Now he must decrease the pile of work on his desk in preparation for his upcoming travels.

A knock sounded on the door, which annoyed him. He worked best without interruption. "Come in."

Mr. Riddle, the usual pencil behind his ear, strode in carrying a note and closed the door. "I have several matters for you," he announced. "One is particularly good news."

Peter leaned back in his chair and closed his eyes. He didn't relish another problem to solve. "Tell me the good news first."

"Mr. Henderson sent a message." He held up a piece of paper. "Officials have captured the Union spies who stole the train from Big Shanty. They are being held here in Chattanooga. Officials now refer to the band of spies as Andrews' Raiders."

Mary Beth would relish the information.

"Also, there is a Confederate officer here to see you. His name is Lieutenant McDonald. I tried to send him away, but he insisted he knew you, and Mr. Sadler seemed to know him."

How interesting. What would make the lieutenant come here? He glanced at the mound of files surrounding him, yet the lieutenant's request intrigued him. Besides, Peter could send him packing if the matter was trivial. "I've met him. Please send him in."

When Riddle opened the door, Lieutenant McDonald marched into the room, a stack of papers clutched in his hand. "Mr. Chandler, have you heard the news? The military captured the thieves who stole the train. The North will learn it's useless to interfere with Chattanooga. We're quite prepared."

"Indeed. Surely you didn't come just to give me this news?"

"I would not waste your time, sir. As a loyal Confederate, you'll be interested in several investment possibilities I have available." He slapped the stack of papers on the desk. "The first opportunity is a group of blockade runners I've contracted. Of course, that's a lifeline for us since the Union is cutting off imports. These men work hard to get around the ships blockading the harbor and bring in necessary goods."

Peter nodded. "I'll look at that proposal."

"I appreciate that, sir. The second is a high-yield Confederate bond set up only for banks. The fund supports salaries for upper-level military staff. These bonds earn seven percent more than the usual Confederate bonds. Any loyal citizen would want to invest."

Peter sat up straighter. No. Military men didn't sell bonds, especially those bonds benefitting them personally. "Our bank deals only in gold. According to Confederate law, we're not required to buy or sell government bonds."

"As I said, these are special bonds. Every bank may carry them. Furthermore, all bankers who have Confederate interests at heart will do so."

"You are an agent of the Confederate Treasury Department?"

"My older brother works for them." Lieutenant McDonald avoided eye contact. "I'm sure you agree we must support our officers. It would be foolish not to do so."

Peter detected a threat in McDonald's words. Southern newspapers spoke of men devising fraud to procure income. Money in the bank belonged to those who deposited funds. Peter saw himself as a steward of each client's money. "I must study these documents carefully, Lieutenant."

"You'd best call me Fritz. We shall be good friends."

"We shall see." Peter rose and firmly ushered him to the door. "Mr. Riddle will show you out."

Peter's curiosity compelled him to study the material. The blockade runners might be legitimate. He could check at the Savannah harbor. The bonds, however, appeared contrived. The prospectus didn't sound professional.

Did McDonald come because he learned Mary Beth's father owned the bank? She might be in danger.

Everyone wanted the bank's money. Shaw might find a way to rescind the bank's charter, but McDonald made veiled threats about Peter's loyalty. Did he also have friends in the government? If he accused Peter of disloyalty, would more of the bank staff rebel?

God help me.

Chapter Seven

Friday Afternoon
April 18th
Roper Kitchen

Mary Beth found the silence daunting as she sorted the herbs in the immaculate kitchen. Her household servants had the afternoon off, and she used the time to prepare medications for the following week. Would emptiness soon become a way of life?

No. She must refuse such thoughts. The drugs she prepared gave Papa relief from discomfort. First, she'd cook the fennel for cough syrup. Next, she would use lily of the valley to make an elixir to strengthen Papa's weakened heart.

She chopped fennel leaves into bits and dumped them into her mortar. How pleasant to throw her weight into the grinding process. Crushing the plants released the healing oils, and brought her a sense of relief. She could *do* something.

"That McDonald man be askin' after you." Elsie stepped in from the back door. "He's out front."

How annoying. "Maud told him I couldn't see him today."

"I be tellin' him the same," Elsie said. "He's sittin' on the porch like he's gonna wait."

"Is he delivering a message from the boarders?"

"No, ma'am. I believe he's wantin' to court you."

Fennel soiled Mary Beth's hands. McDonald's desires only annoyed her, but maybe Elsie didn't know that. She worried too much, especially after Eddie proved false. "How irritating. I have work to do, and I do not care for him anyway. Tell him to leave."

"I done tried that. What else can I be doin' for you?" Elsie said.

"You aren't taking the day off?" Mary Beth grabbed a nearby saucepan.

"I done made my deliveries and got my money. But this here stove is not hot enough to cook. Lemme get some wood out back."

"I would appreciate that." Mary Beth peered into a tin she took from the shelf. "Oh, dear. There's barely enough sugar. I'll have to use it all."

"Ain't no matter. Those tonics be more valuable."

"Father requires sugar in his coffee. So, I must purchase more." Elsie didn't know how tight the household budget had become, and Mary Beth could not face telling her. At some point, she might need to buy herbs from Nelson's grocery because of the extra rainfall this year.

The bank's income had dropped too. Soon the rising expense might not be just herbs and sugar. The war was making her safe world crumble. Her world, and perhaps everyone's.

Friday Evening

Peter stood inside Mr. Roper's room, where the older man sat, propped up in bed. His eyes resembled pools of stagnant water, and his cough rattled like a thunderstorm. "I promised Maud I would not stay. So, I'm keeping an eye on the time. She told me Mary Beth fetched the doctor for you again last night."

"My illness is nothing new. I asked for a report on the bank, and that is what I want. Pull up that chair and sit down."

Peter wished he could devise an excuse to spare his partner. "Mr. Sadler upset our newest employee."

"Yes, that sounds like Gustav. What did he do?"

"I hired a woman to fill the bookkeeping vacancy when Mr. Strong left for the military. Sadler dislikes her and torments her. When I spoke to him, he questioned my political position."

"It sounds as if you're learning how to manage people. Pray for wisdom, and you'll do fine." Roper smiled. "What else?"

"It seems everyone wants the bank's money."

Roper laughed until he coughed.

"I shouldn't be bothering you, sir." Peter rose to leave.

"Nonsense. I'm enjoying this. Who wanted money?"

Peter told him about Shaw and McDonald.

"All kinds of people will make requests, and some will even demand. Attempt to stay neutral till the war ends. You may have a bit of a mystery to unravel. Someday I'll tell you about one I untangled when I first came here. Such an interesting time to be in banking."

What a perspective! He called their quandary a mystery. "Maybe I worry too much."

"Yes. If you worry at all that's too much. Pray instead. If you need help, talk to Mr. Henderson or Dr. Milo Smith. Both serve the city and are trustworthy."

"The Confederacy is at war. Few men are available to enforce the law."

"I have confidence in you, Peter. Rely on the Lord."

Peter couldn't argue with such advice. Trusting God sounded easy, but he found it much harder to do, especially now.

"This conversation seems backward," Peter said. "I should be encouraging you."

"I've lived long enough to see God work. If you trust him, he will provide. I look forward to seeing my dear wife and meeting my Savior. I believe God called *you* to run this bank."

Peter realized their voices had dropped to a whisper. What an intense topic. Banking without a seasoned partner would be difficult for Peter, but Mary Beth would lose a parent

Mary Beth came in. "Peter? Are you disturbing Father?"

"No." Mr. Roper exchanged a look with Peter. "We just chatted."

"How likely is that?" She huffed. "I know you both. You work too hard."

"I'm leaving now." Peter returned Mr. Roper's knowing look as he followed Mary Beth out the door.

Moments Later

Wearing a stormy expression, Mary Beth closed the door to her father's room and turned to face Peter. His galloping pulse reminded him he needed wisdom for this encounter, and he sent a silent prayer to heaven.

"What were you doing?" Her piercing gaze met his. "The only reason he appears energetic today is that the doctor gave him a stimulant. It won't last."

He chose honesty. "Your father and I talked—"

"Business?" She rolled her eyes. "I thought so. Peter, I want him well again, and should you mention the bank might fail, the stress might kill him now."

"What? The bank fail? What made you worry about that?"

"I've been helping Papa this week, and the documents I saw indicated income had dropped."

"We are no longer receiving payments from our Northern investments. That will make the balance sheet appear to be shrinking."

"How can you be confident they are doing well? The North is a foreign country now."

"Information gets to me. And as for your father, I was trying to leave, but he would not let me. Either way, our conversation lasted but a few moments."

Her face softened as she grabbed his arm, pulling him down the hallway to the stairs. "That doesn't sound harmful. I apologize. It's so easy for me to worry."

His heart slowed as he followed to the sitting room. "He insisted I share my concerns and seemed to enjoy my visit."

"That sounds like him. He loves banking."

The hardened look on her face had vanished. She was so much prettier when she wasn't so tense. "Of course. I am sure you would like good news."

"Indeed, I could use some." She perched on the brocade sofa and motioned for him to sit too.

He sat down on the other end of the sofa. "Mr. Henderson said officials captured the Northern spies. Chattanooga is safe."

"That is good news." She smiled. "Thank you."

He said another fervent prayer for the proper words. "Your father recently brought up a topic we need to discuss."

She frowned, seemingly baffled. "Really? What?"

Suddenly, Peter's mind refused to produce language. What if she refused him?

"Go ahead."

"Your ... father believes his life is coming to an end, and he would like us ... to marry. I believe he wants to know you'll be safe and cared for."

A few tears welled up in her eyes. "He's such a wonderful father."

He kept his gaze on her face. Overloaded with emotion, her expression told him she had more to say. He'd best wait.

"I know ... I caused you pain, earlier ... with Eddie. I'm sorry."

Her voice and body language revealed humility. She was being honest. But could he trust her after what she'd done?

"That's in the past. Let's consider the future."

"Right now my time centers on caring for Papa. The future looks foreboding. A wedding should take place amidst happiness."

Peter often wondered if she wanted a decisive man. He leaned toward being the thoughtful type. "What should we tell your father? Your wellbeing means everything to him."

"Papa will be anxious, and that's not good for him." She fingered the gold chain around her neck. "What if we assured him we are discussing it?"

"If we tell him we are thinking of marriage, then we should actually consider being wed. I prefer honesty."

She nodded.

"I have misgivings too. Could we agree to try courting again, with the understanding that either of us could opt out?"

Her face broke into a smile. "Absolutely!"

"It sounds as if we agree," Peter said. He hadn't expected the conversation to go this well.

"Yes. To this point, anyway."

At this moment of openness, he would best express one big concern. She'd matured while caring for her father, and this might reveal how much. "I have one request."

"Of course. What is it?"

"Watch out for Lieutenant McDonald. He's trouble."

"What do you mean?"

"The day I met him, he appeared to be flirting with you, but I don't think that's where his intentions stop. I believe he's selling bogus bonds. He's dangerous."

"Dangerous?" Mary Beth's eyes widened. "That sounds ominous."

Mary Beth gazed into Peter's eyes. He might think she was interested in McDonald, yet he had the courage to warn her. Her respect for Peter grew. "How did you find out?"

"He came to the bank with a prospectus which appears to be a fraud."

Given enough time, she would have seen though McDonald on her own, but now she'd be watching him. His behavior had already made her suspicious. "I'm so glad you told me. Upon reflection, he reminds me of Eddie with his profuse compliments."

He glanced at his watch and stood. "It's getting late, and I don't want to keep you from your father."

Peter was and had always been considerate. "If there's more, I'd like to know."

"I suspect he may be targeting you since your father owns the bank, but at this point, I have no evidence."

"Unbelievable!"

Peter shrugged. "Remember, I'm only guessing, but he came to the bank soon after I met him here. He presented two possible investment opportunities that I intend to check while I'm in Savannah."

"Papa said you'd be going there. He used to go at least once a year." She accompanied Peter to the front door. "Let me know how I can help."

He nodded and headed down the porch steps.

Mary Beth pushed the door shut with her body. If the bank closed, she would lose everything her father had accomplished. Considering that, she must be careful who she trusted.

Chapter Eight

Saturday Morning
April 19th

Mary Beth yanked out another weed and tossed the unwanted plant aside only to discover an herb tangled with it. She carefully extracted the herb's roots and replanted them in the soggy soil. If only the plant would recover.

"You have planted in an area with poor drainage."

She jumped at the unexpected voice. When she turned, Dr. Bell stood behind her. "Oh, you scared me."

"I had noticed the drying herbs, and I wondered where they came from."

"Oh. I make all the herbal preparations my Papa takes."

"I commend your efforts. Has his doctor given him a prognosis?"

Mary Beth did not want to repeat the doctor's words to a man who was almost a stranger. "I don't know. He's quite sick."

"Isn't that lily of the valley? He must have a heart problem."

She nodded.

"But I'd best get back to the hospital." He turned and walked toward the road.

She brushed the hair out of her eyes with her forearm and watched him leave. Was he right? When she returned her gaze to the garden, the unwanted plants seemed to leer back at her. If only she could maintain what she envisioned, a neat garden bordered by her collection of smooth stones.

Perhaps she could obtain a few fresh sprigs from a friend and start over. Giving up would not provide medicines for her father.

"Mary Beth?"

She looked up to see Ruth Chandler approaching with a large cloth-covered basket.

"Good morning!" Mary Beth wiped her hands on her apron.

"I convinced Mums to let me bring a treat. There's jar of strawberry jam just for you, and Cook included some pastries."

Mary Beth hurried across the distance between them and enveloped Ruth in her arms. She had become the little sister Mary Beth had always wanted.

"I hope you like it."

A peek under the pretty checkered cloth revealed flaky pastries surrounding a jar of jam. "What a thoughtful gift."

"Mums said your daddy is not improving." Ruth's brown eyes glowed with compassion.

"He's still very ill. Growing herbs for medicine gives me something tangible to do, but I still worry."

"I don't blame you."

"You know how that hurts, right, worrying about your father?" Mary Beth led her toward the house.

Tears pooled in Ruth's eyes.

"How are you?"

Ruth shrugged and looked away.

The two of them ambled up the steps into the kitchen. Mary Beth washed her hands and turned to Cook. "Please put the kettle on for tea. And serve these pastries Miss Chandler brought."

"Yes'm."

Mary Beth led her guest into the sitting room. "Have you made any new friends?"

Ruth offered the ghost of a smile. "Yes, one."

Pulling her down onto the brocade cushions beside her, Mary Beth said, "Tell me about her."

"Her? Oh, hmm. Maybe later on."

"What's on your mind, hon?"

"We'll be leaving for Savannah soon, but I wish I could stay here." Ruth's shoulders sagged.

The Chandler family came from Savannah, and Mrs. Chandler often visited her sister there while her late husband did business. "Is this a vacation?"

"No. Peter is worried about the war and said we would be safer there. Mummy wants me to attend the school Auntie opened. I won't be able to visit you or Papa's grave." Ruth dissolved into tears.

"There now." Mary Beth drew her close. "Your Auntie taught me for years, and she became one of my favorite people."

Ruth continued to sob.

"I have a lovely pair of shoes I purchased recently. They are a tiny bit snug on me, but they'll be perfect you. I'll give them to you, and you can think of me when you wear them in Savannah."

The weeping girl clung to Mary Beth. If only she could find a way to provide comfort. After all, Ruth was still a child. Savannah might be safer than Chattanooga, but no one would be safe until the war ended.

Monday Morning
April 21st
Peter's Office, C&R Bank

Peter sensed bad news. Mr. Grant stood before him shifting his weight from foot to foot. Peter motioned to the plush chair for office visitors. "Please, feel free to sit."

"I shouldn't be taking your time, sir."

"Very well." Peter rose and settled on the edge of the desk so he would appear less intimidating. "What's bothering you?"

"You're very kind, sir. It's just that last Friday Mr. Sadler approached me, and ... uh, I guess I thought I should ... speak to you."

Peter offered his best reassuring smile. He didn't want his employees afraid to share their concerns. "I appreciate you coming to me."

Grant looked down at his feet. "Sadler believes he should … run the bank."

Alarm bells went off in Peter's head. Grant was correct. He didn't have experience managing a bank. Peter's father had planned for him to work with supervision for a year. However, his father died, and the plan never materialized. "Is there more?"

"I guess the truth is, I'm worried Sadler might be correct."

"Let me understand. You worry the bank is vulnerable in some way. Is that correct?"

Mr. Grant nodded, his face relaxing a little. "Mr. Sadler said we are doing nothing to promote the Confederacy. Considering that the North might attack us at any time—"

Peter interrupted. "Even if I loaned money to the Confederacy, that money wouldn't prevent a Union attack." Peter wanted the real issue. "Go on. What was Sadler worried about?"

"Banking in a national crisis calls for finesse. Perhaps C&R Bank should be supporting our new government." Grant rubbed his neck. "He wants me to ask Mr. Roper to place Sadler over you."

Grant's trepidation was legitimate. Peter inhaled to calm himself while he formed an answer. "Yes. Sadler has worked here longer than I have. However, I'll make up for my lack of experience with hard work."

Grant didn't look convinced, but he shrugged and left the room.

Peter stifled a groan. Fear of failure already haunted him. Should the bank go under, he couldn't face telling his employees he could no longer pay them anymore.

Chapter Nine

Tuesday Evening
April 22nd

Mary Beth tried to ignore her discomfort as she matched her stride with Peter's. Their footfalls clattered on the wooden sidewalk as they walked down Main Street. Everyone who saw them would understand they were courting again. At the same time, they would likely recall her ridiculous infatuation with Eddie, and the gossip after his death. If only darkness had already fallen, she and Peter could interact with more privacy.

Tonight, she and Peter would try courting again "to see if they truly belonged together" as Peter had said.

"You seem rather quiet." Peter glanced in her direction. "Are you worried about leaving your father?"

"No. Papa seemed stronger today. He'll be fine for an hour or so. I just wish everyone wouldn't gawk."

A smile tweaked the corners of his mouth. "Indeed, that's a *terrible* crime. We should blindfold the entire city while we have dinner."

Mary Beth erupted in laughter. "I'm not accustomed to your humorous side."

"That's exactly what I would say about you." Peter chuckled. "Your opinions surprise me. Is there any reason people shouldn't see us?"

"Our assignation might remind them of my past stupidity," she whispered.

"I have good news. Today you demonstrate brilliance." He tilted his face down closer to hers. "Going out with me will correct all previous indiscretions."

The glow in his eyes made her heart beat faster. She didn't deserve his kindness. "I surely hope so."

When they arrived at the café, fabulous aromas swirled about her, and her stomach growled with pleasure. She must forget her past embarrassments and enjoy this time with Peter.

The host seated them at a table for two spread with a linen tablecloth.

"This is much better. No one's paying attention to us here. I no longer have the desire to run."

"I'm glad you didn't act on your whim. I shall enjoy your company all the more."

Compared to both Eddie and Lieutenant McDonald, Peter's compliments rang true. How he'd teased her in the past about her crazy ideas. "I've improved. I don't often act on impulse anymore."

"Indeed, you have. When we were young, you always wanted to change the scenario the moment I finished getting organized. Remember the time we were going to play riverboat? Once I set up the dock, you wanted to play dressmaker."

"It took you forever to get ready. Playing should not be so hard. Besides, it was starting to rain, and I wanted to go indoors."

"I wanted you to help me set up the dockyard."

"Dockyard sounded dull. I could not devise a role for my dolls."

"What?" Peter put down his menu. "I can see we will have to work on communication."

Mary Beth glanced over her shoulder. "Oh dear, here comes the waiter. Everything on the menu looks wonderful. I don't think I can choose."

"Do you mind if I order for you?" Peter asked. "I've eaten here with clients, and I know your tastes."

She nodded her approval as the waiter arrived.

"What would you like, Miss?" he asked.

Peter spoke up, "Miss Roper would like the chicken dish with green peas and potatoes. I'd like the roast beef with the same vegetables. We both want iced tea."

"A salad comes with each," the waiter said.

"In that case, please give us the house dressing," Peter replied.

"Very good, sir." The waiter left.

"You remember my favorites. Even down to green peas rather than green beans."

"You love to feel them pop in your mouth. When you told me that, I realized I liked them too."

"When did I tell you that?" She didn't recall telling anyone, even her father.

Peter shrugged. "I don't know when we had that conversation, but your wording was endearing. I'll never forget."

She let out a giggle.

The waiter placed a salad before each of them. She grabbed her fork and took a bite. "Umm. This dressing is excellent."

"I knew you'd enjoy this place."

She took her knife to cut a large piece of raw carrot, which resisted. She added pressure. Without warning, the carrot soaked in dressing, flew across the room, landing in a man's lap.

The man, who wore a dark suit, stood, brushing the mess off his pants.

Mary Beth snatched her napkin from her lap and covered her face. She wanted to disappear. All the patrons stared at her. "I'm horrified."

"Never mind." Peter rose. "I shall take care of it."

Peter was a treasure, indeed. She had let him down before, and she hoped she would never hurt him again, ever.

After Dinner

Mary Beth closed the door behind Peter. If only the evening had been as long as those evenings she sat up with her father. Now she must turn her attention to nursing. Papa needed several medications before retiring for the night.

After a gentle tap on the door, she entered his room. He was in bed, and his head had slumped to one side. In his hands, he held a sheaf of bank papers. She reached over to ease the documents away.

"No." His eyes flew open, and he tightened his grip. "I was reading those, and they must go back to the bank tomorrow."

"Very well." Mary Beth hurried to the dresser where she kept a medication chart. "Your medicines are due. Let's see. You need cough medicine and heart medicine."

"Leave off that cough preparation."

"That's fine." She added his heart medicine to a lump of sugar and carried the concoction toward the bed. "Here."

"Before I take anything, I want to know about your dinner with Peter."

"I'm so terribly clumsy, Papa. He's not going to want a lady like me."

"I daresay Peter won't care." He lowered his bushy eyebrows. "Tell me what happened."

"Accidentally, I made a slice of carrot sail across the restaurant. The errant vegetable landed on a man's trousers. They were dark trousers, so the mess was obvious."

Her father exploded into laughter until he had a coughing fit. "That's ... a story you'll ... tell your grandchildren."

The excruciating noise of his coughing made her cringe. "Papa, you need your medicine."

His coughing died down a little. "Fine. But it tastes horrid. At least, the heart medicine is mixed with sugar."

Mary Beth went back to the dresser and measured the cough medicine. She placed both on the table beside him. "I don't care which order you take them."

Her father frowned as he swallowed. "Dreadful stuff. What did Peter do?"

"Peter?"

"What did Peter do after the carrot sailed past him?"

"Oh, that." She recorded the medications on her chart. "Peter offered to replace the soiled clothing."

Her father nodded. "He's worth gold, Mary Beth. Hang onto him."

She might not have a choice about keeping him. "Shall I turn off the gas lamp so you can sleep?"

"No." He pulled the bank papers closer. "I must finish these tonight."

Mary Beth tried to push away her fears. All three of them worked harder and harder, going beyond reasonable limits to keep the bank functioning. The cost of constant stress and worry could impact them all, even Peter.

Early Wednesday Morning
April 23rd

Mary Beth pasted on a smile for the soldier standing before her. She didn't think well in the morning, and yet McDonald stood before her, pontificating. Flirting might be appropriate at certain times, but not when she was so sleepy. He must think women liked elaborate speeches. Boring!

"Of course, our noble soldiers deserve whatever we can do for them, so I'm sure you understand. Should they appear later in the day, I informed them you would have your cook prepare whatever they request."

She opened her mouth to object, but then stopped. *Investigate. Gather facts.* "I apologize, Lieutenant. I've never been at my best in the morning. What time is it?"

"Oh, dear lady. I shall leave you to rest. Though nothing dulls your beauty, I have no desire to cause stress."

Several months ago, she might have found this flirting fun, but compared to Peter, McDonald lost the contest. "Stress? Oh no. I'm sleepy. That's all."

He smiled. "In that case, if you would perhaps consent to take the air with me before lunch, I would be grateful."

The words were hard to say. "I shall be honored."

He bowed and turned to leave.

When he returned, she would pose numerous questions to see what she could learn.

Later Wednesday Morning
Chandler Home

Anna Chandler's mouth tightened as she returned her quill to the inkstand and blotted the list of chores. She was losing patience with her daughter's resistance to the tasks that must be completed for their trip. "Come. You must do these chores. Now."

"But, Mother ..." Ruth dropped her book and rose from the sofa where she had been reading. "I have only a few pages left, and you always want me to read. Couldn't I do these chores later? Please?"

Anna took a deep breath and almost choked on her daughter's eau-de-toilet. That topic could wait. She must convince Ruth to pack, and today she would not give in. Peter had never been this difficult. "Stand up, dear, and watch that posture."

"Yes, Mama." Ruth stood and straightened her shoulders.

"Peter purchased our tickets." Anna maintained a no-nonsense tone. "Go now. You must start sorting your clothing."

"But—"

"Are you saying you don't want to visit your favorite aunt? You don't want to shop in Savannah?"

"No, Mama. I prefer staying here and sleeping in my own bed."

Surely, someone must have taken her child and replaced her with a stranger. "We will leave this week. Ruth Inez Chandler, go and do as I asked."

She slunk out seemingly to obey.

Anna turned back to organizing at her desk, alert to her daughter's footsteps in the hallway. The squeaky hinges sounded and then a door closed. No mistaking the sound. She'd at least gone to her room.

Wednesday at Noon

Walking along with Lieutenant McDonald's, Mary Beth focused on the questions she had prepared. The breeze kept the temperature pleasant. *She* hoped to remain pleasant and relaxed in order to learn something about her escort. They walked along Mary Beth's road, which was still damp from a recent rain. The hem of her dress would suffer, but she hoped her reputation survived this walk. "Lieutenant, where's your home?"

"Home is a place where you are loved, and I can honestly say I've felt such love and loyalty from these officers who surround me here. I enjoy Chattanooga. The river and the mountains are breathtaking. Don't you think so?"

He must have a low opinion of her if he thought this talk would deceive her. Men didn't enter the military to feel love. Growing up alongside Peter and her cousin Ben, she'd learned men enjoyed plotting a good fight. "I was asking where you were born, and where you family lives now?"

"Oh. How kind. My brother owns a large plantation in New Orleans. Have you ever been there? It's quite the place to visit."

"So your family came from there?"

"New Orleans? I think not. The McDonalds are Scottish, but that history is long and dull."

"No. I'm truly interested." She offered him a smile for that tidbit. "That explains your red hair. Did your father immigrate?"

"Hmm. Much earlier. How about you? Is Roper a British name?"

"I'm not sure. I plan to research my family someday, and I'm rather curious how others have done that."

"I see. That explains your interest. I shall speak with my officer friends and learn what I can to assist you. Although that sort of thing will be difficult in wartime."

Did McDonald have something to hide? "How many siblings do you have?"

"I come from a large family." He fished out a pocket watch. "I fear I'm out of time. I'm terribly sorry. Let me deliver you back to your home. How fortunate we didn't go far."

They hadn't gone far enough to reach the Haskell home, so perhaps Jane wouldn't think poorly of her. "I wouldn't want to keep you from your duties."

He picked up his pace, and she had to work to match his stride.

"Ah, here we are." They hurried up to the porch. "I shall leave you here, dear lady."

Mary Beth glanced toward the floor clock in the foyer. She and McDonald had hardly walked five minutes. Perhaps he had a sudden urge to leave because her curiosity.

"You bein' out with that officer again?" Elsie stood at the top of the stairs.

"I have. I daresay he's not an honest man." She still had no proof.

Late Afternoon Wednesday

Arms full of bank documents, Mary Beth hurried down the stairs to the sitting room. She couldn't wait to see Peter. All day, she'd wondered what he thought about their first outing. In the sitting room, however, an older man stood with his back to her. She must have misunderstood Maud. "Uncle Sadler?"

"Hello, Missy." A huge smile blazed across his thin face as he turned toward her. "It's been too long, but I brought you some caramels. You still like them, right?"

"I do. Your mama's candy is my favorite." She extended her hand for the gift. "I was expecting Mr. Chandler much earlier."

"He's quite occupied today, as you can well imagine." He pointed to a pile of papers on the occasional table. "I believe your father wanted these."

"Yes." She handed him the stack of documents she had retrieved from her father's room. "And will you return these, please?"

"My pleasure." A frown crossed his brow. "I do, however, have one other matter of business."

Business? She could not imagine Mr. Sadler asking her about a banking matter. "You must be wanting to see my father."

He shook his head with a grimace. "No .I understand he's very ill. I'd be so grateful if you would give him a message. Please?"

"Yes, of course." Her father had fallen asleep, and she wouldn't have aroused him for anyone, not even Peter.

"I'm concerned for the bank." His stance was rigid, and his cheeks flushed. "Your father's illness left young Mr. Chandler in charge. That boy has no idea how to manage, and I'd like to suggest your father give the reins to me as soon as possible. Chandler will ruin the bank."

The room began to spin, and Mary Beth grabbed the wing chair beside her to steady herself. "Excuse me? I don't quite understand."

Sadler raised his voice. "It's not pleasant news, Missy, but we must do what is best for you. Mr. Roper and the elder Mr. Chandler wouldn't want their efforts wasted. I fear young Peter isn't qualified to do his job."

"You're saying Peter is incompetent? That's rather difficult to accept. He certainly earned the highest scores in school. His mother said he graduated with honors."

"Your former playmate is a good man. I daresay he's honest and intelligent. However, he's never run a bank, and I assure you, it's much harder in wartime. His father had planned a tutorial of sorts for the boy. Obviously, that never happened."

"We all grieved after Mr. Chandler died. The terrible train accident—"

"And your father fell ill once Peter returned from Europe." His frown wrinkled every inch of his face. "It's not Peter's fault, but we must remedy the situation."

"I understood Peter inherited half the bank from his father. Isn't that correct?"

"The elder Chandler held fifty-one percent, which I assume Peter now owns." He waved a finger in her face. "Listen to me, Missy. Owning a bank doesn't mean one can manage a bank." Mr. Sadler sucked in his cheeks seemingly displeased.

All the years she'd known him, Sadler had never said an unkind word to her. Today his words didn't sound like the man she knew. His description of Peter made no sense.

She tried to recall what her dad owned. He once told her he had the deed to the house, and he owned all the furnishings. They'd sold the horses and carriages when his heart failed. She'd have a place to live, even if she had no income.

Her legs became rubbery, and she dropped into the chair, confused and afraid.

Moments Later

Mary Beth stood in the doorway of her father's room, gazing into the semidarkness where he lay abed. His eyes were closed, and a wheezing, rattling sound accompanied each breath. His pale, thin face tugged at the deepest part of her soul. She didn't know how long she could keep him. Despite the fear tormenting her mind, she couldn't wake her him. Rest might give him a few days longer.

Trust. A simple word carried so much importance.

She ran her fingers along her smooth gold necklace as she pondered the future.

Oh, God. I trusted Papa, Mr. Sadler, Peter, and the bank. Sadler said I can't trust Peter or the bank. I won't have Papa long. I need to trust you. Somehow. Help me.

Chapter Ten

Thursday Morning
April 24th
C&R Bank

Mary Beth hurried inside the bank. She didn't want to waste a moment getting the job done so she could get back to Papa. After a quick wave to Mr. Riddle on her right and Mr. Grant at the teller window, she bolted toward the stairs. However, as she put her foot on the first stair, a hand grabbed her arm.

"Ma'am?" A slender lady held her back. "The teller window is to your left."

Mary Beth looked over the too-attractive lady who wore her tresses up in ringlets. Doubtless, this was the new employee. "I am going to the office."

"Do you have an appointment?"

"No. I am Mr. Roper's daughter," Mary Beth said.

No light of recognition lit her face. "You must have an appointment."

Mr. Sadler approached from his office. "Mrs. Phipps, you must finish this."

When she turned away, Mary Beth fled up the stairs.

Peter took Mary Beth's bonnet and shawl before he guided her up to his office. He'd been on his way down to speak with Mr. Grant when he overheard the conversation with Mrs. Phipps. The look of terror on Mary Beth's face convinced him she needed to talk. Once he settled her in a comfortable chair, he handed her shawl and bonnet to Mr. Riddle. "Would you like something to drink?"

"No." Her hand trembled as she dabbed at her forehead with a handkerchief.

"What is bothering you?" When they were young, she often lost her perspective, and he'd mastered ways to calm her. He pulled his chair up to face her and took her hand.

"I so upset that I barely slept last night. Mr. Sadler came … yesterday."

Peter kept his voice light. "Yes, I meant to come myself, but a client dropped in to see me."

"Mr. Sadler thinks … you're incompetent." Her voice was just above a whisper.

Peter inhaled to clear his mind. Since Grant reported something similar, he must know details. If this was Sadler at work again, her anxiety was justified. This accusation could be quite serious. "What did he say, exactly?"

"He said banking during a war us hard, and he believes you will 'ruin' the bank."

Peter rubbed the back of his neck. She'd touched on his greatest fear. He'd devised contingency plans for several scenarios, like an invasion. But if too many citizens demanded cash at one time, he would close rather than go out of business. He hoped and planned to keep the bank running. The bank was his father's legacy, too precious to lose.

A man needed his woman to believe in him, and he wasn't sure Mary Beth did. He chose to be honest, opening up his heart. "I lack experience. That's true. Your dad said to pursue investments that pay in gold. I'm following that advice, and I'm also pursuing God. He's the gold I want. I believe He'll guide me."

Mary Beth gazed at him for a moment while fiddling with her necklace. "I don't understand Mr. Sadler, but I trust you."

He wanted to whoop with delight and embrace her. Instead, he allowed a big smile. Her confidence meant a lot. "Thanks."

No longer fidgeting, she rose to leave. Surely, he could keep his word. He couldn't imagine losing Mary Beth again after such a failure. She would be destitute, and he'd be at fault.

Friday Morning
April 25th

Anna Chandler's heart flopped about in her chest as she gazed at the steps leading to her husband's office at the bank. Andrew would never again descend those stairs. If only she could feel his arms around her once more—but she must wait for heaven.

She chose to forget her pain and live in the present. The bank manager stood behind the teller window, and Mr. Riddle still occupied the front desk to her right.

"Mr. Grant." Wearing a smile, she advanced toward the counter. "How are you?"

"Mrs. Chandler, it's good to see you."

"I must speak to Peter. We leave for Savannah tomorrow."

He nodded. "Peter told me he would be traveling."

"How is business?"

Grant lowered his voice. "I have never had to handle politics and banking at the same time."

"Politics?"

"You know how much I dislike bickering. It interferes with business."

"Indeed, I do. How did politics come up here?"

Grant looked around. "Mr. Sadler is very pro-slavery. All of us knew his stance, but the subject never surfaced. Of late, he provokes everyone. Just this morning, I overheard him debating Mr. Riddle."

"Anyone else?" *Not Peter.*

"He dislikes the new employee Mr. Chandler hired." He raised an eyebrow. "Let me assure you, I've chosen to stand by your son, but Sadler dislikes him."

"Has Sadler questioned Peter?"

Mr. Grant leaned toward her. "I would never tell anyone else this, but Sadler's trying to undermine Mr. Chandler's leadership."

The bell sounded behind her, and Mr. Grant stepped from behind the counter. "Welcome to C&R Bank, sir. How may I assist you?"

Heat exploded inside Anna as she dashed to Peter's office where he sat in the huge leather chair. He looked like Andrew as a young man. She closed the office door and marched toward him. "I understand Mr. Sadler's creating problems. I tried to convince Andrew and James to fire him, not once but several times."

Peter's mouth fell open. "Mother? Why are you here?"

She brushed a bit of dust off her husband's leather-bound books occupying the shelves by the door. "I apologize. Sometimes I forget your father's gone. We talked about everything, even personnel he hired. This bank feels like mine."

Peter closed the portfolio on his desk. "Who spoke to you?"

"Matthew Grant told me Mr. Sadler is undermining you, and I lost my temper. Mothers must protect their young, and it's impossible to stop when they grow up."

Her son inhaled. "So Mr. Sadler has caused problems before. Tell me what he did in the past."

"He's never easy to manage, but when he chooses an enemy, he's impossible." She straightened a stack of papers on Peter's desk. "I suspect he would impale a saint if he labeled the man incompetent."

Peter ran a hand over his jaw. "Interesting."

"Your father used to say that also." How distressing. Her son couldn't handle Gustav Sadler like she could. "What do you intend to do?"

"I must consider my options."

"That's exactly how Andrew always answered. Oh, dear. I'm sorry. I mustn't pry into your business."

"Mother, you still have not told me why are you here"

"It's Ruth." Anna sat on the edge of a wing chair. "I think you should cancel the trip or at least go alone. I know you must check on investments there, but Ruth will give us trouble."

"I'm taking you and Ruth to get you out of the city. Chattanooga is a Union target."

"They want the entire South, even Savannah. We would only be a bit safer." She groaned. "I hate war."

"Savannah isn't at the top of their list. Please, Mother. Ruth still needs mothering. Protect her. Make her leave with me."

"You're probably right, but Ruth can be stubborn." She turned and left the office.

She would go to Savannah with Peter, but she wouldn't stay long.

The Chandler Library

Peter leaned back from his notes and checked the time on his pocket watch. Nine thirty p.m. He still had so much to do before leaving town tomorrow, but a commotion in the hallway disturbed him.

A female voice mingled with Billy's. The woman wasn't his mother or sister. He stood and eased toward the open door with a sense of foreboding. Something was wrong.

Whoosh! Mary Beth rushed into the room, pulling off her cape, with Billy close behind. She was breathing hard.

"Excuse us, sir." Billy accepted her bonnet and cape in one wadded bundle. He smoothed the fabric across his arm. "Miss Roper had to see you right away."

"Yes." Mary Beth added a grimace seemingly to emphasize the urgency.

The butler left and Peter held out his hands to Mary Beth. What now? She was easily distressed these days. Life with her would never be dull if they married. "You appear troubled. Is it your father?"

She walked straight toward him, her face stiff and her jaw clamped. "When did C&R Bank decide to issue *paper* money?"

"Paper money?" His gaze locked with hers. "Never. Our fathers agreed the bank would always trade in gold. It has intrinsic value, so gold coins are the only safe medium of exchange."

"That's what I thought." She grabbed his arm and squeezed. "I ... found one of those things that masquerade as money."

Only last Tuesday, she spoke of how she seldom acted on impulse. Perhaps she was still maturing in that area. She had a wild gleam in her eyes. "Mary Beth, you'll have to explain. Give me facts."

"I found dollar bill among my household funds. The bill read it was issued from C&R Bank and bore your signature. My father will be livid if he finds out. I don't know what to do."

"You must be mistaken." His mouth was too dry. "I never authorized that."

"Oh, but I do know your handwriting. Remember the time we played wedding? We signed our names repeatedly on the pretend church registry. Your hand improved over the years, but I always recognize it."

"Yes, I remember."

"You see; I cannot be mistaken."

"Do you have the bill handy? May I see this?"

"Yes." Her drawstring purse dangled from her arm. She yanked it off and rummaged, producing a handkerchief, a scrap of paper, and a small pencil. "I thought I had it here, but I shall find it."

"It's vital that I see it." *Surely this can't be!*

She dug around in her pocket. "Here it is," she said waving a wrinkled slip of paper in his face.

His heart rate sped up. "Let me see."

She hurried toward Peter's desk and flattened the wadded bill. "See, it reads, 'Present at C&R Bank, Chattanooga, Tennessee, to redeem for five dollars in gold.'"

Peter stiffened. This couldn't be happening, not when he was leaving town.

"Are you ill? Your skin is clammy. Shall I ring for tea?"

"This is not from our bank." He pulled the oil lamp closer, examining every inch.

"Someone forged your handwriting?"

His chest constricted, making him aware of every breath. "Yes."

"Your handwriting is perfect. Who? Who would do such a thing?"

"The facts. We must gather facts. Counterfeiting is very serious." He drew a breath against the tightness in his chest. "People can bring this to the bank and demand gold. If we can't cover the bills presented, we go out of business."

She thought of the impact to the bank and shivered. "Can't we claim we didn't print it?"

"Banking is all about trust. If our clients do not trust us, they go elsewhere." Peter placed both hands on her shoulders. "We must find the culprit. Right away."

"What about calling the sheriff? Forging a signature is against the law."

"That won't matter to our clients, Mary Beth. People are already nervous because of the war. If they sense a threat, they'll take their business elsewhere."

"What do you suggest?"

"We work together to find who did this and stop them. Do you recall where you got this?"

"I should be able to." She touched her forehead. "I've had so few of these new-fangled bills."

"You must be sure." He strengthened his grip. "We cannot accuse lightly."

She sighed. "I must think. Hard."

"Very well." He released her and stepped back.

She ran her hand over her face. "Maud handles most of the money now, but I have been using this new money when I pay the tradesmen. My boarders paid in this new currency."

He willed himself to calm, rational thought also. "Anything else?"

"The three soldiers exchanged paper money among themselves before handing any to me."

Peter's thoughts raced. These were important facts. "All three?"

"Yes." She extended her lip and put a fist under her chin. "I never thought much about it, but I think they were changing large bills. But why? Why would they do this?"

"Whoever is doing this wants our bank to close or else wants to take over. Let us consider the soldiers suspects along with Sadler and Grant. Add in everyone close to us. Whoever did this comes from here or knows someone in town who could obtain my signature."

She nodded. "None of the soldiers came from the area, so they seem unlikely suspects unless they have friends or relatives here. I'll investigate McDonald. He comes around enough."

"We must work separately for a while." He made a face. "Tomorrow, I accompany Mother and Ruth to Savannah. Our clients there expect me, and I *cannot* trust anyone at the bank now."

She stared at him. "You're leaving? This timing is terrible. What if—"

"I shall be gone less than a week." Peter moved closer. "That is all."

Her mouth dropped open. "You tell me the bank could go out of business and then announce you must leave. I can't find the counterfeiter on my own."

"What excuse could we give to cancel the trip?"

She nodded. "We must keep this quiet."

"Yes. We don't want our customers to panic. *That* would ruin us. Should a large crowd show up and demand their deposits, the bank would go bankrupt." He pictured telling Mr. Roper the bank folded. Peter's face burned with shame at the thought. What a nightmare to confess failure. He'd have to tell his mother. Mary Beth would despise him. They'd be destitute. Never, never, never. He'd rather die.

Chapter Eleven

Saturday Morning
April 26th
On the Train

Despite Peter's noble intentions, Anna dreaded this trip. The hiss of steam, the clatter of passengers, and the general chaos added to her anxiety. Ruth wouldn't be happy, especially after the three-day journey. Anna would do her best with her, offering as much encouragement as possible. Her consolation would be assisting them both, particularly helping Peter with the bank.

Ruth settled into the seat by the window, while Anna occupied the middle seat between her children. As the train pulled from the station, Peter removed a document from his briefcase

Anna saw her opportunity. "Peter, I met the lady you hired. She's quite attractive."

He nodded.

"She told me Gustav believes he should run the bank. I believe he wants employees to side with him."

"Sadler won't have Mrs. Phipps. They despise each other." He ran a finger along his collar.

"What do you plan to do?"

"I shall deal with Sadler once I return. In the meantime, I can consider various strategies."

Ugh! She wanted to *act*, not wait. Peter responded to stress like his father. If only she could participate in banking decisions. "Have Mr. Roper fire him in your absence. If he stays, I doubt the bank will survive long."

She watched as her son blanched. The bank must already be in trouble. Anna wouldn't allow anything to destroy the legacy Andrew left her son. She had several helpful ideas, and Peter would never know.

Tuesday Morning
April 30th
The Roper Library

Mary Beth took in the tall visitor with his lanky frame and thin, solemn face. He bowed as she entered. She slid behind the desk, searching for the name Maud had given her. "Good morning, Mr. …"

"Mr. Gray, Miss Roper." He inclined his head and pulled a sheaf of papers from his briefcase. "I'm Mr. Chandler's lawyer. I've never had the opportunity to meet you before, and I want to offer you my deepest condolences on your father's illness."

She'd never conducted business with a lawyer. Her heart sped up. "Indeed. What brings you here?"

"Mr. Chandler asked me to draw up certain documents and deliver them to you. He gave you the power to sign material for the bank should the need arise."

Mary Beth held onto her chair to steady herself. What a huge responsibility. At least, Peter had a degree. She had no experience and no education beyond her father's tutelage. "I feel sure my father could manage whatever might occur."

"But what if he were too weak to sign a document?" Gray raised his bushy brows. "Mr. Chandler chose to consider every contingency, and he placed incredible confidence in your abilities."

"I see." She didn't have that confidence in herself. "What do you need from me?"

"If you will sign here, on this line." Gray placed a document before her.

Mary Beth read the document, which repeated all the lawyer had said. She signed and pushed the paper toward him.

"Now that you've signed, I have this for you." Gray placed a thick folder before her. "I wish you good day, madam."

As Gray left the room, Mary Beth scanned the folder.

If everything depends on me, the bank is doomed.

Wednesday Morning
April 30th

Mary Beth stopped reading a Psalm to blot a tear trickling down her cheek. She had been sitting in her father's bedroom reading. Her father's head had slumped forward on his chest. She placed her Bible on the bedside table so she could prop his head into a more comfortable position.

If only she did not have to watch him suffer. When she was a child, she'd depended on him to keep her world intact. He chased away the nightmares and fears.

But for now, she needed to focus on the job, not waste time on tears. Her new routine seemed less and less onerous. Now, she wrote banking-related letters and read bank documents while her father slept, and sometimes she would darn. She intended to juggle all her new jobs and leave nothing undone. Daddy's girl would do her best.

If only Papa could recover, she'd make almost any sacrifice. Reorganizing this room had been one of her most painful tasks. She'd never intended to disturb her mother's decorating. The handwork was all she had left of her mother. The brocade bedspread now resided in the closet, and Mother's knickknacks had been displaced by numerous medications.

She slid the heavy draperies closed, and the scraping sound made her wince. Her father moaned but remained asleep. Her foot had gone to sleep, so half-limping, half-tiptoeing toward the dresser, she bumped the bedside table and tipped over his tea. She watched the liquid spread across the wood floor.

Her mind froze as she watched the puddle inch toward the cherry bed frame. Any cloth she used to absorb the liquid might not come clean. Noticing a thin blanket at the foot of the bed, she blotted the stain just before the creeping fluid reached the rug.

Elsie's voice came from behind her. "That be a fine mess, honey chile. I be headin' downstairs, so I take your papa's tray."

Mary Beth's fingernails were absorbing the tea stain, and she snatched her hands away. "Please alert Maud. I have no idea how to clean this."

Elsie stopped and turned. "She ain't here. I guess she done moved out. I thought you knowed Maud was gone."

Her mind reeled. What would she do without Maud? How could she add one more chore to her life? "I had no idea. Did I offend her?"

"There ain't none much kinder."

Mary Beth stood stunned while Elsie contained the mess on the floor. "This is unbelievable."

"You be paying attention, honey chile. There be more to this than you be knowin'."

Mary Beth followed her companion outside the room and pulled the door shut. "She is a free woman and has the right to leave. But I'm worried. So many in the Confederacy have no respect for the Negro."

"She done left, and I be a thinkin' yous have many chores, what with nursin' your papa and all. I be a-helpin' all I can."

"I appreciate your offer but what about your sewing business?"

"What you thinkin' chile? You be needin' me." Elsie shook her head as she eased toward the stairs. "I ain't sewin' all the time."

No how tempting, Mary Beth must not rely too much on Elsie. She hurried to her bedroom where she paced. Her father always brought in a slave, trained him or her and then offered freedom. She could not stand that option. That involved enormous amounts of work, and she despised the slave market.

Reverend McCallie always admonished his flock to pray about their troubles. She closed the bedroom door. As she dropped to her knees, her mind filled with all her doubts and fears from the past few months. She needed a severe scolding for allowing such thoughts to remain in her mind, but despite her efforts, she couldn't drive them away.

She forced her eyes shut and ran a hand over her mouth. "Almighty Father ... if you are there. I'm so selfish, and I need help. Forgive me—if you can."

Her eyes flew open. How could she pray for her troubles to vanish? That's exactly what God promised would come. She stood and brushed off her skirt while determining to make a plan.

Savannah
Wednesday Morning
Aunt Keller's Home

Peter shoved back the bed sheet and pulled himself to a sitting position. He'd come to Savannah to conduct business and to investigate fraud, not to empty his stomach every hour during the night. His aunt had a knack for untangling such issues, and she believed he'd eaten spoiled food while traveling.

He managed to stumble to the mirror hanging on the wall. His face was whiter than Mr. Roper's. Getting sick would never do. Mary Beth shouldn't have to handle emergencies in his absence. Sadler might attempt even more mischief.

He whispered a prayer for the bank as dizziness sent him back to bed.

Wednesday
Mid-Morning

Anna Chandler walked toward the brass bed where her daughter lay. Her sister, Louise, had given Ruth the guest room with the lush hand-crotched bedspread. Eyes closed, cheeks flushed, Ruth took deep rhythmic breaths, as if sleeping, yet she'd slept on the train during the trip. Did this lethargic state signal an illness? "Ruth?"

No response.

"How is she?" Louise, appeared at her elbow, a deep crease forming between her brows.

Anna touched Ruth's forehead. "The child has no fever, at least not yet. Since Peter's been ill, I want to be careful."

Louise shook her head, causing hairpins to slide from her upswept coiffure. "Peter's uneasy stomach came from eating rancid food. He'll be fine tomorrow. Come with me. I have an idea." She led Anna down to the kitchen, shoving the loose hairpins back in place. "How long has it been since she's eaten?"

"She downed a hearty meal before we left. If she doesn't wake, she will miss the tea party you planned with your students."

"She's been in bed almost thirty-six hours." Louise fingered her upswept hair, checking for more loose hair pins. "I think that's sufficient. You remember, she's stayed with me before. If she wants to avoid something, she pretends to sleep. I think we should assume she's doing that again. What's her favorite breakfast?"

Anna massaged her neck, still sore from the long trip. "She adores pecan pancakes."

"Let's have the cook prepare a large batch." Louise winked. "The aroma will fill the house. Her appetite should bring her around."

Anna bit her lip and hoped her sister's ploy would work. If all else failed, she'd return home, but Peter would be livid.

Wednesday Afternoon

Anna Chandler wondered what her beloved Andrew would say about what she was doing now. Concealed behind a thick fern in the sunroom, she peered through the fronds into the open sitting room. The leaves prickled her cheeks and irritated her nose. Sitting in this position made her legs cramp.

Ruth sat in the next room drinking tea with two girls, Sally Marie, and Josie. Sally Marie sat on the sofa facing the window. Giggling filtered in from the sitting room, and Anna's heart jerked, sending an ache through her chest. She saw nothing funny and hoped Ruth wasn't the brunt of a joke. Anna longed to sit in the room with them. If only Ruth would talk to the girls around her.

Louise walked in from outside. "Anna, where are you?"

"Sh-Sh."

"I thought you wanted to walk in the garden," Louise said.

Anna held her finger to her lips as she untangled herself from the greenery. "I wanted to watch a moment," she whispered.

"How are they doing?" Louise lowered her voice as well, and Anna gave silent thanks.

"I can't say yet." She held her breath as the room grew silent again. "I need to go back in there."

"I think not." Louise shook her head, dislodging yet another hairpin. "You mastered the art of conversation years ago. Ruth must learn now."

"Sh-Sh."

"Sister, they know someone's watching. We should go to the library and leave them alone," Louise said.

"We'd have to go back through the sitting room to get there."

Louise rolled her eyes. "We could go around the house."

"Mama? Is that you?"

Anna groaned. Perhaps she was too old for spying. "Yes, honey. I've been waiting for your aunt."

Louise gave her a shove, and Anna led the way into the sitting room. "We shall be in the library if you need something," Anna said.

Ruth took a large gulp from her cup and looked at the floor. Sally Marie giggled. Josie met her gaze and smiled.

Once in the library with the door closed, Anna collapsed into a soft chair and massaged her neck. "You should have kept your voice down."

"Nonsense." Louise patted her upswept hair. "You overreacted. The girls don't want you watching."

Anna crossed her arms, hugging herself. "Sister, you saw how difficult it was to get her out of bed. Ruth does not want to be here for some reason."

Louise chuckled. "But the pancakes worked."

"Yes. You were right. She doesn't want to be here, so she feigned sleep." Anna sucked in air, attempting to achieve calmness. "But Ruth would not even look at those girls. She used to be full of fun before her father died."

"Those are my top students. They will do fine together."

"I hope so." Anna closed her eyes and tried not to think about what was going on in the sitting room.

Friday
May 2nd

Mary Beth adjusted her bonnet to keep the sun off her face as she and Elsie bustled down Market Street. Papa had been very ill yesterday, and Mary Beth worried all night. Today he seemed more himself. She was embarrassed at succumbing to anxiety and chose to venture out to search for clues at the printer's shop. She must learn something useful—maybe find clues to the counterfeiter. The documents she perused from the bank had turned up nothing so far. "There's the printer," she told Elsie. "I shall scurry inside. I hope I'm not keeping you too long."

Elsie pointed to the store across the street. "I be shoppin' for thread."

"This shouldn't take long. I'm working on a project for the bank." She pushed open the printer's door and the smell of ink greeted her inside.

The balding man who approached her wiped his hands on his ink-stained apron then pushed his glasses up on his nose. "Can I help you, miss?"

Would Papa be angry because she did not inform him of this visit? She didn't check the client's name before leaving home. "I'm Miss Roper of C&R Bank. My father is quite ill, and I'm visiting a few clients for him. I'd like to know how your business is going."

"I cannot complain. A few businesses left the area, but the military placed several orders, so our income remains stable."

"My father will be pleased." She plastered a huge smile on her face and plunged further. If only her mouth were not so dry. "I am interested in having stationary printed, as well as calling cards."

"What sort of type would you like?"

"I'd like to use my signature."

He shook his head. "That requires an engraver, and we cannot do that."

Mary Beth's heart picked up speed. Exactly what they needed. Peter would be thrilled at what she learned. "Why? Is engraving difficult?"

"I use moveable type or letterpress printing. You choose from the font and designs I have available." The man pulled out a chart displaying various types of printing. "These are the most common fonts we use. We have almost every style one could wish for."

She touched one type of font. "If I selected this one, what would you do?"

"Once you pick the wording, we'd drop the type into trays and load them into the printer." He pulled out another chart. "You can add decorative scroll work to give that extra touch."

Perhaps one of these on display would match the design on the bills. She moved closer and peered at the chart while wracking her memory of the counterfeit bill. Some of the designs resembled those on the bill, but nothing matched exactly. "How do you print signatures or pictures?"

"Both must be engraved on plates. See these?" He went behind the counter and pulled out a small metal plate. "My father had this done so we could print his signature in the editorial column. He's retired now, so I show them to customers like you who need information."

Mary Beth ran her finger along the cold steel. "I'm rather surprised you can't do this."

"None of the businesses here require that." He shrugged. "I do almost all the printing in the area."

Her mind buzzed. If he was telling the truth, he had no part in the counterfeiting scheme, but she must keep firing questions. Maybe she could find a discrepancy in his story. "What sort of things can you do?"

"I've done brochures, trains schedules, fliers, menus, advertisements, even newspapers." He pointed to various stacks of documents. "You're free to look at these."

Mary Beth fingered a train schedule and the newspaper he handed her. The decorative work along at the top and edges looked nothing like the forged bill. Maybe she was wasting her time. "If I found an engraver, could you print the cards?"

"Printing isn't the problem. Engraving requires special tools and equipment. The clients I service in this area require basic printing."

"How much should I expect to pay for engraving?"

"That depends on what you have engraved. A photograph is the most difficult, but a signature would require a good bit of skill."

She pulled a tiny pencil and a scrap of paper from her purse. "Could you give me the name of someone in Chattanooga who could engrave for me?"

"You'd have to go to Atlanta. That would be the closest place, perhaps the only place for engraving of high quality."

Someone in Atlanta might want to destroy their bank. She must find out who, and soon.

Monday
May 5th
Savannah Dockyard

Peter combed his fingers through his hair to repair the damage done by the salty breeze. Bankers must look neat and organized. He was more likely to get answers if he didn't look like the tide washed him in. He'd lost enough time to illness. His stomach still cramped some, but he had to conduct business. If anything happened to the bank, he'd need to be back home.

The dockyard office, a long brick building, stood several hundred feet away from the dock. He entered the quiet office and approached the only occupied desk.

An older man with white hair had a handful of papers, but he put them aside as Peter approached. "I'm Mr. Doss, secretary to the owner. May I help you?"

"I am Peter Chandler, a banker from Chattanooga. I came looking for investment opportunities. A friend informed me I could ask Mr. Cox for a list of blockade runners."

He nodded and pulled a sheaf of papers from a cabinet. "Mr. Cox is in a meeting, but we have a list here."

Peter opened his portfolio and pulled out a file. "I need information on the 'Firefox,' 'Glowing Dawn,' and 'Blade Runner.'"

He donned a pair of glasses. "Give me those names one at a time."

"'Firefox.'"

"I don't have to look for that one. A friend of mine owns it, but it's a shrimper."

"That's interesting," Peter said. "Could it be used for both shrimping and blockade running?"

"No, sir. That's the only ship by that name here."

"The other name is 'Glowing Dawn.'"

The man wrinkled his brow as he flipped pages. "That doesn't sound familiar. No. We have no ship by that name."

Peter had a feeling the next ship was fictional too. "How about 'Blade Runner?'"

"No. It doesn't exist. You must have received inaccurate information. If you still want to invest, I can have the clerks list our best blockade runners."

"I appreciate that. May I pick that up this afternoon?"

"Sure. I can arrange that."

Now Peter was certain McDonald was dishonest, but he was not sure what he hoped to obtain. Peter did not want Mary Beth to deal with him alone.

Chapter Twelve

Monday
May 5th

After glancing up and down the hallway, Mary Beth stepped inside her room and yanked the letter from her pocket. McDonald had slipped the epistle into her hand during their walk and muttered something about privacy. Afterward, he cracked a joke, so she never questioned him about the letter. Did this contain some message meant only for her, or did the missive contain a secret?

The oil lamp on her dressing table should provide enough light to examine the paper. She took a seat on the stool and turned up the wick so she could get a good look. The handwriting proved the message came from a friend who'd moved to New York. Her penmanship had a backward slant, not easy to mimic.

She slit open the letter and glanced over the contents. Her chum talked about ball gowns and handsome men. The writing transported Mary Beth to the past. She recalled how often she and her friend chatted about those topics a year ago. Now they seemed trivial in the light of her responsibilities.

Nothing here explained the lieutenant's actions. She didn't know what he wanted nor did she know if the military had access to the mail. How did mail get here from New York in a time of war?

She strongly suspected the lieutenant was dishonest.

But she must have proof.

Savannah
Thursday
May 8th

Standing outside Savannah's Bay Street Bank, Peter took a deep calming breath. This interview could prove valuable as well as painful. The bank manager and his father had shared a friendship. The man could advise him on investments that paid in gold as well as McDonald's bonds. He hoped Mr. Field would become a trusted colleague.

Once seated inside the bank office, Mr. Field, now gray and portly, entered. "Peter, my boy. I'm glad to see you. How is your father?"

Peter's mouth went dry. "In the past few months, I've operated the bank alone. My father died a little over a year ago."

The smile vanished from Mr. Field's face as he eased into his leather chair. "I'm terribly sorry. And what about James Roper? I remember he brought his daughter to the office to learn bookkeeping."

"He did, and Mary Beth still enjoys keeping books. I'm sorry to say Mr. Roper is ill."

"Ghastly news."

"I received the letter you sent my father. He would be glad to know you got this position. Let me offer you my heartfelt congratulations as I know he would also do."

"Thank you. I dreamed of being president of a large bank, but at times, I wondered if I would manage to do it."

"My father would commend your diligence."

"Your father was a brilliant man, but he refused to leave his hometown. I came across several lucrative jobs, but he turned them all down. What can I do for you?"

"I wonder if you have heard of a special Confederate bond that yields an extra seven percent interest."

"What?" Mr. Field's eyes widened. "Did you say *extra* interest?"

"I did."

He whistled. "No, I've not heard of it, but there's a fair amount of fraud."

"I don't trust the man who gave me the prospectus. Nothing he gave me sounds legal."

"Have you made inquiries at Richmond?"

Rubbing his chin, Peter continued, "Being new to the banking industry, I'm not sure who to approach. Do you know who I could consult?"

Mr. Field pulled out a sheet of paper and dipped his pen in ink. "I can make some discreet inquiries for you. I know all the right people. Give me some time, and I shall see what I can find."

"I appreciate that. One more thing. I need to invest in ventures that pay in gold. We aren't fond of the new legal tender being issued today and prefer to use gold coins."

"I can help you there." Field pursed his lips. "Do you have any particular businesses in mind?"

"I'm interested in any good opportunity, even blockade runners."

"I do know several reliable sailors who make a tidy profit. They give you a percentage of their earnings." Mr. Field tapped a pile of papers. "The more you invest, the higher the profits. Are you interested?"

"As long as they pay in gold."

"I shall have my secretary prepare portfolios for you. We own stock in railroads, and I strongly recommend you to invest there. It's the way of the future. With the steam locomotive, we pay dividends much faster than before."

In these uncertain times, Peter wanted exactly that—reliable income. He would examine the portfolios with care, but at least he had a recommendation. "How often do they pay?"

"Each quarter. We also back a textile mill. As you know, in the absence of the Union factories, we cannot make our own clothes. This mill is a great opportunity."

"No." Peter frowned. "I'm not comfortable supporting an industry relying so closely upon slave labor. That's one I'd have to refuse."

"There's no slave labor in the factories."

"That's true, but slaves tend and pick the cotton. Until that changes, I won't invest in the textile industry."

"What a shame! Your high standards will prevent you from earning a lot of money."

Thursday
May 8th
Roper Home

Glancing at her watch, Mary Beth scrambled toward the staircase to the library downstairs. She'd tried all day to get to the documents Mr. Riddle delivered yesterday. They needed to go back to the bank as soon as possible. So far, none of the material she combed through looked suspicious. But these might prove different.

An odd sound came from her father's room. Mary Beth paused and ran there instead.

She burst into his room and gasped, "Papa?"

Mr. Roper lay in a heap beside the bed, panting. "I tried to reach those files."

"Files?" Her heart protested with vigorous thumping. "Are you injured? Does anything hurt?"

"Those files." He motioned to the bedside table. "I knocked off the letter opener while trying to reach them. Didn't you have some letters for me to sign?"

She draped his robe around him and helped him stand. "I do, but this wasn't necessary. All you have to do is call me."

"I detest being waited on" With shaky hands, he tied the belt to his robe. "Now help me to the chair, and bring me those papers."

"But you've had no breakfast."

"I'm not hungry."

"Nonsense. You must eat. And look your lips are getting dry. Dr. Smith gave me something. Let me find that ointment."

"You can do that later."

She moved bottles around on the dresser until she located the medication. "Here it is. This medication will take just a moment, and then I'll get you something to eat."

"That smells nasty." His face turned red as he pushed her hand away. "I want the files."

Mary Beth settled him in the armchair and placed a blanket over his legs. She retrieved the papers, which had scattered behind the table, and put them on his lap.

"My reading glasses are on the other side of the bed."

Mary Beth grabbed his glasses and handed them to her father. If only he would allow her to soften his lips before they cracked and bled.

"Have we heard from Mr. Allen?"

"Mr. Allen? He's the one Peter asked you to check on. You said he was difficult. I do not think he answered."

"Write him another letter."

"I'll do that if you'll dictate."

"Wait." Her father didn't look up. "There's a serious discrepancy in the math here. Get this to Mr. Grant today as you send a message to Mr. Allen. This problem needs resolution right away."

Mary Beth glanced over his shoulder. "That must be Mrs. Phipps' handwriting. I recognize Mr. Sadler's. He never makes a mistake."

His concern gave her an idea; one she should have thought of already. Until now, she and her father had poured over client accounts, reviewing loans and interest payments. Now she would obtain the general ledger and check the math.

Monday afternoon
May 12th

Clouds masked the late afternoon sun as Mary Beth hurried down Market Street. A few citizens still strolled about, and Mr. Nelson pulled the shades as she passed the general store. She would clear up the mystery of the letter today. Perhaps she'd also find a relationship between the lieutenant and the bank. Elsie trotted alongside her with a grimace on her dark face. "I apologize, Elsie. I am hoping to finish while Papa sleeps, plus I must arrive before the post office closes."

"Old bones be movin' a bit slow today."

Mary Beth nodded to the left. "I shall run in—"

"And I be waitin' right here." She plopped onto a bench beside the café, fanning herself

"Thanks for coming on short notice. I have business to clear up." Mary Beth waved to Elsie as she stepped inside.

Mrs. Scott stood behind the counter. "Hello, Miss Roper. I hope your father has improved."

Mary Beth's gut clenched. Could she never escape describing her situation? "He's still quite ill, but I am mailing letters for him while he sleeps."

"Good girl. Your efficiency always impressed me."

"Have you heard from your sons?"

"Alas, no." A tear dangled on her bottom lashes. "I send packages and keep praying."

"Don't we all need to pray?"

Mrs. Scott bustled to the door. "It is one minute before closing, so you are my last patron."

"Wonderful." She handed the postmistress both letters and coins.

"You are busy, honey. I hear you are caring for your father and keeping house."

Mary Beth didn't mention her work for the bank, or growing herbs, and mixing medications. "Yes, I am. But I'm rather curious. Does mail pass between the Union and the Confederacy?"

"Yes, a few things come through. I have heard rumors about how that happens, but I'm not sure."

"Does the Confederate military have any dealings with the mail?"

Mrs. Scott's eyebrows scrunched together. "I don't think so, but I'm not sure. Why?"

"A lieutenant brought me a letter, and I thought it rather strange."

"Does he have red hair?"

Mary Beth's body grew hot. "Yes, he does."

"He mesmerized my daughter, Liza, and I see him hanging about when she's been working. He flirts with everyone, even me."

"Would Liza give him my mail?"

"I think she might, even though I wish she wouldn't."

Once again, Mary Beth suspected McDonald but could prove nothing.

Chapter Thirteen

Tuesday Morning
May 13th

Mary Beth tiptoed about the house, glancing around each room and peering outdoors. No tradesmen approached. Elsie sewed a uniform, and Cook worked in the kitchen. Her father had dozed off over bank documents. Since her boarders came just as she discovered the counterfeit money, she'd been meaning to search their things. At last, she had an opportunity to do so. Today she'd start with Sergeant Glass.

She stepped into his room, and her chest tightened. Was she protecting her family—or breaking the law? No, they needed clues, and she could say she was making sure the cat kept away rodents. After all, this was her home.

Inside the bedside table, she found a pipe and bag of tobacco. A pile of money rested on the dresser, and she examined the notations on each bill. One came from Alabama, two from Georgia, and one from Mississippi. In the top drawer, she found handkerchiefs and several clean shirts. She ran her fingers along the smooth fabric of each. Where did he get such nice clothing? The next held expensive pants, underwear, and socks. Ammunition and metal cleaner resided in the bottom drawer. The washstand held a comb, shaving soap and mug, and a razor.

How odd that he had so few personal items.

Of the three men, Glass seemed evil enough to be the forger, but nothing here proved that. Maybe one could make a case with his costly clothing, but clothes could be a gift. If only she knew the contents of his pockets. Surely, whatever he carried with him would reveal something valuable about his character.

She glanced about to see if anyone had come in the house.

"Mary Beth? Mary Beth?" Papa called.

Tuesday Noon

Mary Beth suppressed a grin as she entered the bank and didn't hear the bell. Each time she arrived to exchange documents, Mr. Sadler hurried out of his office to greet her, perhaps alerted by the ringing. What memories she had of riding on his back or bouncing on his knee! Now, however, she sensed he shielded something from her. What could that be?

Mr. Grant had promised to assist her. She wondered if he achieved his objective.

"Here you go, Miss Roper." Mr. Grant sent a surreptitious look behind him as he walked from the teller window to hand her the ledger book. "Mr. Sadler will have a fit if he knows it left the bank."

"I shall cram it into my straw bag. How did you silence the bell?"

"I removed it for cleaning." He beamed. "No one argued. I'm the bank manager."

"I appreciate your efforts, and I know Papa will too." She nodded to Mr. Riddle as he entered the foyer. "How's business?"

"Since the rumors died down, business is brisk. I suppose you've heard from Mr. Chandler?"

"No, and that concerns me. He thought he'd be a week or less. I'm getting worried."

"Business often takes longer than we expect." Grant inched toward the counter. "I'd best be back to work."

"Thank you."

Mr. Sadler's desire to maintain control of the general ledger made her wonder what he was doing.

Savannah
Wednesday
May 14th

Peter whispered a prayer as he bent over the mound of files at Bay Street Bank. Mr. Field hovered at his elbow, waiting for an answer. After reviewing his criteria for investments, he picked the businesses that fit. "I want to invest in the railroads, and the button factory, as well as the blockade runners you recommended. I'm eliminating Tessler's munitions factory."

"Excellent. The railroad will bring in a tidy profit. Are you sure you want to exclude Tessler and Wren? Tessler will bring in plenty, and Wren will be a safe investment that will pay well."

"I can't agree to producing weapons, and I prefer to watch Wren for rising profits before buying in."

"Ah, but you'll miss the highest earnings by waiting."

Peter grew warm. "I'm seeking less-risky clients."

"You're quite conservative, like your father."

"That's the way I prefer to run the bank during the war."

"Very well. Here's a special pen to sign your contracts. The company is testing the design." He placed a small rectangular box before Peter. "Take it home and use it. These pens have a reservoir for ink, eliminating the need to dip your pen every few words. And if you decide to sign with the Cross Company, I'll give you several more."

Peter took the new pen from its box and flipped the mechanism that pulled ink into the barrel. "What a useful invention."

"Yes. One you may wish you had invested in."

Peter's smile wilted. The man needed to learn when to quit.

Chattanooga
May 15th

Mary Beth put away her budget and rubbed her eyes. She'd spent a couple of hours on household bills. Even without paying Maud's salary, she would have to stretch the money to finish the month. On another slip of paper, she listed ways to cut back. Maybe she could plant vegetables too. Of course, her herb garden hadn't been a great success.

She pulled out the right-hand drawer of the roll top desk and lifted out their cash. Once she counted the money, she pored over what her banker-father would call legal tender or paper money. Two bills, one from a Georgia bank and three from Virginia lay in her hand. One Confederate Treasury note. Once she'd failed to notice the counterfeit bill with her bank's name, but she wouldn't fail again.

Elsie appeared at the open door. "Bookkeepin'?"

"I'm balancing the budget, or trying to, anyhow."

"It's a giftin', chile, like your papa."

Mary Beth rubbed her neck. "Everything costs more, so I find it difficult."

"Sewin's bringin' in money for me. I could be paying some rent. You may be needin' such after your pa dies."

"Oh, Elsie." Her lips trembled. "I don't want him to die, nor can I think of living here alone."

Elsie embraced her. "Don't you be goin' there yet. I'm sayin' my income's growin'.'"

"Yes, but should Papa … die …" The thought sliced through her like lightning.

She patted her cheek. "We be takin' a day at a time."

Mary Beth closed her eyes and considered living like a pioneer. She would have to learn to slaughter animals, make candles, and weave her own cloth. The thought made her shudder.

May 15th
Savannah Depot

Where are they? Peter looked over Aunt Louise's head to scan the milling crowd. The huge train stood behind him, bustling with people. He hated to leave without a goodbye, but he must return home to Mary Beth and the bank. The whistle blew, and passengers pushed past him to board. Peter inched toward the entrance. Mother and Ruth promised they'd come.

Aunt Louise grabbed his arm and pulled him back. "I feel sure they will arrive at any moment."

"I cannot wait much longer, Auntie."

"You could catch the next train, Peter. I've hardly seen you. Ah, there's Anna." She released a sigh. "But I don't see your sister."

Peter looked up as his mother ran toward them, panting and waving. He threw his arms around her and planted a kiss on her cheek. "You almost missed me."

"I'm terribly sorry to be late." His mother fanned herself. "Ruth sends her regards. She couldn't dress in time."

Aunt Louise raised an eyebrow. "We had her out of bed."

"Have no worries about me, Mama. I'm concerned for Ruth. In addition to safety concerns, we brought her here to make new friends and attend Auntie's school. She must learn some discipline."

Aunt Louise crossed her arms. "I agree. You allow her too much freedom."

"I promised her a week for vacation," Anna said.

"Even on vacation one must keep regular hours." Aunt Louise pressed her lips together.

Peter never dreamed the two sisters would clash over Ruth's antics. They'd always seemed to share the same values. "Start today, Mama. Get her on a schedule."

"I do indulge her from time to time." Anna screwed up her face. "She's been so sad and restless since her father died, and—"

"That was months ago, sister. The child must move on with her life, and I want to help her do that," Louise said.

"All aboard for Atlanta," the conductor called.

"I agree, Mama, and Father would also. Write me so I know how she's doing." Peter hugged them both and boarded the train. He hoped his plan to leave his mother and Ruth in Savannah would work.

May 16th
Roper Library

Boredom! McDonald was on bended knee before her. Knowing him, he wasn't about to suggest marriage, and his flirtations grew loathsome. If she had her choice, she'd bury herself in one of the leather-bound books filling the walls about her. Perhaps she could learn some useful tidbit. "Lieutenant, did you come to give me a message?"

"Oh, indeed, ma'am. I'm here on business, of course, but I treasure every one of your smiles."

The more he complimented, the less sincere he sounded. "Really now! I never know when you are serious."

"Then no one else has ever been honest about your beauty."

She saw Eddie, not McDonald, and she wanted to scream. "But, you said you came on business. What can I do for you?"

"Your boarders will miss dinner tonight. Both, however, request a hardy breakfast, and they sent me with a menu."

"I shall see you out." She looked over the so-called menu as she guided him to the front door. "I shall notify the cook. I cannot be sure what we have on hand, and if she can obtain certain meats."

"I am certain you will do your best. Give my best to your father."

He'd never mentioned her father before, and his comment stirred her curiosity. "He's a little better today."

"Should anything ... happen, who would inherit his share in the bank?"

He cared about the bank. "Sir, you must excuse me. I cannot bear to think of such."

She hurried back inside, shutting the door with more energy than necessary. McDonald's actions made her think he wanted her money, not her.

Chapter Fourteen

Friday
May 16th
Chattanooga Depot

The train slowed. Peter shifted his weight, hoping to relieve the tingling in his left foot. After seven hours, the padded seats didn't provide much comfort.

The Chattanooga depot now stood on his right, and he longed to visit Mary Beth to find out how much she'd learned. He checked the time—seven p.m. Peering out the window, Peter observed Mr. Shaw ambling toward the station. Since he wanted to avoid him, he waited for the other passengers to leave first.

Cool spring air and misty rain greeted him as he stepped off. A porter pushing a large container of luggage passed between him and Shaw. He prayed the official would not see him.

"Oof!" He stumbled as a Confederate soldier, surely not more than sixteen, rammed into him from the left

"Hey, watch where you're goin', man." The young man scowled and puffed out his chest.

"Excuse me," Peter said, backing away. A fight would attract attention, and he wanted to disappear.

"And what if I do not excuse a man who won't serve his country?" He shoved Peter and then raised his fists.

Peter gave the boy his sternest glare and backed off.

"Hey, here's what I think of cowards." The soldier jumped forward and swung a left hook.

Peter ducked and reached for his pocket knife as a crowd formed around them.

The boy punched again, but Peter sidestepped. "Do you want time off for medical care?"

A Confederate officer broke through the crowd. His brow crumpled. "Private Peel, I thought I heard your voice."

Peter slipped the knife back into his pocket. "I shall be fine, sir."

The soldier shrank away. "I didn't start it."

"You said that one too many times. You are under arrest." The officer shoved the man toward the depot.

"Hey," the soldier yelled. "My brother's dying right now because men like that won't stand up and fight."

Peter had already melted into the crowd. He was living in dangerous times.

After sending his luggage and portfolio home, Peter hurried toward the Ropers' with the brown package his mother sent. He yearned to see Mary Beth. His banker's mind tried to count the days since they last talked, but he kept forgetting the numbers. The separation seemed like months.

As Peter neared the Roper home, Mary Beth ran onto the huge front porch, smiling and waving. She'd left her hair down. "You look wonderful."

As he approached, he offered the gift. "Mother picked out fabric for you."

She grabbed the package he handed her. The huge grin on her face reminded him of earlier times. "I didn't expect you today, but I'm thrilled to have you home."

"You didn't get the telegram?"

"I got one cryptic statement about arriving in Savannah. That came days ago."

"I asked Mother to send another saying I was returning. Maybe something went wrong." He shrugged, wondering if Ruth had way-laid his mother. "I want to hear what you've been doing."

"I've so much to tell you. Let's hurry inside. It's too warm to talk out here."

Holding his hand, she pulled him inside. Courting was going well. He prayed no young man interfered this time.

As they entered the sitting room, she tore open her package and squealed. "Blue silk and white chambray—beautiful. Thank you. How much do I owe you?"

He shook his head. If only he'd brought a gift of his own. "Can you find someone to watch your papa tomorrow? If you let me walk you to church, we'll call it even."

Mary Beth tucked her chin and giggled. "At today's prices, you are cheating yourself. Fabric is expensive now."

"Look at it this way. I look forward to seeing you in the frocks you make."

"Then I must start sewing right away." She ruffled the curls about her face. "Papa wants me to go. Perhaps Elsie can look out for him."

"I'm delighted to help you obey your father."

"What did you learn?"

"In Savannah, counterfeit bills abound. The authorities are understaffed because of the war and do nothing to prosecute. So, you can imagine Chattanooga will have even fewer resources."

"What will that mean for us?"

He ran his finger along his collar. She didn't understand the danger they might face. "We probably should find the criminal ourselves, then report."

"I visited the printer here in town. He's a client, so that gave me an excuse to check on his finances."

"Your father allowed that?"

"I didn't tell him. He sent me to the grocer first, so I felt like I knew what to do."

"Please be careful. Our grocer would harm no one, but this war brings out evil people. A soldier accosted me here in Chattanooga, but fortunately, I had a knife and could defend myself."

Her eyes widened. "How frightening!"

"You need to take precautions."

"I was fine until the grocer offered me his son for a husband. His proposal was embarrassing, but I encountered no danger."

"Don't be afraid to mention we are courting. His son is much too young anyway."

"I agree, and I prefer you." She reached over to touch his hand.

A knock sounded on the door, and Elsie stepped inside. "Dr. Smith is here."

The elderly doctor walked in, holding his black bag. "Peter Chandler, I am glad to see you. When did you arrive home?"

"About an hour ago." He stood and offered his hand. "It's great to be home."

"Would the two of you like some time alone while I see to Mr. Roper?"

They both laughed because nothing would please them more.

An Hour Later

Mary Beth gazed at Peter over the café menu. He had always been handsome, but he had never looked better. The restaurant had a larger crowd than the last time, but the waiter seated them near the back, so they were almost alone. Since the doctor had stayed with her father, she could relax.

"Are you sure you do not mind eating here again? Don't feel obligated just because the waiter seated us."

"I have fond memories of our last visit here. I want to make some more memories together."

"Then we'll do that," he laughed. "I apologize for the length of my stay in Savannah. While traveling down there, I ate something that didn't agree. The first few days, I spent recovering."

"How dreadful for you, and here I was worried about train accidents."

A shadow passed over his face, engulfing the smile. What a mistake. She'd best get on another subject. "I have something I need to talk over with you before I forget."

"Yes?" The sparkle returned to his smile.

"I found some errors. Sadler made them, which I thought was interesting. Papa always said he was amazingly accurate."

Peter leaned closer. "Your father is correct. Tell me more."

"I got the idea from Papa. He found a discrepancy in the math on a client account, so I thought I'd look over the general ledger. That's when I found it. Mr. Sadler marked out several deposits Mrs. Phipps made and recorded them again as a lump sum. However, further along in the book, he reduced each deposit by ten or fifteen cents. That continued through the entire ledger."

"That's good information." He reached over and squeezed her hand. "Thank you."

A warm glow filled her heart. Her father used to praise her. His illness now made him grumpier than usual. "Mr. Grant had to assist me to obtain the ledger. He said Mr. Sadler would become angry if the ledger left his control."

"I wonder if he'll still have that attitude when I show up Monday." He rubbed his chin.

She shook her head. "Surely not. That's dreadful."

"When we return to your house, get that ledger, and I'll return it tonight."

Her respect for him grew. "Thanks, I wondered how I would get it back. When I was a child, Mr. Sadler used to let me ride on his shoulders. I can't imagine him as a villain."

Peter sighed. "You might find him different now."

"What are we going to eat tonight? Didn't you say you like everything?"

"I think we should both have a plate of raw carrots." He smiled playfully.

She dissolved into laughter. "No. No. I'm not doing that again."

"But you said you had fond memories of this place. This time, I'll compete with you to see how far the carrot might go."

She doubled over laughing. "You know, Lieutenant. McDonald tries to be funny. You actually are."

"I think I'll allow the waiter to choose. That way I can't be blamed for such accidents."

"And I won't have anything uncooked, which might be cheaper since you won't have to replace anyone's clothes."

A longing in his eyes made her hope.

Chapter Fifteen

Saturday
May 17th

Peter slipped into the dining room, where a single place setting awaited him. He had dressed with haste so he could head to the bank before visiting Mr. Roper. As he slid into his chair and grabbed the linen napkin, Maud entered with a teacup in her hand.

He blinked and ran his hand over his eyes to convince himself he wasn't dreaming. "Maud? What are you doing here?"

"Excuse me, sir. Billy done told me you be home. McDonald. What an awful man. He bein' pure evil, he is. I be thankin' the good Lord for my Billy. He'd been askin' for my hand. Yes, sir, I be needin' escape."

Peter held up his hand. At a moment like this, her chatter could unravel him. "Please, start at the beginning. Why are you here?"

She lowered her head. "Billy and I's married now."

"What?"

"My Mr. Roper be sayin' Billy's a fine man. We been courtin' thereabouts a year."

Peter shook his head, needing basic facts before she launched into another speech. "Does Mary Beth know?"

"No, sir."

Billy entered with sugar and milk. "I'm sure Mr. Chandler would like his breakfast now."

"Wait. When did this happen?"

"Tuesday last month. You done left for Savannah. I be packin' my clothes and met Billy at the church. He 'ranged for the preacher to marry us there. He asked me over and over till I finally promised to marry him. I couldn't bear to leave Miss Roper till I saw how that reptile be flatterin'—"

"I'm sorry, sir," Billy waved her back to the kitchen. "She tends to talk on and on. But she's a fine lady."

"Maud just left the Ropers? Whenever you make a change, you must inform your employer. I know Mary Beth is worried."

"We will apologize, sir."

"What does your wife know about the lieutenant?"

Maud returned with Peter's breakfast. "Billy be telling me not to talk about McDonald, but I see bad things in his eyes. I be knowin' there's no honesty inside him. He be nice on the outside to hide the nasty innards."

Perhaps he didn't know Maud as well as he thought. She must be a master at watching people. "Do you know anything specific?"

"I be overhearin' him talkin' with another man in the graveyard. I took flowers to Mrs. Roper's grave like Mr. Roper requested. I be carin' for that sweet lady in her last days. God rest her soul. And that's when them men be whisperin'."

"Can you recall what they said?"

Maud frowned. "I better be rememberin'. Now, I will be thinkin'. Oh, dear. The lieutenant be talkin' rough like, not smooth-tongued like he be around Miss Roper."

Peter pushed aside his plate, no longer hungry. Sometimes Maud tangled up the facts if she got upset. He'd have to learn more. "Maud, if you recall what you heard, please let me know. Now, I'd like some fresh tea, please. This tea is no longer hot."

"Right away, sir."

"This afternoon, I'll discuss arrangements with you and your wife, Billy."

"Yes, sir. We'll take your advice and speak to Miss Roper."

"Speaking of advice, I might need yours on courting." Peter stood. "But for now, I'd best head toward the Roper house."

Maud darted around Billy with a steaming cup. "I do recall hearin' somethin' about a half-brother and Mr. Roper, I think. They be speakin' in whispers. No, he be speakin' of a cousin, and it was Mr. Chandler or somethin'. Both being sneaky like. It gave me a turn, I tell you. Scairt me to death."

Peter had proved McDonald's deceit. Now he must speak with Mary Beth.

Later That Morning

Peter's neck and shoulders hardened into rock as he perused Mr. Roper, who occupied a chair by the bed. Roper had aged, and he was thinner. Peter hoped to chat without endangering his health. "Are you able to talk for a few moments?"

"Of course. I forgave my daughter for not sending you up right away last night. However, I was thrilled you took her out to dinner."

"Before I left for Savannah, a soldier named Lieutenant McDonald asked permission for two medical men to reside here. The lieutenant is not trustworthy. He is the one who brought the prospectus on blockade runners and Confederate bonds. After sleuthing about in Savannah, I know both are fake."

"Superb work. What else?"

"It's so alarming I almost hate to tell you."

Roper chuckled. "You can't hurt me now. I'm on my way to heaven. I insist you tell me."

"Mary Beth found a counterfeit bill issued from C&R Bank with my signature."

"That's serious." He tapped on the arm of the chair. "What's your plan?"

"Mary Beth and I intend to search for the culprit."

"I've known Dr. Milo Smith for years. He can be trusted. Just don't make an official complaint until you have tried to find the culprit. We want to protect the bank, so if several months go by, you may have to report."

"That won't endear us to our clients."

"If someone forged your signature, the person involved is close. Start looking, but be on your guard. Keep Mary Beth from getting too heroic."

As if I could. A picture of Atlas flashed into his mind. Within a short time, he'd be holding up the entire world. If only God would heal Mr. Roper. "I'll do my best, sir."

"What else, Peter. What about investments?"

He took a deep breath. "I met with Mr. Field, and he gave me several portfolios. I invested in the railroad. He also had several blockade runners that do well. I chose them also."

"Good work." Roper coughed several times. "And how are the clients there?"

"The shipping clients have suffered because of the ships guarding the harbor. That's to be expected, I suppose. The ship building is down also, but the fishermen are making more. That almost makes up the difference."

"All of those are fine choices. What about my girl?"

"We've been out twice, which we both enjoyed."

"I prefer to believe my daughter learned something from Edward Teal. He hurt her badly." Mr. Roper banged on the armrest with his fist. "Demonstrate true love. She'll respond."

"I did that last time, sir." He massaged a knot in his temple. "She deserted me for someone else."

But again, Peter was taking a chance.

Sunday
May 18th

The morning air was damp and chilly as Mary Beth and Peter headed off toward the morning service. She'd eagerly anticipated talking and was more comfortable being seen with him. They had so much to discuss about finding the counterfeiter.

Peter glanced at her. "Would you like my jacket?"

"Yes. Thanks." Unlike Eddie and McDonald, he was attentive.

He draped his coat over her shoulders.

"Ooh, that feels better. We must do more investigating. Any ideas on what to do next?"

A wry chuckle escaped Peter's lips. "This morning, Elsie reported your father's care is becoming more demanding. I doubt you have time."

Despite Peter's coat, a shiver went up her back as she imagined the bank failing. "A woman tends to see the subtle things that men might miss. Please, tell me how I can help."

"Keep your eyes open. Try to find out if others have similar bills."

"Yes. We need to get an idea of the number circulating. I can initiate conversations about the designs on bills. No one would suspect my motive."

"We must learn who got my signature. What did they do with it afterward? Who printed the bills? How many fake bills exist?"

"I could ask around about large shipments at the railroad station or even at the docks."

"Please be careful. You might encounter trouble, and I do not like the risk. Your father will certainly agree. Let's hunt inside the bank—go through desks." Peter rubbed a hand over his eyes. "I never imagined one of my employees would stoop to this."

"But Peter, if one of the workers stole your signature, would they keep the document?"

"Maybe. We can't be sure either way."

"Let's search for a missing document or anything out of place."

He smiled. "You are determined."

She squeezed his arm. "I'd like to investigate together. And that gives me another idea. Perhaps I could come by the bank and poke about. I grew up there, and I might catch something amiss."

He pulled his watch out of his pocket and glanced at it. "We must hurry."

"I've tried to get information from McDonald, but he seldom shares anything. I also searched Sergeant Glass' room and found nothing. I've got to investigate the doctor's room as well. Do you think any of those three men could be guilty?"

"We can't rule that out yet." His face wore his get-the-facts expression. "But how would they get access to my signature?"

"I guess that's a problem. But I won't give the idea up until we rule them out."

They rounded the corner, and the small frame church stood before them. Friends who were gathering for church stood about outside or climbed the steps to the foyer. "I am sure we can solve this problem if we work together."

"Mary Beth, I think we'd best stop discussing—"

"Yes." She looked Peter in the eye. "We should talk later."

Chapter Sixteen

Sunday After Church

A humid breeze and blazing sunshine greeted Mary Beth as she and Peter passed through the heavy oak doors of the church. The buzz of voices mingled with laughter, which Mary Beth usually loved. She normally enjoyed conversing with friends, but today she wanted to be alone with Peter and talk. So far, she had failed to discuss what she knew about the lieutenant.

Ellen McCallie, the pastor's wife, came up to Mary Beth. "My husband told me your father is still very ill. How can I assist you?"

"I wish I knew what to ask for."

Ellen hugged her. "I've done a bit of nursing. Perhaps I could give you a morning off now and then."

"That would be wonderful." Guilt gnawed at her heart. This wonderful woman wanted to help her, and she wanted to brush her off to return home. "Peter would like assistance at the bank, but I cannot get away."

"Let me speak with Thomas," Ellen said. "Tomorrow morning works for me. My husband usually spends Monday with our little one."

Mary Beth's gaze met Peter's, and her heart skipped when he nodded in return. Maybe God did answer prayers. "Superb. Thanks."

Jane, one of her best friends, squeezed her arm. "Mary Beth, I'm so sorry I couldn't come to your tea. Papa thought I should remain home at least until the rumors died down. I hear your father is sick."

A pang radiated through her chest at the unwanted reminder. "Papa is quite ill."

"Our family prays for you daily." Jane nodded her head toward Peter. "I'm glad to see you together again."

Everything Jane said made Mary Beth want to cry, even though Jane didn't intend harshness. Crying in public terrified her. She grabbed Peter's arm.

He leaned close. "Do you want to stay and chat more?"

She shook her head.

"Then let's go." He steered her through the crowd and down the street until they rounded the corner.

She kept her gaze on the ground as her sniffles accelerated. "Thank you. Once I start to cry, I keep going. I feel silly sobbing in public."

He pulled her into his arms, and she relaxed, sobbing into his jacket. When she gained control again, she pulled away and tapped the damp spot. "Will this stain your jacket?"

Peter shrugged and offered her his handkerchief. "I leave that sort of problem for Billy. He's pretty good at fixing what I do. Do you feel better?"

"Yes, but Papa's going to need me. We should head back. With the war and Papa's illness, I am always uneasy. Why is all this happening at once?"

"I don't know. If I could alter circumstances, I would. I hate to see you cry."

Her head hurt, and all the fear she crushed inside her soul wanted to rush out. "Is God really love? Is he, Peter?"

"God must be sovereign and powerful. He must be."

The lines about his eyes and mouth worried her. "What?"

"May I be honest with you?"

Peter seemed a tower of strength. They hadn't had a serious talk for a while, and she longed for a peek inside his mind. "Please do."

"If I put aside the counterfeiting problem, I still must keep the bank solvent in the middle of war. That's not easy. I seek the Father's guidance daily."

A heaviness settled into her heart. All her concerns focused on herself, yet Peter carried burdens too. She patted his arm. "Have you spoken to Papa?"

"Indeed, I have, but you'll recall he had been unable to guide me at times." He took a deep breath. "Besides, your father has never operated a bank during a war."

She'd always respected her father's wisdom, but he was a man, and, therefore, limited. *To whom, then, will ye liken me, or shall I be equal? saith the Holy One.* The sentence rang true. Sure, she'd believed in God's power before, but now she understood. Neither her father nor Peter possessed all knowledge. If only God would answer prayer. Or perhaps he was teaching her. Her faith must rise to the challenge. "True. Give me some details so I can pray."

The tension in Peter's face melted into a smile. "The Confederacy seeks income to cover the heavy expenses of battle. Government officials request loans repeatedly, and their appeals grow more and more demanding."

"I assume you refuse."

"Indeed, I do. Plus, we are supposed to give farmers larger and larger loans based on their future crops. Successful farming depends on many factors. The crop must get enough rain and sun while avoiding insects or disease."

"Giving loans on future crops? What if the crop fails?"

"If they can't pay off those loans, banks go under. Each Confederate state allows banks to print paper money rather than using gold, which the banks loaned to the government. Then if a bank is unable to back their paper money with gold, they can go under too. Most banks right now are printing huge quantities because of inflation."

"And if everyone went to them with the dollars and demanded gold?"

He rolled his eyes. "If too many people come and demand their money back at once, bankers call that a run on the bank. Such an event would close the bank."

"What can we do?"

He took a deep breath. "I have to increase the amount of gold the bank owns. That means looking for business ventures that pay in gold or in commodities we can sell for gold. The banker I visited in Savannah offered me several opportunities."

"Let's find our counterfeiter."

Chandler Home

Peter sat on the edge of his father's executive chair in his library, where he once conducted family business. He focused on the Negro couple who stood before him. "Maud, I am now your employer. You and your husband may continue to live here. I shall alter the downstairs apartment to accommodate you both. Please present a written request within a month. I'll match the salary you received from Miss Roper."

"I commend your generosity, sir. Thank you." Billy took his wife's arm as if preparing to leave.

"I'm not finished. Even though I pay you, Maud, I request you return to Miss Roper. She will define your duties and set your hours."

"Oh, please, no. I could never return there and leave Billy. He is my husband now. The Bible says you should not separate a man from his wife. Folks in the South do that, but it's wrong. I feel sure your heart is not so wicked as to do that to us. Please, sir. I beg you."

She dropped to her knees.

"Maud, please get up. You will live here, but I'm sending you back as ... my spy."

She gasped. "Sir?"

"First, I want you to observe Lieutenant McDonald. He's a dangerous man—"

"See there, Billy. I told you so. I've a special sensitivity about these things, and you should listen to me."

"At this time, the lieutenant attempts to influence Mary Beth. I have warned her, but I still feel responsible for her wellbeing. Keep track of how much he comes and tell me if he becomes over bearing.

He could be part of a counterfeiting scheme that could sabotage our bank."

Maud rolled her eyes. "Land sakes! He is that dangerous? You just gave my stomach a turn like I have never had in years. I knowed the man had a bad streak, but it must be wider than the Mississippi."

Billy laid his finger on Maud's lips. "Let him speak, honey."

Maud looked at Peter. "Mr. Chandler, I am wishin' I could say I could be a spy, but I must be tellin' you I just be sayin' what I think. I have no bone that would sneak about and pretend. I jus' don't rightly know if I can do what ya ask."

Billy took her hand. "I know you can, Maud. Please promise."

"The lieutenant frightens me, and I—"

"Remember Mr. Chandler's kindness," Billy said.

Peter stood. "Watch out for Mary Beth, and I shall pay you extra to go back during the day."

She clamped her lips together and closed her eyes. "Very well. Only for a short time. I'm so afraid that my heart be wantin' to pop right outta my body, but I can live with this for a little while. Maybe."

Chapter Seventeen

Sunday Evening After Church

Hot air was stifling as Mary Beth and Peter stepped inside her house. The two of them had walked from church, and she longed for a glass of tea.

Maud descended the stairs into the foyer waving something in the air. "I be lookin' for you from the window upstairs. Praise the good Lord it not be dark yet. I be findin' one of them bills. Land sakes, I be thinkin' the master signed this at first. One look and I knowed you wanna see."

"Another counterfeit bill?" Mary Beth removed her hat and extended her hand. "Where did it come from?"

"See for yourself. I knewed you and Mr. Chandler would be wantin' it the moment you arrived. I been watching for you."

Mary Beth went to the oil lamp beside the sofa to examine the bill. "It says 'C&R Bank.' And Peter's signature is there. This one looks a bit different, though. Is that a smudge on the backside? I wish I had more light."

"I be likin' gold cause every one of them there paper-things look different. Even different sizes."

"You are correct. They vary in size, shape, and color depending on which state prints them. Notes produced by the Confederate government have another design." Peter took the bill. "Maud, where did you find this?"

"Tomorrow's the day for the butcher, so I be wantin' to see how much money we had in the household expense jar. It be sittin' in there."

"I've been through all our cash, and I failed see it," Mary Beth said. "I gave Bessie money for the jar a couple of days after Lieutenant McDonald brought Bell and Glass here. They paid me with a roll of bills rather than coins."

"I knowed it. That lieutenant is bad—very bad." Maud slapped her apron as if dusting off something unpleasant. "This is proof. I don't trust any of them soldiers. We must be a-callin' the sheriff."

Peter turned to Maud. "We must proceed with caution before we make serious accusations. Mary Beth, I'd like to talk to Bessie. It's possible she received this when someone gave her change."

"Yes, that's true. Maud, would you fetch Bessie?"

"Right away, ma'am." She darted from the room

Mary Beth collapsed on the sofa. "How could I have missed this?"

"You've been nursing your father. How could you monitor every transaction in the house? If we have it, then it's out of circulation."

"That doesn't make me feel better."

Bessie bustled in, wringing her hands. Her brow wore a deep crease. "Miss Roper, did you need me?"

Peter handed Bessie the dollar. "We're trying to solve a puzzle. Maud found this bill among the kitchen funds. Do you remember where it came from?"

Her eyes widened. "Did I do somethin' wrong?"

Mary Beth rushed over and put a hand on her shoulder. "No. We need information. Try to remember if someone gave you a dollar bill for change."

Bessie's thick lips trembled. "I don't like handlin' money, but I did as Miss Roper asked. I tried to give exact change. Her father always preferred coins, and if I gave correct change, I would not have to refuse the bills."

Peter took the dollar. "We aren't angry, but we do need to be certain no one gave you change."

"No one did."

"That's all. You may leave."

"Thank you, ma'am." She zipped out of the room.

Mary Beth sighed. "We still have no information. Nothing."

"Actually, we did learn something," Peter said. "This bill didn't come from anyone making deliveries here. Who has given you bills recently?"

She closed her eyes and probed her memory. "The grocer gave me an interest-bearing bond on one occasion. I still have that. The butcher gave me a bill, which I used for flour. I told you the three soldiers exchanged money among themselves before handing anything to me."

"Then any of the three could be guilty. Keep trying to remember," Peter said. "You are coming to the bank tomorrow, correct?"

"Yes, Ellen McCallie said she could sit with Papa in the morning. She can stay several hours."

"I shall say your father wants information on our financial position. That should give you time to talk to the employees and poke about."

"Do you want help searching through desks?"

"We can do that only when the bank is closed."

"Let's go now."

Peter nodded.

Thirty Minutes Later

The bank would be empty, but Mary Beth checked each room to make sure no one was there. Afterward, she went to Peter's office. "We are ready to search."

"Good. Let's begin with Mr. Riddle's desk."

"But he could never do such evil."

"We can't leave him out."

"Very well. You check his desk, and I shall go through Mrs. Phipps.'"

Mary Beth entered the office next door, and Peter followed. Neat stacks of papers and files covered the top of Mr. Riddle's desk. One pile had files of incoming letters. He'd fastened Peter's reply to each letter and put them in order by date. None had signatures. Most likely he had mailed the ones he'd signed. If anyone had complained about not getting an answer, Mary Beth would have suspected Mr. Riddle, but there was no such note.

Another stack contained bills the bank owed. He had circled the due date in pencil and organized them by date. Bills paid formed another stack. Records of client conversations sat in a file under the bills. Mr. Riddle had no problem with organization.

The drawers had pencils, India rubber erasers, pens, and an assortment of nibs. She also found blotting paper, a sheaf of white paper for letters, and bottles of ink. Two calendars sat in the bottom drawer: one for 1861, the other 1862. Mary Beth found personal items too: three handkerchiefs, a comb, and three letters from his sister. Nothing threw distrust on the secretary.

When she finished Mr. Riddle's work area, she didn't see Peter at the other desk, so she hurried downstairs. "Peter? Where are you?"

"I'm in Mr. Grant's office."

She scurried toward him. "Mr. Riddle's desk had a lot to sort through. Are you finding anything?"

"There's nothing unusual here. He keeps track of the warehouses where we store wheat and cotton that farmers pay loans with. Those books are here along with the main ledgers."

"I shall work on Mr. Sadler's office."

"I looked through his already. He keeps his scrupulously clean. Not even a speck of dust."

The serious look on Peter's face made her laugh. "We aren't searching for dust."

"No, but the man cleans up every night. It took five minutes."

"Let's check your desk next."

"Mine?"

"What a great place to hide something—right under the owner's nose." She dashed back up the stairs.

"Wait. I'm coming with you." His tread pounded rapidly up the stairs behind her, much like their childish races. She seldom won because her shorter legs couldn't compete. A giggle bubbled up while she dreamed up an appropriate taunt. She reached the top and waved her arms overhead. "I won."

He frowned. "We were racing? You did *not* play fair. I get to torture you."

She squealed and ran into his office, and he followed, laughing. Once again, she was a girl, and he was her playmate. How fun! Today she'd tease about being the winner. She dodged him and ran behind his chair.

Laughter felt good. She couldn't remember how long since they had acted silly together, and the joy on his face made him even more handsome.

They danced around the chair and desk until he finally grabbed her around the waist. He tickled her neck, and she collapsed giggling. Every time she almost pried herself away, he managed to reestablish his hold. Her stomach muscles ached. "I surrender."

He pulled his hand away from her neck. "You admit to cheating?"

She managed to catch her breath between gales of laughter. "Yes, but it was fun."

"Fun? Does that mean I haven't punished you enough?" He smirked, holding his hand aloft as if ready to throttle her.

"No, no. I'm repentant."

He ran his fingers through his rumpled hair. "What would our clients think?"

Mary Beth plopped a hand on her mouth and doubled over laughing. "We could tell them we've been doing this for years."

"And I'm sure that will make them trust their banker all the more."

Trust. That was exactly what she had in Peter, and she hoped he could trust her now as well.

11:30 p.m.

Darkness swathed the city, and the only sound came from the crickets. Peter wrapped his arm around Mary Beth's waist as they ambled toward her home. His pulse kept a brisker rhythm than his feet. Tonight the two of them enjoyed each other again. He and Mary Beth had always worked well together.

"We worked for over an hour," she said.

"And played." He pulled her closer. "Don't forget that part."

"I wish we'd discovered something useful."

"Don't get discouraged. We searched the desks without knowing exactly what we might find."

"But it had to be done. It was a starting place. There's much more to do. I enjoyed that—a lot."

"So did I. It was better than our childhood."

She turned toward him, the shadows hiding her face. "Papa's illness makes me appreciate people more, Peter. I treasure every moment now because I know life comes to an end."

Right now he appreciated her, and he wished this walk could last longer.

"When Mrs. McCallie sits with Papa tomorrow, I must see Mr. Sadler's work. Mrs. McCallie also offered me Friday morning."

He'd look forward to both days. But during office hours, they must act like adults. "We need an excuse."

"Excuse?" She stopped at her front porch.

Her father would expect him to protect her. "Yes. Everyone will want to know why you're coming, and one of those could be the culprit."

"Come up with one, Peter. I'm going in to check on Papa."

"Goodnight, Mary Beth." He dropped a kiss on her forehead before she hurried inside.

Chapter Eighteen

Monday Morning
May 19th

After a difficult night with her father, Mary Beth, accompanied by Elsie, hurried down Main Street to the bank. While she needed rest from constant nursing, she had hated to leave her father to Mrs. McCallie's care. If only she could possess the warm security of her past. Today, however, she must focus on unraveling issues with the bank, not her father's illness.

"Leave it be, chile," Elsie said. "Your papa's in God's hands."

"You are correct; I was worrying about Papa. I've always been Daddy's girl and done what I should. Now I feel God abandoned me, and I want to lash out in anger."

"Honey chile, without God, you ain't got hope," Elsie said. "You knowed that."

"Oh yes. I've heard trite phrases and admonitions and I've given a few of them myself. For some reason, I'm angry. I don't want to be an orphan at twenty-one."

"Tell God," Elsie said.

Mary Beth couldn't believe what she heard. But when she glanced at Elsie, her face had an I-told-you glare.

"Miss Roper?"

Mary Beth turned at the sound of the familiar voice. McDonald trotted behind her. His eyes held a hint of humor. In her mood, she wanted to slap him. With a chuckle, she wondered how he would like hearing what she just said to Elsie.

He pulled off his hat and bowed. "This is a pleasant surprise. I assumed you would be hard at the task of nursing your dear father."

"I have business at the bank."

"So the bird is set free from her cage. Spread your beautiful wings, my lovely one."

She managed to suppress a shudder. He probably found her attractive because her father owned the bank.

"I'm heading there also. Perhaps I can escort you."

"Certainly." She hated to say the words, but she'd do anything to solve their mystery. "Elsie, you may go on to your appointment."

Elsie shook her head. "No, ma'am. I be stayin'."

"But there's no need—"

"Your father would prefer it." Elsie's dark eyes smoldered.

Protesting would obviously be fruitless. When Elsie had that look, argument accomplished nothing. She did not understand Mary Beth's purpose in allowing McDonald's attention. Elsie was more protective, especially after Eddie.

"And I don't mind having two lovely ladies to escort." He fell into step beside her.

Mary Beth held back a groan. The lieutenant didn't respect Negro women.

The weather offered a useful topic. She'd see what else surfaced. "Don't you just love the sunshine?"

"You have been inside too long. Military maneuvers in this kind of sun and humidity can kill a man."

How interesting. He likes the comforts of life. "I assume you weren't a farmer before the war."

"Indeed not. Your companion would be great working in the sun, not gentleman or ladies."

"Now, Lieutenant, surely you believe the Bible. It teaches the value of hard work."

"Oh, yes, madam. But one can work inside. Negros were made for the grueling labor."

Slavery was a dangerous topic, especially with Elsie present. "If you had your choice, what would you like to do?"

"Oh, maybe banking, or perhaps running a business."

Her anger rose, but she must control herself. If he thought he might get the bank by marrying her, she would make him very unhappy. "But there are so many types of businesses. Which suits you best?"

"A plantation owner sounds attractive though, I have often thought of the law, or running for the legislature."

He likes to be in charge. Plantation owners made their living off slaves who worked the fields. She liked him less and less. "What office would you run for?"

"I'd start with the Senate. Ah, we've arrived." McDonald put one hand on the brass doorknob.

Elsie touched Mary Beth's arm. "Will Mr. Chandler be accompanying you home?"

"Yes, Elsie."

"There's no need to cut your appointment short. I have the time if Miss Roper doesn't mind."

"Peter will see me home." Mary Beth had enough of McDonald. If she wanted more information about this man, she'd have to ask others.

Mary Beth managed to slip inside the bank and upstairs without attracting attention. After the unwanted escort, she needed time to cool off. She stepped into Peter's office and collapsed into the chair by the door. Peter stood with his back to her studying a ledger. "Peter."

He turned at once, his face lighting up. "Good morning."

She walked toward him. He put his arms around her, and she placed her head on his shoulder.

"How's your father?" he whispered.

"He's very sick. I was up several times. When he coughs until he can hardly breath, it frightens me."

His arms tightened. "Is there anything I can do?"

"You're doing great, Peter." She pulled away and looked in his eyes. "I think I'd like to work in Papa's office. He gave me the key."

"Let's go in."

Mary Beth's pulse raced as she followed Peter inside. Papa's huge oak desk and her mother's ornate inkstand looked empty and sad.

"Nothing looks out of place. Start searching for supplies, and I shall fetch the ledger you had last time."

Memories filled her mind. She could see her father here working. Would he ever come here again?

She perched on the edge of her father's wooden chair and opened the top drawer. Here she found a selection of pens and pencils. The right-hand drawer contained a small painting of her mother on top of a stack of clean paper. Whoever dusted the room had broken the frame, and her father had never bought a new one. As she gazed into her mother's face, Mary Beth toyed with the gold necklace around her neck and then touched the replica in the painting. The gold cross disappeared before her birth. She guessed Mother must have been about eighteen when she sat for the painter.

The next drawer down held files and contained numerous contracts with her father's florid signature. The dates started in 1859 and went through the summer of 1861. The last date was August 1861—the month of his heart attack. Thoughts of the event made her heart as heavy as a boulder.

"Mary Beth?" Peter's voice drifted in before him. "What did you find?"

"I just thought of something. The person who forged your signature knew you ran the bank alone. A few months earlier, and he would have needed my father's signature."

"You're correct. I've only signed documents since your father's heart attack, five months ago. But who might have access? Surely there are fewer samples of my writing than your father's."

"That's what we have to learn. Did you bring the ledger?"

"Yes. Plus, I included the next one." He placed them on the desk.

"Thanks. I'll get to work." She chose the general ledger for 1862 and started reading. Early entries bore Mr. Sadler's handwriting. Another hand appeared about halfway through. The numbers were small and simple. Mrs. Phipps's elegance didn't extend to her penmanship.

"Mrs. Roper, do you have everything you need?"

Mrs. Phipps stood in front of the desk. Her intent gaze bored into Mary Beth's soul. What did this woman want? As the newest employee, she might have a hand in their troubles. "I'm *Miss* Roper. And I can find anything I need. Am I keeping you from your work?"

"Oh, no." Mrs. Phipps didn't leave. "I felt the need to apologize for what I did downstairs the first day you came. I had no idea."

"All is forgiven. You have such a nice, clear hand." She returned to the book before her. The whole point of this visit was to investigate, and she had to search without company.

"Compared to Mr. Sadler, my writing is miserable. He produces such lovely figures."

"Very ornate."

Angela leaned close and whispered, "Do you find him frightening?"

She stared at the woman's widened eyes and tight frown. Odd. The woman went from terse to confiding. "Frightening?"

"Yes. I've never seen someone so angry. He hates abolitionists." She placed a well-manicured hand on Mary Beth's arm, seemingly to protect her. "You have never seen him in that light? I warn you—be careful. Very careful."

"There you are, Mrs. Phipps." Suddenly, Mr. Riddle came in. "I looked everywhere for you."

"Miss Roper had questions. What do you need?"

"There are customer accounts." Mr. Riddle's face had that let's-get-the-job-done look he often wore. "They must be balanced to-day."

"I shall see to them now."

Bank employees seemed to have access to any part of the bank, anytime. When her father was still here, no one came upstairs except Mr. Riddle. Maybe the change in policy had something to do with bank problems.

Chapter Nineteen

Monday Evening
The Haskell Home

Peter entered the sitting room with Mary Beth and gazed with longing at the red velvet cushions of the settee. Several sumptuous chairs stood in a semi-circle around the sofa, seemingly in preparation for the evening. Mary Beth greeted her friends, and Peter nodded to each.

At the bank this morning, Mary Beth informed him she'd received an invitation for this evening. She asked Peter to accompany her. Of course, spending time with her delighted him, but he'd prefer a small dinner party to a game-night.

Mr. Haskell walked up. "Good evening, Mr. Chandler. We appreciate you coming tonight. We planned this party at the last minute for Mary Beth."

"That's very kind of you, sir." Peter shook hands with him. "Is there an occasion we celebrate?"

"Several weeks ago, Mary Beth planned a small tea party. With the disturbing rumors going around, I preferred Jane to stay home. Given Mr. Roper's illness, we felt we should make up for our daughter's absence that night."

"I understand your wife is sitting with Mr. Roper tonight," Peter said. That fact weighed in favor of his attendance at this party. If only he could endure whatever game they might devise.

"Indeed, she is. Jane is quite fond of Mary Beth. Because of Mr. Roper's illness, they've hardly seen each other this year. She's done a wonderful job caring for her father," Haskell said. "If anyone deserves this, she does."

"Everyone come and find a seat. We're going to play charades until dinner is served." Jane's older sister, Mrs. Black, clapped her hands. "Come now, don't be shy. This game will be fun."

Peter took Mary Beth's arm and guided her to the settee which captured his attention earlier.

"We're passing around a basket with slips of paper." Mrs. Black held up a small gray basket. "Each person takes one and passes to the next person. The word on the slip is your charade. Don't open them until I tell you to."

Mary Beth's eyes glittered with joy as she handed him the small basket. Anything that made her so happy was worth the effort.

"Now that everyone has their paper, my sister will choose the first person to present. You may not use words of any kind, only gestures to demonstrate. The rest of us must guess."

"Miss Roper," Jane said. "You go first."

"But I haven't looked at my paper," Mary Beth said.

"Once you stand before the circle, you may look." Mrs. Black motioned for her to come forward. "You will have a moment to think."

Mary Beth stood in front of the group and unfolded the tiny paper. A slight blush colored her cheeks. "I'm ready."

She knelt on the floor, adjusting her skirt about her, and she pretending to be holding something and stacking.

"Making candles," a young man said.

Mary Beth shook her head.

"You are laying bricks," Peter said.

"That's correct." Mary Beth glowed.

"Wonderful," Mrs. Black said. The others clapped.

"Yes," Jane agreed. "I had no idea. You are truly suited for one another."

Peter smiled.

The Same Night

Anna Chandler sighed with relief as the cab pulled up at her Chattanooga home. She had not expected the journey back to be so hard, but Ruth had behaved well. Billy should have retired for the night, and Peter would be going to bed soon. If she encountered him, she had prepared an explanation for her return.

She was glad to be home, but the late-night encounter she planned made her nerves jittery. If only she could complete her unpleasant task tonight. This escapade would be a secret she intended to take to her grave.

But first, she must be gracious to the cab driver who transported her here from the train depot. She handed him a large tip as he placed her luggage inside the foyer. "I appreciate being able to find transportation this late at night. I thought Chattanooga was too small for such service."

The man smiled. "Yes 'm. Soldiers come in at all hours."

As he pulled away, she turned to Ruth, who had slept during much of their evening journey. "Are you ready for your own bed?"

Ruth nodded.

"The house is dark, so everyone must be in bed. Let's be quiet."

"I promise."

She carried their baggage upstairs and tucked Ruth in bed.

Mothers took care of their children. Once Ruth had gone to sleep, she made preparations. Gustav Sadler would not ruin her husband's bank.

After dressing in black and donning soft shoes, she added her husband's pistol to her drawstring purse. As she headed for the city, she stayed in the shadows as much as possible, not that anyone would be out at this late hour.

Once at the bank, she reached into her bag and drew out her husband's spare key. From the lobby, she went straight back to the offices behind the teller counter. She was pleased to see the oil lamps burning in Gustav's office. A trip to his home would have more difficult. A few strides led her right to Sadler's office where he wrote in an open ledger.

"Gustav."

He gasped. "Mrs. Chandler? What are you doing here at this hour?"

"I could ask you the same." The shocked expression on his face pleased her.

"I have a job here, and I do it well."

"Do you?" Her mind went to the pistol in her bag. She couldn't use it, but it kept her from losing her determination. "Trying to undermine my son isn't wise. He owns fifty-one percent of the bank."

"Your *boy* doesn't know how to operate a bank. His expensive education is worth nothing. I've been here long enough to do all the jobs, without errors, mind you."

Anna yanked off her hat and cloak, dropping them at her feet. "I'm going to say this once more. Be sure you understand. Don't ever speak evil of Peter again. In fact, why not go ahead and resign? You've done enough harm already."

"Woman! You are a disgrace coming here late at night. Your son—Petey— is a babe. He will ruin the bank."

How dare he use her precious name for her baby? This man learned other's weak spots so he could use them. His twisted body reflected his warped soul. Her hand fingered the pistol in her bag. "Gustav A. Sadler."

"What?" He stepped backward.

"How dare you violate our trust so completely! Remember Andrew? My husband couldn't stop talking about the accuracy of your work."

"I respected your husband."

"You did? Then how could you treat our son so badly? Your wife was my dearest friend. I cried for days after she died. Your actions betray our family."

His shoulders drooped, and his hands hung loose.

She had him.

An Hour Later

Peter guided Mary Beth down the street, so glad to be alone with her at last. He was also thankful for the cool May breeze. The Haskell's home had been stuffy.

"Well, what did you think of the party, Peter?"

The outing wasn't the topic first in his thoughts. The two of them never had a chance to discuss her work on the ledgers today. An acquaintance met them as they left the bank and walked with the most of the way to the Haskell's. All night, he longed for a few seconds to whisper a quick question to her. "I'm overwhelmed and grateful. Jane is the best kind of friend."

"It was so good to see her. I don't think we've interacted at all since Papa's heart attack."

Footsteps sounded behind him, and he turned. "There's Miss Haskell."

Jane Haskell ran up, breathing hard. "I didn't know if I could catch you. Here's something you'll want."

Peter accepted a slip of paper from her, and his stomach hurt. "Is this what I think it is?"

Miss Haskell nodded. "It's a twenty-dollar bill issued from your bank. Mary Beth always told me about using gold rather than bills, and I worried this wasn't right."

Mary Beth groaned. "Not another one."

"I appreciate this. Where did you find it?"

"My father found it," Jane said. "I asked if I might share it with you. He agreed."

"Tell your father I shall call on him very soon."

She nodded and turned back.

"How dreadful." Mary Beth rubbed her temples.

"The Haskells are friends," Peter said. "I have a high opinion of him."

"I'm terribly fond of Jane." Mary Beth shivered.

"Here." He wrapped his jacket about her. "I shall look into this later. Right now, I really want to know what you learned at the bank today, if that meets with your approval. I wanted to ask all night."

"Of course." She smiled up into his face. "I wanted the same thing, but of course, I had to go to the party they threw for me."

"What did you uncover?"

"Well, Sadler is still changing the deposits."

"How much are the discrepancies?"

"Now they are a dollar or two less than the original deposit. Some pages he didn't make any changes, and I thought he had quit. Then suddenly he'd redo every deposit for the day."

"How sad."

"I feel that way too."

"Inheriting father's business placed a huge responsibility on me. I recognize my father's lifelong work, but on the other hand, I need to own it myself. Given all those facts, I prefer not to fire Mr. Sadler. It seems as if I'm undoing what my father chose."

Mary Beth laughed. "I know that wasn't meant to be funny, but I understand what you mean. I feel as if I have a priceless gift, and I fear defacing it in some way."

"Yes. That's true for me too. I tell myself a business is more like a living thing requiring continual effort. If things don't change, I'll have no choice to deal with Sadler."

They came to the Roper's picket fence, yet he didn't want this conversation to end.

Elsie came out onto the porch. "Mary Beth, you have a message from the McCallie's."

"Oh, thanks." She ran up the stairs to accept it. "Hmm. Mrs. McCallie will come tomorrow. Her husband needs her Friday, so I'll see you tomorrow."

Peter tipped his hat and smiled.

Chapter Twenty

Tuesday
May 20th

Mary Beth groaned when the alarm went off. During the night, her father had one severe coughing spell that brought up his last meal. She had changed his sheets at three in the morning. If she hadn't planned to go to the bank, she'd remain in bed. But an image of the first counterfeit bill passed through her mind, and she rose.

After throwing on her robe, she hurried to the kitchen. Bessie was there preparing coffee. "I'd like some warm water for washing up."

"Yes'm. I be doin' it for ya." Bessie handed her a cup. "You be needin' some coffee."

Mary Beth preferred tea, but coffee woke her. She ran upstairs to dress.

Voices came from the foyer, and Mary Beth dashed downstairs to find Mrs. McCallie had arrived.

"Mary Beth, I appreciate you allowing me to change my plans. How is your father this morning?"

She didn't want to say the words, but she must face the truth. "He's not doing well. You might prefer not to stay."

"Stuff and nonsense. It appears you need a break even more than yesterday. Be assured, this doesn't frighten me."

"You will alert me should anything—"

"But of course. Leave your father to me. Remember, even the timing of one's death is in the hands of God. Besides, I have cared for many sick and dying."

"I'm so grateful."

The pastor's wife beamed. "I brought some lotion I concocted to prevent bedsores, and I have some tea that improves appetite. Yesterday, I left both at home."

"I wish someone would invent a cure for anxiety."

The pastor's wife embraced her. "I've struggled with anxious thoughts so many times. For me, the pain of loss makes having faith harder. My dear aunt suffered so long before her death, even though the entire church prayed. It helps me to remember God sees from a different perspective."

"I don't understand what you mean."

"Whenever I am grieving, I think of Ruth and Naomi. What a terrible thing Naomi lost both her sons and her husband while she lived in Moab. When Naomi returned to Israel, she requested her friends call her 'bitter.'"

Bitter. Mary Beth turned the word about in her mind. She might not call herself bitter, but she was angry. The one emotion could produce the other, given enough time.

Mrs. McCallie continued, "Yet when the story ended, Ruth was in the genealogy of the Messiah. Sometimes God has a higher purpose for life than we could ever imagine."

A higher purpose. What a heavy thought requiring consideration!

Peter rubbed his eyes as he entered his foyer. His mother's hat and shawl hung on the coat tree. Funny. He didn't recall seeing her outerwear when he came home from Savannah. Besides, that's not where clothing belonged. Before retiring at night, Billy's job was to make sure the housemaid had returned clothing to the bedrooms. Maybe having Maud about made him less efficient. Plus, Peter was leaving for work earlier than usual and leaving without breakfast.

Upon waking this morning, he had a strong urge to hurry to Mary Beth's and escort her to the bank. He'd never done so before. Doubtless, his mother would pronounce him in love, but he wasn't ready to agree.

The night before played in his mind as he closed the distance to the Roper home. Mary Beth's face, her laugh, her smile brought pleasant visions on this cool morning.

At last on the Roper porch, Peter raised his hand to knock, but the door swung open. "Hello?"

Mary Beth and Elsie stood before him in the doorway. Mary Beth wore her hat and shawl. "Peter? Did you say you'd come for me?"

He shook his head. "No. I decided this morning I should accompany you."

"I be doin' some sewin'," Elsie said, turning back toward the house.

"And I'll be going with you." Mary Beth came onto the porch and linked her arm with his.

Peter couldn't hold back a smile as they walked toward the picket fence.

"Papa is much worse. I had to convince myself to leave him today."

This might be the reason he had felt the urge to escort Mary Beth. He sent a prayer of thanks to heaven. "I'm sorry."

"I thought about you as I cared for Papa. Everything you shared last night made me think. May I ask a question?"

Her mood was different today, but perhaps she was tired. Maybe they could talk about issues below the surface. Sometimes, when a person is not feeling rested, their guards come down. "Of course."

"How did you feel when Eddie flirted with me?"

The episode with Eddie wasn't his favorite topic, but she wanted honesty, so he'd try. "I found myself angry. He wanted to conquer you and list you among his possessions. You were a trophy he could display."

She huffed. "Why didn't you tell me?"

What a simple question without an easy answer. An analogy would help.

"Peter?"

"Give me a moment."

"I apologize. This topic should probably be off limits."

"Have you ever given your father medication that made him groggy?"

"Yes." She nodded. "I think I know what you're going to say."

"You've probably guessed it." He laughed, "One cannot reason with a groggy person."

"And I was groggy from Eddie's enchantment. Correct?"

"That's a good way to put it. I had experience with a family member who appeared honest, but once his mask was stripped off, he wasn't worthy of trust. I wanted to warn you about Eddie, but I knew you'd think my comments self-serving." He had no desire to hurt her, even though her actions had almost killed him.

"How can you forgive me?"

"I could see what was happening. You could not. Most men like that toss the woman aside when a bigger challenge comes along. I knew he would probably hurt you, but at that moment, you could not hear, even though I wanted the best for you."

"I learned my lesson. I hated being deceived. If I could go back and do it over—"

"You don't have to. I believe you have learned people are not always what they appear. People are sinners, and they act like it. Almost everyone has to face man's true nature at some point, if they grow up. Those that do not keep making the same mistake."

Mary Beth pressed her lips together.

Her silence worried him. She faced so much these days. "What is it?"

"My thoughts get tangled up with emotion. Mrs. McCallie and I had spoken before you arrived. She said things I must sort through, and so did you."

"When you get ready to voice those thoughts, I would like to listen."

"Hmm. I like the way you put that."

"You are growing."

A Few Moments Later

Peter shielded his eyes from the morning sun as he unlocked the bank door. The moment he gazed inside, a jumble of papers came into view, scattered around the clerk's desk. The mess had not been there when he left last night. "Mary Beth, wait here."

"Why?"

God help me. He stepped in front of her to protect her. "Something's terribly wrong."

"What? Records dumped on the floor? What—"

"Please stay here." The situation alarmed him, and he must gain control.

"Peter, you've got me worried." She grabbed his arm. "Have we been burglarized?"

"I won't know until I look." He tugged free, making sure his touch was gentle.

"Whatever happened impacts us both. I will inherit my father's share."

"Very well." He flung open the door and let her enter, but his stomach complained because he sensed something was wrong.

Mr. Sadler lay prone behind the desk, documents splayed all around him. His legs extended up the steps, while his chest and head lay on the floor beneath. His head was cocked at an unnatural angle. As if gasping for air, his mouth was open, his dark eyes glassy, and his features waxy and hard.

Mary Beth gasped and paled, creeping toward him.

The room spun as Peter stared. Death didn't belong here.

"This is terrible." She covered her mouth with a trembling hand. "Was he murdered?"

"Surely not. I suppose he dropped those when—" He couldn't finish the sentence. Reaching over, he put a protective arm around Mary Beth's waist. For several moments, time stopped while his head continued to spin. Peter's heart walloped against his ribs with each breath—in and out, while Sadler's chest didn't move.

Mary Beth gazed up at him. "What shall we do?"

A dream-like unreality clung to his mind. "We must summon a doctor, maybe Sheriff Campbell."

"Yes, I agree."

"It appears he fell, but maybe someone struck him. When he landed, everything in his hand scattered. From the position of his body—" His mouth was too dry to talk.

"Possibly." Mary Beth moved closer to Peter. "Maybe someone pushed him. I wish we could be sure. Something about this does not seem normal. But he had arthritis, and steps posed a challenge. It would be easy to stumble."

An image of Mr. Sadler's recent pro-slavery tirade appeared in Peter's mind. Plus, he'd been soliciting to gain control of the bank. He wasn't the best-liked employee. "Yes, his joints were stiff, so he might not look the same."

"His back was bent. Poor Uncle Sadler." Tears hovered on her bottom lashes.

"That is why we must call Dr. Smith. We are so fortunate he's the town doctor, not just the mayor. He knows us and yet can handle city business." He stepped forward and touched Sadler's face. "His skin is cool."

"But his hands were always cold. I hated it when his hand brushed mine, even as a child. Could someone else have been here? A burglar?"

Peter shook his head and raced for the front door. They would have no customers today. "This door was locked, and I want to keep it that way."

As he reached the door, Mr. Riddle walked in. "Thank goodness you are here. We're closed today. Stay at the door and don't let anyone in. When Mrs. Phipps comes, send her for Dr. Smith, immediately."

Mr. Riddle frowned and looked past Peter. Eyes bulging, he gasped. "What …?"

"Mary Beth and I found Mr. Sadler. He's dead."

"God protect us." His face turned pasty white. "That man … How? Why?"

Peter shook his head. "I don't have answers, but I need your help."

"I'll do whatever you require, sir. Mrs. Phipps will fetch the doctor. Perhaps you'd like the employees back later?"

"Yes. Arrange for them to come back in a couple of hours after we move the body." Peter touched his shoulder. "Thank you."

He hurried back to Mary Beth. Her face ashen, she leaned against the front desk, but her gaze focused on Mr. Sadler. Perhaps she could not stop looking. "Since this is a bank, we will need Sadler's key. A bank must always consider security. Come. Let's search Sadler's desk for clues and see if he left the door key there."

Peter held her hand as they tiptoed around the body to Sadler's frugal desk. His chair was scooted away from the desk. An oil lamp on his desk cast a narrow, flickering beam. Peter turned the knob, spreading light about the room. Sadler's pen lay beside an overturned inkbottle. The dark fluid had dried, forming a stain. "He'd never leave a mess like this. Wonder where the lid is?"

"It's here, on the floor by the desk. Maybe he dropped it."

"Perhaps, but the Sadler I know would never have stopped searching until he found it." He returned the top and continued examining the desk. An open account book displayed rows of neat figures and a tiny smudge at the bottom. "He was quite careful with ink. Did someone interrupt him?"

Mary Beth pulled open the top drawer, which contained two quill pens and a tiny knife.

"Sadler used that to sharpen quills." He opened the rest of the drawers. "No key here."

"What about his pockets?"

Peter clenched his teeth. "I think we'd best allow the doctor to examine the body first."

Mr. Riddle hurried in. His eyes snapped with energy. "Mr. Chandler, Dr. Smith is here."

Peter nodded and hurried toward the front of the bank where Dr. Smith knelt by the body. "Who found him?"

"Mary Beth and I."

His head popped up. "She's here?"

"Yes. Mrs. McCallie is with her father."

"I have been training her to care for her father. Your Mary Beth has the makings of a fine nurse. But there's nothing we can do for this man."

"We worried about the position of the body." Peter pressed his lips together. Something prevented him from saying the word— *murder*. Nevertheless, the word would not leave his mind. Sadler annoyed everyone, but enough for this? Surely not. His father had trusted each employee except Mrs. Phipps, who was new. She seemed too timid to do something so bold. "Something about him … does not look natural."

Dr. Smith stood and met his gaze. "After death, the muscles become flaccid for a time, but the muscles in his face and arms are hardening."

"Does that account for his position?" Peter's heart wobbled about in his chest.

"It could. Allow me to finish my post mortem. In many cases, death reverses disfigurement from arthritis, unless contractures are present."

"Do you know the cause of death? I am worried we should call the police."

"It seems likely to be a fall. Sadler's health was not robust. He could have had a heart attack, which would have caused him to topple down the stairs."

Mary Beth appeared and slipped her hand in the crook of Peter's arm. "Dr. Smith, did you find a key in his pocket?"

"I haven't searched his clothing."

Peter turned to her. "Thank you for reminding me. The bank was locked when we arrived. We've examined his desk but didn't find it. For security reasons, we'd like all the keys in our possession."

The doctor nodded. "I shall check once I remove the clothing."

"You will let me know." Peter stuffed his hands in his pocket. Now that he had the situation under control, he could not stop the tremor.

Mary Beth gasped. She stood upstairs in Peter's office. The door to her father's office stood ajar. Yesterday when she left, she'd closed and locked the door. Given the audit she conducted, the material must be safe, even from bank employees.

Peter came in behind her. "I need you to—"

She latched onto his arm. "Did you open Papa's office this morning?"

He shook his head. "I have not been up here yet, with all the chaos downstairs."

"Nor have I, yet the door stands open."

He groaned and shook his head. "This situation grows darker still. Mr. Riddle has the only other key. I shall ask him. Right now, I need you to gather the papers around Sadler so they can remove the body. We'll talk about the contents later. When you finish, come and search your father's office for anything out of place."

Mary Beth bustled down the steps. The papers lay all over the steps and even covered part of Sadler's trunk. But what was this? Something thick and soft. A clump of cotton lay underneath the papers.

Chapter Twenty-One

An Hour Later

Mary Beth sank into a chair in Peter's office, trying to recover from the shock. The doctor and his assistant had covered Mr. Sadler and carried him out. Images of Uncle Sadler playing with her as a child and offering her treats came to her mind.

She must wear a black dress to the funeral, and she shuddered as she realized she might wear the frock more than once. Her eyes burned, and she sniffled. Peter pulled her into his arms as tears broke from her rigid control. He held her for twenty minutes or so as cried. She pulled away, hoping she had not ruined Peter's coat. "My childhood is disappearing. Uncle Sadler was such an important part of it."

Peter looked pale also. "I remember him, but I spent most of my time here with my father. Sadler was a distant figure, though someone I admired for his abilities."

"Now he's gone. And my father may soon be gone also." She was so tired.

"Things change, even if we do not want them to. I certainly did not want this."

Mary Beth returned to the chair in front of Peter's desk. She longed for life to return to normal again, even if doing so meant ignoring reality. She had learned Uncle Sadler wasn't the man she recalled.

"Now we have no suspect."

"What shall we do?"

"Plan our new strategy." He grabbed a sheet of paper. "We will see what the doctor says about the cause of death. But first, we must speak with the other employees. How long can you stay?"

She believed she'd been here for hours, but the clock didn't agree. "Mrs. McCallie will stay until noon. It's only ten."

"Okay, here is one problem." He pulled up a chair to sit in front of her. "I need someone to take Sadler's place."

The very thought of work made her weary. "Your mother can do it."

Peter's eyes widened. "My mother?"

"She once told me she and your father ran the bank together until my father came."

"I thought of you."

"Yes, I can do Mr. Sadler's job. Let me think about how I can rearrange my chores at home. With Papa ill—"

He put his hand to his forehead. "Your father. How could I forget?"

Mary Beth wished she could forget. The circle of those close to her was shrinking.

Peter rubbed a hand over his eyes. Somehow he could not absorb the tragic events, yet he saw everything—Sadler's vacant gaze, his ice-cold skin, and the hearse that carried him away. Could this sudden death be a nightmare? The bank was slipping away as impossible circumstances mounted. Selling the building and assets might be his only option. He almost gagged. His father would have been very displeased.

No. He had to gather information and work through the problems, no matter how difficult. He would pay any cost to hang onto the bank. His father's business was his legacy.

The bank employees waited downstairs to talk to him.

Peter glanced at Mary Beth, who sat across from him. "Do you want to be here as I interview each of the employees? I think I can finish before you need to go home."

"Yes. I asked Mr. Riddle to send a message to Mrs. McCallie. I shall stay as long as I can. Perhaps I could ask a few questions and take notes."

"Good. I want you here."

Mr. Riddle appeared in the doorway. "An official at the train depot said your mother arrived.

"What?" He thought of the hat and shawl on the coat tree. "She's in Savannah."

"See for yourself." Riddle shrugged and handed him the paper. "This note said she's there."

Peter needed to get over the shock and solve problems. That's what a man did. "Is Mr. Grant here?"

"Yes, he is here. Shall I send him up?"

"No. Ask him to go to the depot and take Mother home." Everything he tried to accomplish crashed about him.

"I'm sorry," Mary Beth said.

He took her hand in both of his, hoping she didn't think him a failure.

Riddle came in again. "Mr. Grant is on his way there."

Peter scooted closer to the desk. "Thank you. Come in and shut the door."

"Me?" Mr. Riddle said. "You want to interview me also?"

"Yes," Mary Beth and Peter said together.

Peter looked at her. "We think alike."

Mary Beth pulled an empty chair next to hers and turned to the secretary. "You may sit here."

Mr. Riddle took the seat. "What do you need to know?"

Peter spoke up. "Did you notice anything unusual in Mr. Sadler's behavior?"

Mr. Riddle groaned. "He is ... was never an easy man. You are aware of his perfectionist tendencies and his temper. Recently he took me aside and suggested he was best qualified to run the bank. Plus, his relationship with Mrs. Phipps became more explosive."

Mary Beth started writing. "Explosive? In what way?"

"He did not like Angela Phipps," Mr. Riddle said. "The lady is new and asked numerous questions. He hated giving her detailed explanations, but he also lost his temper when she made errors in the books."

"Did he dislike all questions, or just hers?" Peter asked. He glanced toward Mary Beth, and she nodded. They both wondered why Sadler didn't want anyone observing him.

"He never responded like that to me," Mr. Riddle said. "Miss Phipps set him off. He said he didn't like having a woman underfoot."

Mary Beth said, "He must have been very different than my memories."

"He was quite fond of you," Mr. Riddle said. "But the tension between Sadler and Mrs. Phipps continued to escalate."

"Did anything happen out of the ordinary yesterday?" Peter asked.

"No. Mr. Sadler said his books were off by a few cents or so, and he would work late."

Mary Beth spoke up, "Was that typical?"

"No, but it did happen from time to time."

"What about you?" Peter asked. "How did you get along with Sadler?"

"The man respected me. We never had a problem."

"Can you think of any reason why someone would want him dead?" Peter asked.

Mr. Riddle frowned and lowered his voice. "Do you suspect something?"

Peter looked down. "It's a question I'd like you to answer."

"We all found him unpleasant, even before the war, but no one here would wish him dead," Riddle said.

"That's all for now."

Mr. Riddle bounded from his chair. As he opened the door, Mr. Grant paced in the hallway outside.

Peter rose. "What's your news, Grant?"

Mr. Grant said, "It was a mistake. Your mother wasn't there."

Peter sighed and motioned for Grant to come into the office. "What a relief."

"No, sir. She came home last night. The ticket clerk found a note someone wrote when she arrived."

"I saw her hat and shawl on the coat tree this morning when I left for work. Now I know why." He was unhappy she came home right away. Later today, he'd have a chat she might find uncomfortable.

"I'm glad she arrived safely, sir," Mr. Grant said.

"I appreciate your help. If you will sit down, I have some questions." Peter jotted himself a couple notes.

"I find Mr. Sadler's death very unsettling because it brings back my past. My wife became distraught after we lost our baby. The doctor put her on laudanum. She fell and died," Grant said.

"Of course," Mary Beth said. "We understand."

"Mr. Grant, we want to know if Mr. Sadler's behavior seemed odd or unusual the past few weeks," Peter said.

"Nothing about that man was normal."

Mary Beth leaned closer. "What do you mean?"

Mr. Grant wiped his face with a handkerchief and shoved the cloth back in his pocket. "As the bank manager, I worked around Sadler, not with him. He would not allow me to see his ledgers. I checked his work after he left for the night."

"This was recent?" Peter said.

Grant shrugged. "He was less volatile in the past. Since the war started, he's been angrier. I had to avoid any talk of the city or government, and we never talked about trivial matters. He was not friendly."

"Were you aware that he planned to stay late last night?" Peter asked.

"Yes." He sighed. "I wanted to stay until he left, but my mother is ill. A friend from church helps with her care, but I could not stay all night."

"Did Sadler often stay overnight?" Mary Beth asked.

"Sometimes he did." He shook his head. "I discouraged that and often stayed in the bank until he left. I never trusted him completely."

God help me. Peter's heart plummeted to his ankles. How disturbing. He assumed his employees could be trusted. Now he must make considerable changes. Perhaps Mr. Roper had some thoughts on why they hired such a dangerous man.

Mary Beth sat across from him with her mouth open, seemingly surprised.

He inhaled as he chose and discarded words. "Please explain yourself. I'd like to know why you never let me know about this."

Mr. Grant nodded. "Your father had a unique ability to handle people."

Peter gritted his teeth. If only he could have learned from his father, this might never have happened. "So I've been told."

"Sadler respected him, and I believe he earned your father's confidence," Mr. Grant said. "After Mr. Chandler's death and Mr. Roper's absence, Sadler retreated into himself. He seemed uneasy. I wondered if he concealed something."

"What did he do to make you believe that? Peter asked.

"Here's an example. One day last week, I stepped into the file room to fetch him, and he startled and dropped the armful of ledgers."

"What was he doing?" Mary Beth said.

"I cannot be sure. Nothing was out of place. Maybe he had just walked in himself."

"How often did this happen?" Peter said.

Mr. Grant shrugged. "Two or three times since Mr. Roper's illness. I decided I would mention his behavior to you today."

Mary Beth leaned back in her chair and groaned as the bank manager left the room. Who was this man she called Uncle Sadler? Mr. Grant's description sounded so different from the man she adored. How could he claim such affection for her and rob the bank at the same time?

"Peter, all this horrifies me. This man played with me when I was young, and I adored him. Now I know he undermined your position here and embezzled money."

He rubbed the back of his neck. "I'm upset too, but we must remember Sadler faced judgment the moment he died."

She pictured her childhood friend before God's throne. "Surely he received a hearty scolding. Or much worse."

Peter took her hand and squeezed.

She put her other hand atop his. "What will Papa say?"

"I cannot imagine." He stood. "I shall interview Mrs. Phipps at her desk."

"Why can't she come here?"

"I prefer not to upset her. She should be calmer at her desk."

Angela's attractive face popped into her mind. Because Peter was so gracious to women, he didn't catch their tactics. "We know she disliked Sadler, so why should his death unsettle her?"

Peter headed for the office door. "It happens that way sometimes."

She grabbed her paper and scurried to follow. "I am coming too. You need me to see through her."

"See through her? Do you think she's hiding something too?"

"I won't know until after we talk to her. Maybe this spat between them was for appearances. She could be in league with Sadler."

Moments Later

Mary Beth pulled up a chair by Peter's, in front of Angela Phipps's desk. Angela sniffled and twisted a lace handkerchief, but Mary Beth noted the lady's dry face.

"I appreciate your willingness to talk with us. Are you calm enough to answer a few questions?" Peter asked.

"Yes."

"Please describe your relationship with Mr. Sadler," Peter asked.

"Beastly. Revolting. I almost resigned last week to get away from him."

Mary Beth leaned closer while gazing into her face, looking for clues to her motives. She might be glad Sadler was dead or maybe even played a part in his demise. "We need details," Mary Beth said.

"He scolded me continuously."

"Could you be more specific? What actions caused him to treat you badly?"

Peter nodded. "I agree with Miss Roper. Please share one incident."

"Yesterday evening, I picked up a ledger, and he yelled at me to put the book down immediately. I protested since Mr. Riddle had asked for that particular one, but he yelled louder."

"Do you recall the exact ledger?" Peter asked.

She rubbed her forehead. "I think it was the general ledger from this month."

"Excellent." Mary Beth said. She exchanged a look with Peter. She would examine the ledger for clues to Sadler's behavior.

Chapter Twenty-Two

Tuesday Afternoon
May 20th

Peter locked the bank door and glanced around the darkened bank, now empty of employees. One unpleasant job remained now, and he must tackle that before considering future changes. He trudged up to his office, where Mary Beth awaited him.

She came toward him as he entered. "You look exhausted."

He collapsed into his chair. "I am, and it's too early in the day for fatigue."

"I prepared a cup of tea, adding a heaping teaspoon of sugar, just the way you like it." She set a cup before him.

"Perfect! Thanks."

"What should we do next?"

Mary Beth used the word 'we' and he loved the sound. So far his record as a banker did not look great. His schooling never dealt with such a crisis, and he had missed the internship with his father. "I must take the bad news to Mr. Sadler's mother."

"I shall accompany you."

"Do you have time?"

"I do. Maud will sit with Father if Mrs. McCallie must leave."

Her decision surprised him. "Are you sure? Your father's care takes a toll on you, and I wouldn't be offended if you went home."

"I am quite sure."

The task seemed less distasteful now. She couldn't imagine how grateful he was. He rose and offered her his hand. "Let's go."

She walked past his hand and embraced him.

Sadler's Home

With Mary Beth at his side, Peter waited in the dimly lit sitting room. What a difficult job he faced. He prayed for the right words. If only his mouth wasn't so dry. The heavily draped and dollied suffocated him.

At last, the door opened, and chubby Mrs. Sadler hobbled in, supported by a crutch. She wore a black crepe dress and a shawl over her stout body.

Peter stood. "Good morning, ma'am. May I help you to your chair?"

"Morning." A gnarled hand waved him away. "Please sit. I always need a moment."

He eased back onto the sofa, and Mary Beth slipped her hand into his. As much as he disliked Mr. Sadler, he never wanted to announce his demise.

"So you're the young Mr. Chandler. Such a shame to lose your father suddenly like you did. But then, I'm surprised those deadly steam engines don't kill more."

"Yes, Mrs. Sadler. I'm here with Mary Beth Roper, Mr. Roper's only child."

"Humph. She should be home caring for her father, not gallivanting about town. But these young ones never listen to reason. My son's wife was like that too. I called her obstinate, but Gustav married her anyway."

Peter swallowed hard and glanced over at Mary Beth, who blushed. "I've come to speak to you about your son."

"He's at the bank. That's all he cares about, you know. I seldom see him these days, and when I do, he talks bank business."

Mary Beth spoke up, "Has he talked about the bank recently?"

"Counterfeit money."

Peter exchanged a glance with Mary Beth. "What did he say, exactly?"

"He said counterfeit bills would destroy all the banks in the Confederacy. All the Sadlers have strong opinions, you know."

"Did he mention our bank, Mrs. Sadler?" Peter hoped they were about to get something tangible.

"I told you what he talked about. Why did you come to see me?"

"I'm sorry, Mrs. Sadler. There's been an accident." Peter forced his lips to move. "We found your son this morning. It appears he fell, and … he's …"

"What? What's wrong?"

"I'm very sorry." He must not be abrupt.

"I cannot hear you, young man." Loose skin on her face trembled.

"He must have fallen down the stairs. We found him ... he's dead. An accident."

"No! That can't be true. No!" She screamed, and her dark eyes disappeared in folds of wobbly skin.

Mary Beth jumped up and patted her back. "Mrs. Sadler, we are so sorry."

The door sprang open, and slender lady ran in. "Now, Mrs. Sadler. You've worked yourself up."

Mrs. Sadler continued to scream.

"I'm available to help in any way I can," Peter said.

"I'm Miss Fitch, her nurse-companion and niece." She held Mrs. Sadler's hand. "I assume you brought unpleasant news."

"Yes, ma'am. We're from the bank. This morning when we arrived at the bank, we found her son. He'd had an accident."

Miss Fitch gasped, "Oh no. Is Gustav okay?"

"No. I'm sorry to say he passed away." Peter shook his head. "We assume he had an accident. I'm so sorry."

Mrs. Sadler shoved Mary Beth away and screamed louder.

"There, there, Mrs. Sadler." She turned to Mary Beth and Peter. "Aunt has a neurological disease and loses control. All we can do is sedate her. Can you stay with her while I get her medicine?"

Peter went to her chair and placed a hand on her shoulder. "Mrs. Sadler, I'm terribly sorry."

Mary Beth came close and took her hand.

Mrs. Sadler shook off Mary Beth's grip and cried louder.

Moments later, Miss Fitch returned with the butler. She carried a tray with a glass syringe. "We have something to relax you, Auntie. Be very still."

Mrs. Sadler thrashed and screeched more. The nurse turned to Peter and Mary Beth. "You see how difficult she is."

Peter hated to see her suffer. Mrs. Sadler was upset, but a mother should be sad when her son died. "Is this necessary?"

"Perhaps some warm tea might help," Mary Beth offered.

Miss Fitch deposited her tray on the coffee table and nodded toward the butler "Not for Auntie."

The butler pinned Mrs. Sadler down while Miss Fitch injected the medicine.

Mrs. Sadler swatted at her, but Miss Fitch jumped out of the way.

"She's unreasonable when one of her spells come. We cannot control her." She turned to the butler. "You can put her to bed now."

Peter scowled at the harshness.

The old lady went limp, and her head lolled off to the side. The butler threw her over his shoulder and left the room.

Mary Beth trembled as the door closed behind Miss Fitch. "I had never met the family until today, but people said Mrs. Sadler threw fits. That was dreadful."

He pulled her close. "I'm so glad you came. The task was daunting, but I was not alone."

She nodded. How she enjoyed working with Peter. "Maybe we can learn something from her niece. Sadler must have known about the counterfeit money."

"Or printed the bills himself," Peter suggested.

Mary Beth released a sigh. She was hesitant to believe him to be so evil.

Miss Fitch returned. She dropped onto the chair Mrs. Sadler had vacated. "Now, I want the whole story. What happened to Cousin Gustav?"

"We arrived at the bank just before eight-thirty," Peter said.

"You and your wife?"

Wife? Mary Beth's heart leaped to her throat. Maybe someday she'd have the title.

"This is Miss Roper. She assists her father with bookkeeping."

"I apologize, Miss Roper," Miss Fitch said. "I assume you called the doctor?"

"Yes. Dr. Smith suggested a heart attack."

Mary Beth spoke up. "Mr. Sadler—that is, his body lay at the foot of the stairs, quite cold."

"We believe he fell." Peter glanced at Mary Beth. The intensity of his gaze seemingly begged her to say no more.

"We were wondering when he came home last night," Peter said.

"He didn't."

Mary Beth was startled. "Not at all?"

"No. I managed to keep that from Aunt Sadler. As you saw, she's quite volatile. These fits are frequent."

Peter nodded. "Did he say anything about working late?"

"Cousin seldom told me his plans, and I doubt he would tell his mother either."

"I thought they were close." Mary Beth glanced at Peter for his reaction. "He always carried her homemade candy in his pocket."

"He was fond of eating them," Miss Fitch said. "I enjoy them too."

"Had Mr. Sadler done or said anything you thought unusual?"

"No." Miss Fitch stuck out her lips. "If he talked, he spoke of the bank. He was so proud of the business. He had the sort of pride an owner might have."

"Did he ever mention counterfeiting?" Mary Beth asked.

"Indeed. He worried it would destroy all the Southern banks."

"I noticed Mrs. Sadler walked with a cane," Mary Beth said, thinking of Sadler's ornate handwriting. "Does she have arthritis as well?"

"It's a crippling form of arthritis, and yes, Gustav had it too."

Peter stood and motioned to Mary Beth. "We'd best return to the bank. Please convey our deepest condolences to Mrs. Sadler. And let me know if we can assist her in any way."

"Thank you for coming." Miss Fitch accompanied them to the door. "I've had employers who wouldn't make such calls."

Peter frowned. "We are so sorry to bear such dreadful news."

As Miss Fitch ushered them out, Mary Beth wished they could see Mr. Sadler's room. Perhaps she could devise a plan to gain access.

Later Tuesday

Nothing seemed real. Peter settled into his plush office chair and rubbed his hands together. The crisp paper in his hand possessed all the characteristics of reality. But for some reason, the words he read and the message conveyed didn't seem genuine. How things had changed in such a short time.

> At noon tomorrow, employees of C&R Bank will
> gather at the Methodist church and sit on the front

rows with family members for the funeral of Mr. Gustav Sadler. Because of her son's devotion to his job, Mrs. Sadler requested Mr. Peter Chandler say a few words about Mr. Sadler's work. Reverend Fairfax, Sadler's pastor, will conduct the funeral. The graveside service will be at Citizen's Cemetery. Church members will provide dinner at the Sadler home for the family.

With his pen poised in the air, he delved into the past for a commendation. Gustav A. Sadler faced God with his transgressions. At the funeral, Peter would speak of him with kindness. Taking a deep breath, he touched the pen to paper and wrote of the man's reliability. Peter wouldn't, however, state an opinion on Sadler's recent activities.

Tuesday Afternoon

Mary Beth dropped on her bed to sort her thoughts. What a day! Now that she was home from the bank and alone, she wanted to sob, but she couldn't. Except for those moments in Peter's office, she had held tears back all day. Losing someone so close to her family ached, especially when she learned that he was not the friendly man she grew up loving. Maybe he changed as he grew older. She preferred to remember him as Uncle Sadler, the man who carried candy in his pocket.

Her mind went to the visit with Sadler's mother. How interesting Sadler talked about counterfeiting all the time. They needed more information about what he said and even what he knew. He made no secret of his desire to run the bank. Maybe he considered counterfeiting a means to gain control of the bank, a sort of bribe

… "Unless you promote me to bank manager, I'll flood the city with these phony bills."

When Peter walked her home, they agreed to plan. She had so many ideas on what they could do next. Sadler's sudden death brought an emotional upheaval that made the day seem long and exhausting. She was grateful for the reprieve sleep brought

Thirty Minutes Later
The Chandler Sitting Room

Peter's heart pounded as he marched into the sitting room where his mother sat in her usual chair, knitting. This conversation might not be pleasant. His mother's hasty return bothered him. If the Union chose to attack, Mother and Ruth might wish they had stayed put.

"Peter." She dropped her work and came to hug him. "You look incredibly tired."

"When did you arrive?"

"Last night. You were in bed. The house was dark."

He'd been at the Haskell's home at the time. "I got a message from the depot saying you came back today."

"No. Yesterday. The man who manages the ticket desk knew your father. He worried about how I would get my bags home, but I found a way."

"I left early this morning and didn't see you."

"No. We chose to sleep late." She grinned. "And I slept quite well in my own bed."

"I'm concerned about your decision to return. Why did you come back early?"

"I finally got Ruth to talk. She cried and explained she had a friend here who needed her. It's probably a girl at church who is about her age. I pointed her out to Ruth when we had the dinner on the grounds. You recall I tried to talk you out of going."

"I do." He sighed. "Where's Ruth now?"

"She's in her room, reading." His mother sat down and picked up her knitting.

"What will you do if the Union invades Chattanooga?"

"I shall go to your Uncle David's home in Soddy Daisy. It's closer, and we can return when hostilities end. Besides, David's wife and I have always enjoyed one another."

He still felt responsible for his family's safety, but he didn't object to her plan. If an invasion is threatened, he would do everything he could to get them to safety. They were too precious to lose.

He sank onto the sofa, exhausted. "Mary Beth and I found Mr. Sadler dead. The doctor said he fell down the stairs."

"What?" His mother blanched. "I just saw him ..."

"What was that?" Peter asked.

Billy knocked. "Mrs. Chandler, you have a message."

"Thank you." She tore the note open and gasped, "I must leave right away."

Moments Later
Sadler Sitting Room

Anna sank onto the sofa beside Sara Fitch and threw an arm about her shoulder. Only one candle burned, making the stuffy room more depressing that usual. "I'm so terribly sorry about your cousin. I just found out, or I would have been here earlier to help. It seems rumors circulate much more quickly than news."

"We had to keep Mrs. Sadler sedated most of the day after your son brought the news, so I made the funeral arrangements myself. I feel strange being an employee and a family member too."

Anna patting Sara's back. The poor lady would need to talk.

"I think the shock bothered me the most." She fiddled with her sleeve. "Gustav was fine one day and dead the next. Since he's Mrs. Sadler's only child, I do not know what will happen to Mrs. Sadler. Am I to continue as her caregiver?"

"Knowing Gustav, I suspect he had something in his will about that. If you like, I shall go with you to speak to the lawyer tomorrow."

"Oh, would you? What a relief to have someone there with me. I hate to say it, but Mrs. Sadler will be so dreary about all this. She appears to be strong, but she's not."

"You've taken such good care of her." Anna pulled Sara closer. "If I didn't know, I would think she was your mother."

"Oh, how kind." Miss Fitch sniffled. "I don't think Gustav noticed. At least, he never said so."

"He was never happy after Elizabeth died. She was a lovely person and one of my dearest friends."

"Do you think Sadler became bitter?"

Anna nodded, as she thought of their last conversation. "Yes. In her absence, he hardened. He blamed the doctor for Elizabeth's death."

"That reminds me. I should have told you right away. I found documents among Gustav's things. He wanted the Chandler family to have his diary." Miss Fitch stood. "Let's look in his room."

Anna nodded. She loved being useful. "Yes. I am glad to help."

Sara Fitch led the way to a large bedroom upstairs. The room had a huge chest, a desk, bookcase, and a bed. "He kept his clothes there. Papers would be in the desk."

The simple desk had a set of three drawers down each side. She chose the right side and opened the top drawer. A pile of books resided within. When opened, Anna found his elaborate handwriting. "I think we found it. The first page is dated January 1862."

"Oh, he had several." Miss Fitch ran her finger along the titles on the bookcase and held up one. "This one is from 1861."

"Thank you. That's a lot to read." Perhaps now she could understand what motivated that complex man. "I shall start reading these."

Chapter Twenty-Three

Wednesday
May 21st
Sadler's Funeral

Mary Beth could not recall a church service so dreary. The sky outside was overcast, so no sunshine streamed through the tiny windows. A candelabrum stood on each side of the pulpit, but the tinge of light the candles spread seemed to call attention to the shadows. She and Peter sat down front with the family, and the huge coffin seemed bigger than Sadler when he was alive.

She almost sobbed as the organ played "Amazing Grace." Yesterday, her father asked to have that song played at his funeral. If only she could survive this one without breaking down.

Dressed in his black clerical garb, the minister walked to the rustic pulpit. A solemn look on his face, he cleared his throat. "Let us pray."

Mary Beth only half-listened to his prayer. Memories—a lifetime of them—burst like lightning, into her soul. Uncle Sadler bouncing her on his knees, offering her candy. Sadler and her father reviewing bank records. Again, her eyes burned with tears, but she sucked in the grief. She wouldn't cry in public for this man. Anger, confusion, and grief all mingled in her heart.

She and Peter planned to consult a day or so after the funeral. They needed to know if Sadler died from a fall, or if he was pushed. His death might also have something to do with his embezzling or the counterfeiting. They knew he didn't have many friends and thought he might have worked alone, but they were not sure.

"The family has asked Mr. Chandler to speak." The pastor stepped aside.

The muscles in Peter's jaw tightened, and he buttoned his coat as he rose.

Peter spread his notes before him on the podium and whispered a prayer. He did not mind the crowd or the yawning silence of the moment. However, he despised the behavior Sadler displayed toward the end of his life.

He tugged at his collar. "Mr. Sadler worked with my late father and Mr. James Roper for seventeen years. His loyalty and commitment during those years call for the highest praise. Despite the disease that twisted his body, Mr. Sadler's beautiful hand graced our financial records with artistry and excellence. Children never minded a visit to C&R Bank because Uncle Sadler offered them homemade candy from his coat pocket." Peter inhaled and paused to blot the dampness from his brow. The mixture of truth and sorrow tortured his soul. His gaze landed on Mary Beth, who was teary-eyed.

"Today C&R Bank offers our deepest sympathies to Mrs. Sadler and her entire family. May God comfort you and sustain you in this monumental loss."

Peter stepped away from the pulpit. He hadn't compromised his honesty, yet his heart bore a tinge of guilt. The bank employees all knew Sadler's many faults.

He sat down by Mary Beth once again. Their eyes met, and he sensed she understood. He took her hand, and she squeezed.

Evening
May 21st

The letter stayed in Peter's hand. He couldn't put the missive down, nor could he read the words. He tried again and again. His father couldn't be dead. No!

Peter wept as he staggered down the streets of London. A horse-drawn carriage sped toward him, almost running him down. Everything had gone wrong. A stained-glass window from Westminster Cathedral appeared blazing with light, but the image turned to blood.

Right now, he must find passage home, but the trains had been canceled. As he turned, a multitude of train cars passed him, speeding down the tracks. Suddenly they derailed. Screams filled the air and blood soaked the ground.

Peter bolted upright in bed, awakened by the sound of his scream. Sweat soaked his body. He hated the dream. At least, the nightmare came less often now. If only he'd come home when he graduated, rather than touring the continent as his father insisted.

Memories flooded his mind. The telegram had followed Peter all over Europe from hotel to hotel, but when the message finally arrived, he had to wait for passage on a ship. He arrived in Chattanooga months after the funeral. All he could do was gaze at the grave. If only he could have interned alongside his father.

As a child, Peter craved his father's approval. He didn't know how to manage bank employees, and he failed to prevent embezzling, so he still couldn't please his father.

Thursday Morning
May 22nd

Mary Beth turned to her dresser and opened the top drawer. After pushing aside her clothes, she picked up the manila folder from the bank. Peter had asked her to search for clues among the stack of papers as well as the ledger Angela Phipps pointed out. He promised to come by for lunch so he would be here soon. After she had settled herself on her bed, she flipped open the folder and read.

Mr. Christopher Field
Bay Street Bank
Savannah, Georgia
April 16, 1862
Mr. Peter Chandler
C&R Bank
Chattanooga, Tennessee

Mr. Chandler,

Let me say again that it was a distinct pleasure to see you in Savannah recently. I am saddened by the death of your father and by the illness of Mr. James Roper. However, I believe you will prove a competent banker, and I am pleased to work with you.

I have had some time to investigate several fraudulent proposals from bond salesmen and blockade runners. None of them match the proposals we discussed. Do take steps to protect yourself and your bank from such men.

On the other hand, I have some legitimate investment proposals for you to consider. DeShay Bank of New Orleans has a prospectus, which involves moving goods through Mexico to reach European vendors. Banking personnel from Richmond have agreed to take part in this one. It promises a good return in gold, which is what you prefer.

I have also taken the liberty to include several other proposals. These are companies with which I have dealings. I believe they are both sound and honest.

Yours sincerely,
Christopher Field

She flipped through the rest of the pages listing various companies and figures. All the papers must have come from Mr. Field. She remembered when he visited about four years ago. Peter had been in college, but both his father and hers had spent time with him.

Why would Mr. Sadler have these? Mr. Riddle handled Peter's correspondence, not Sadler.

She pulled out the ledger and studied the entries. Nothing appeared out of the ordinary, despite Angela's comment. Perhaps she lied or misconstrued the facts. Mary Beth disliked hysterical women and wearied of clues leading nowhere.

Peter might have lunch at the Roper's home every day. The best part was not the food. Mary Beth wore her hair down, and her eyes glistened. They had finished their meal, and Maud moved the dishes. With the funeral behind them, they could consult on their investigations.

"Peter, what did you think of the funeral?"

"I was uncomfortable praising him since I knew about his embezzling, but I reminded myself he worked hard for many years."

She touched his arm. "Your eulogy was true—when our fathers ran the bank. You didn't need to speak of recent history. His family needs to grieve."

In light of the circumstances, her praise pleased him. "Thank you."

"I've been through these papers but found no clues about Sadler." She held out a manila folder. "This appears to be your mail."

He flipped through the material. "What was Sadler doing with my mail?" He disliked the man more than ever.

"That worries me too. He never handled the mail when I worked there. In fact, all the upstairs offices were off limits to everyone except Mr. Riddle, and our fathers."

"Interesting." Obviously, Peter needed to change a few things because of recent events. "Tell me more."

"I say I worked, but that's when Papa taught me bookkeeping. You were away at college. I recorded ledgers in Papa's office right alongside him. Mr. Riddle shuttled messages between employees and our fathers."

"And I assume Mr. Riddle worked in the office across the hall from our father's."

"Right. And no one ever went into their offices unless Mr. Riddle accompanied them. Sadler and Grant stayed downstairs. And of course, Mr. Strong. He's in the military now."

He rubbed his chin. "When did Gustav Sadler start going upstairs?"

She shook her head. "Mr. Riddle would know. Papa never discussed how he managed his employees."

"This could be the key. I suspect Mr. Sadler took advantage of me since I'm new to the bank. We need to control access to information." An idea popped into his head. "Let's compare how much we know about Sadler. Did he have friends?"

Mary Beth shrugged. "I heard him speak about his mother, but he never mentioned friends."

He'd never seen Sadler outside the bank, and the man never spoke of his personal affairs. "I wonder why he never married."

"Papa said he did, but that his wife died in a tragic way. I do not know the story."

"I never heard that."

"But there's something more I must tell you." She leaned closer.

"More?" He enjoyed unraveling puzzles with her. "Tell me, please."

"Yes. When I gathered the papers around Sadler's body, I found a clump of cotton underneath. It's in my room. I was going to ask you if I should show it to the sheriff."

"Cotton?" The image didn't fit a murder scene. How could cotton have anything to do with Sadler's death?

"Dr. Smith told me some doctors sprinkle cotton with anesthetic when they put someone under for surgery."

"We use cotton for plenty of other things besides medicine. Our office chairs are stuffed with cotton, and it's also used for insulation. What made you think of the medical uses?"

"It resembled cotton I've seen in Dr. Smith's black bag. I've watched him work, and it's unlikely he'd drop something like that."

"We had several medical men in the bank to retrieve the body. They shuffled things about as they put him on the stretcher. Perhaps the stretcher had cotton padding that spilled out. One of them must have dropped it."

She pressed her lips together and shook her head. "Maybe, but I don't think so. Besides, how did it get under the scattered papers?"

Peter was unsettled by the edge in her voice. "I hoped the material scattered on the steps might give us more information on his activities."

"But Peter, I believe I should speak with Miss Fitch again. She might talk more freely if I'm alone with her. It's so interesting that Sadler talked about counterfeiting."

"It seems an unlikely coincidence. He must have known something."

"His mother's condition is so sad. I believe we should talk with Dr. Milo Smith. Since he's both mayor and town doctor. We should share our concerns."

"I agree. I plan on visiting with Mr. Haskell about the counterfeit bill he found."

"I'd love to go with you."

"In this case, I believe I should go alone since he will be more likely to talk."

"Very well, but if you visit anyone else, I am going." She moved closer. "I want you to know you are not alone in this."

His pulse sped up as he ran a finger along her jaw. "Mary Beth, you couldn't possibly know how much I appreciate you."

She tipped her head to the left. "Really?"

"I'm quite serious." Despite his efforts, his voice grew husky. He moved in and pressed his lips to hers, tasting her sweetness.

**Friday Afternoon
May 23rd**

Peter sat on the red settee he'd shared with Mary Beth a few days earlier. Today he was much more comfortable conducting business than he was playing parlor games. Mr. Haskell sat across from him in a velvet wing chair. "I appreciate your willingness to help us, sir."

"Jane said you were quite relieved to receive the bill."

"Indeed, I was. First, let me thank you for informing me right away. Not many people fully understand our position on the new legal tender. I'd like to know the circumstances around obtaining the bill inscribed with C&R Bank."

"This turned up as I prepared a deposit for my law firm. We don't receive money every day, so income might remain in our safe a day or two, maybe more, depending on how busy we are."

"I understand." Following up on this might get messy. "Do you have a list of clients you currently see?"

"I do." Haskell pulled a folded paper from his coat pocket. "My secretary compiled a list of clients, and the amount they paid. I asked him to make you a copy."

Peter took the paper and saw three names. "Mrs. White paid five dollars."

"I know she paid in coin because I walked past as she gave that amount to my secretary."

"And this Private Jones?"

"He was passing through the city and came with a legal question, which I researched and dispatched for him. Afterward, he returned to his regiment. He paid with legal tender."

"What about Sergeant Fuller?"

"Fuller and his family live in Cleveland, Tennessee. I drew up his will. Should you need to speak with him, my secretary can obtain his address."

"Is he currently serving in the military?"

"I believe he is, yes." Haskell narrowed his eyes. "I understand his wife delivered their first child, and his commanding officer gave him a brief holiday."

"Thank you, sir."

Haskell put a hand on Peter's shoulder. "I'm available to help at any time, should you need legal protection."

Legal protection. Such an offer did not ease Peter's mind.

Monday
May 26th

Eating breakfast with Peter might be hazardous. Mary Beth tried to hold the hot tea in her mouth and not laugh, but she couldn't. A full-fledged, belly laugh took over her body. She grabbed her cloth napkin to cover her face as tea splattered everywhere.

Mary Beth sat with Peter at the dining table with tea and biscuits.

Peter sprang to his feet and patted her back. "How are you?"

"I'm fine now; I had just taken a large sip of tea as you requested raw carrots. I … just couldn't swallow for laughing."

"From now on, I shall time my jokes better."

"Thanks. That's less hazardous." She refilled her cup and added milk and sugar.

"Look at all that sugar," Peter quipped. "Perhaps that explains your sweetness."

"The rising price made me cut back, but I have disliked the process of reducing my intake."

"I shall have to increase your salary, and I can if you take Sadler's job."

"Hmm. I had not thought of the income. That makes it even more attractive. Our budget is tight."

"Then I shall campaign hard for you to take the job. Having you in the bank will provide another pair of eyes too. You might catch irregularities I would not see."

"Wonderful!" She gave him a flirty grin. "I've apparently convinced you how clever I am."

"My lack of experience makes me quite humble. I admit I need you." He buttered his biscuit. "Have you had any ideas about what we should do next?"

"Besides chatting with Miss Fitch again, I think we should visit clients together."

"Great idea." Peter's eyes gleamed. "Mr. Haskell gave me a name to visit in Cleveland. He believes a soldier on leave passed the bill Jane gave us."

"Excuse me." Maud stepped in. "Dr. Milo Smith is here."

The doctor walked in, carrying his black bag.

"Dr. Smith, please have a seat." Mary Beth rose and offered a chair. "Would you care for breakfast?"

"No, thank you. I've breakfasted already. I understood you needed me. Billy said something about Peter's headache."

He certainly did not act sick, but men responded to illness in different ways. Her father often hid his ailments. "Peter, are you feeling poorly?"

He rubbed his forehead. "I do have a mild headache again, but it will pass. I suspect it's from concern over our situation. Today we require your expertise as mayor, rather than as a doctor."

Dr. Smith chose a chair. "How can I help?"

"We'd like to know about counterfeiting. What procedures do you have in place to enforce the law?" Peter asked.

The doctor scooted forward in the chair. "Our manpower is being used to protect the citizens because we could be invaded from the North anytime. I know many cities report such problems. Inflation increases the need for cash, and bogus bills flood the market. Counterfeiters can hire engravers to copy bills, which takes considerable expertise."

"That's what I expected." Peter sighed.

"I understand C&R doesn't issue currency," Smith said. "Is that still the case?"

"I've never authorized it." Peter crossed his arms. "However, a number of bills have shown up with my signature."

"Forgery." Smith frowned. "How did you uncover this corruption?"

"I found counterfeit bills among some of the new paper money at my home," Mary Beth said as she stirred her tea. "But we have an additional problem. While auditing accounts at the bank, I discovered Sadler was embezzling money.".

"We had suspected he might be involved in counterfeiting, but we have no proof," Peter said. "We all believed him to be honest. Why all the sudden?"

"You have an interesting problem." Dr. Smith pursed his lips. "Sadler's mother is ill, and her condition has considerably worsened over the last year, increasing his expenses."

"That makes sense," Peter said. "However, I never thought he would stoop to embezzling."

"Nor did I." Mary Beth said.

"I shall send Sheriff Campbell to visit the bank. Maybe he can turn up something on the counterfeiting. In light of the hostilities going on around us, we have few men to enforce the law."

"We are also concerned ..." She found it hard to say the word.

"Yes." Smith raised his brows.

"Could Sadler's death be ... *murder?*" The word left a nasty taste in her mouth.

The room became very quiet. Mary Beth kept her gaze focused on Dr. Smith.

The doctor paused seemingly considering the question. "The condition of the body is consistent with a fall. I cannot, however, account for the cause of that fall."

"You're saying ..."

Peter spoke up. "Someone could have pushed him."

"Yes." Smith rose and ambled toward the door. "As for the embezzling, we no longer have anyone to prosecute, unless the two crimes are connected in some way."

Mary Beth intended to learn if someone else worked with Sadler.

Chapter Twenty-Four

Mid-Morning
May 27th

Peter was dwarfed by Sheriff Campbell, who towered over him. His muscular physique, badge, and weapon seemed out of place amid the bank's paperwork. Perhaps the man could unearth something for them if he could be discreet.

"Dr. Smith sent me." The sheriff's deep voice matched his intimidating figure. "I believe you have come concerns?"

Peter motioned to a chair. "Indeed."

"Much obliged. I prefer to stand."

Thankful to be a law-abiding citizen, Peter got to his feet. "We had an employee embezzling money. While investigating, we didn't report him since we presumed he might be involved in other illegal activities. Unfortunately, he died rather suddenly, and we have no other suspects."

"Hmm. What other activities?"

"Counterfeiting."

"You'd best give me his name."

"Gustav A. Sadler. He lived east of the city."

"How long did Mr. Sadler work here?"

The length of his employment seemed irrelevant considering the circumstances, but Peter paused to consider. "My father hired him in 1845."

"Any problems with Mr. Sadler over those years?"

"For the last month or so, he annoyed fellow employees whom he disliked or who disagreed with his politics. I'm unaware of his earlier work habits since I've been here only since my father died."

"I believe you have a partner."

Sheriff Campbell wrote nothing down, and that bothered Peter. "Yes, but Mr. Roper is very close to death. His daughter will inherit his portion of the bank."

"I'll see him today too. Did Sadler have an account here?"

"No."

"Really?" Campbell lifted his heavy black brows. "I find that interesting."

"Some people don't trust banks."

"They don't usually work for them, though."

Peter cringed. How could he have missed that? "We have made no formal report about the counterfeiting since we don't want our customers to lose confidence in us. I would prefer you keep that information to yourself."

"You do want inquiries made, correct?"

Peter paused before replying. This man was clever, but would he give away the bank's troubles? Finding the counterfeiter to save the bank might make customers lose confidence and leave. Peter hated the quandary. He paused to send a prayer heavenward. "I do."

"The man committed a crime. I'll do my job."

**Thursday Afternoon
May 29th**

A pang of guilt burned inside Mary Beth as her gaze roamed over the girls who sat in her sitting room. What kind of friend would use people like this? While seeing her friends delighted her, she could not relax and enjoy this chat. Not when there was so much at stake. Instead of gossip and fashion, she must steer the conversation toward money, and the transition must be natural since Peter didn't want a large number of people knowing about the bills. Ida and Jane knew and offered their assistance. She searched for a perfect opening

"Mother gave a reception for the officers last week. I met the most handsome soldier. He's a second lieutenant." Fanny's brown eyes danced. "I hope he stays in the city long enough for us to get acquainted."

Sophie raised an eyebrow. "I daresay you'll unearth another man if he leaves. They seem to fall all over you."

Ida spoke up, "How can you be sure he has no sweetheart awaiting him at home?"

"I could make him forget," Fanny said, adjusting a curl.

"That might be harder than you think." Sophie examined her nails, then buffed them on her skirt. "My brother joined his regiment last week. He writes of target practice and missing his girl-friend."

"I would detest a woman parading herself before my fiancé." Jane glared at Fanny. "My intended, Lieutenant Frost, serves in Richmond. He avoids dances so he can stay away from outrageous flirts. Some girls flutter their eyes at anyone in a uniform."

"I know this officer has no fiancé." She giggled. "I asked right away."

A covert look passed between Jane and Ida.

Mary Beth suppressed a sigh. Had she previously enjoyed these conversations? Or had her friends changed? "Sophie, I do love how the dark green dress brings out the color in your eyes. Is it new?"

Sophie pressed her lips together. "I wore this dress in Amelia's wedding eight months ago. Mama and I altered it this week. How I wish we could plan my summer wardrobe."

"Wardrobe. If I get one new dress this summer, I shall celebrate," Jane said.

Fanny fiddled with her almost-straight bangs. "Mother promised me three new dresses. I'm sure the one I wore to the reception brought admiring glances. The lieutenant commented on it."

"How can your mother afford to entertain? Have you noticed the price of sugar?" Ida devoured the last bite of her cake. "My mother says she'll have to stop buying it should the price continue to rise."

"You can safely reduce the amount of sugar in your pastries." Jane commented. "And I've learned to drink tea or coffee without sugar."

"But a lovely rich cake is a great way to snare a handsome young officer." Fanny spread her arms wide. "I spoke to Mother about having a dance for the soldiers in town. How fun that would be."

"In wartime, not many people can afford lavish entertaining." Jane threw a withering look toward Fanny.

Mary Beth's heart flip-flopped. She'd never loved Jane and Ida more. They brought up the subject for her. "With the rising prices, more and more people are now using bills the banks are printing."

Ida spooned a generous portion of sugar into her teacup. "Yes, but my father prefers gold coins."

Fanny flashed a toothy smile. "My parent believes in using the newly printed bills. It shows we support the infant nation. All those good-looking officers need our backing."

With a clatter, Ida put down her cup, and Jane stabbed a slice of cake, a vicious look in her eyes.

Mary Beth pulled several bills from her pocket. She motioned the girls to gather around. "My father never traded in any medium other than gold. But a few days ago, I noticed some very pretty bills. I'm fascinated with their beautiful engravings. These bills resemble the ones I am interested in. Notice how the fancy lines surround the number. The ones I saw had curvy oval lines. So attractive."

"My father won't allow me to have paper money," Ida said. "He said they're worthless."

Jane pulled two bills from her drawstring purse. "Look at these."

Mary Beth wanted to snatch them, but instead, she leaned over for a peek. "The engraving on this one is nice too, but not quite the same. See how the lines make a circle? They weren't evenly spaced."

"Look. These have an oval around the number." Fanny handed three bills to her.

Mary Beth shook her head. "That's close, but not quite the same. I need to draw it."

"I have a pencil." Jane reached into her bag.

"Here's some paper." Sophie offered a scrap.

"Thanks." Mary Beth closed her eyes to visualize first and then sketched. If only she could copy a bill, but Peter had them both. "It's oval, but it has a little flourish at the top and bottom."

"Hmm." Sophie frowned. "The engraver must have been quite experienced. That's difficult to do. My uncle's a printer, and I've watched him etch plates. He owns a shop in New Orleans."

"If any of you see one of those bills, please bring it to me," Mary Beth said, hoping her face looked appealing, yet innocent. "I'd like to collect them. It's fine artwork and may be valuable someday."

Fanny's eyes widened. "Would you exchange the bills?"

"Of course." She hoped they didn't find many.

Thursday Evening
May 29th
Chandler Home

Anna was shocked when Billy announced Sheriff Campbell. She couldn't imagine what he could want. Her quiet trip to the bank on Monday came to mind, but she'd taken precautions. So whatever the sheriff had in mind must not relate to that event. She stood as he strode in. The rigidity of his facial muscles, however, made her heart thump harder. "Hello, Sheriff, what can I do for you?"

"I have a few questions for you about Mr. Sadler."

"Indeed." His serious manner worried her. She returned to her chair, hoping she looked calm. "Make yourself comfortable."

"I'd rather stand. I always think more clearly on my feet."

She stiffened. This interview might be challenging. "Very well."

"Why did you go to the bank on Monday night?"

No! The words seared Anna's soul. She could tell the truth, but leave out what was inconvenient. "I arrived here from Atlanta after dark. Afterward, I arranged transportation for Ruth and me to come home."

"My witness saw you unlock and enter the bank after closing time."

She searched for words as her heart beat faster. Denying her actions might place her in danger, especially since her son had found Gustav Sadler's body. How foolish. Andrew would have been irate. "I do not recall the exact time."

"You have not answered my question."

"I know." She never intended to tell anyone. Maybe Peter would never hear. "Sadler was undermining my son. He … spoke with Mr. Grant and told him … Peter was not qualified to run the bank. Sadler wanted Peter's job."

"Was Sadler there when you arrived?"

"Yes." Tears ran unbidden down her cheeks. "I … scolded him. His wife … was a dear friend of mine. I reminded him of how Andrew trusted him and spoke highly of his abilities. He was betraying our family by attempting to run the bank."

"What else did you do?"

She blotted her tears, wishing they would stop. "I hoped to shake him up so he would support Peter, or at least stop interfering."

"What other activities did he engage in?"

Anna was horrified. Was he ready to accuse her of a crime? "I don't understand the question."

"You didn't know he was embezzling money?"

She gasped, "No!"

"Your son found him dead the next morning." Campbell scratched his forehead. "Can you explain how he died?"

"No. He was meek, but alive when I left." She shuddered.

"Mrs. Chandler, right now, you are a suspect in Sadler's death and subject to arrest. Please do not leave town."

She nodded. Her whole body trembled.

He left the room without comment, and Peter walked in. His face was white.

She bit her lip. "Peter, did you hear?"

"Yes, Mother. I did. You had better tell me everything because it sounds like the sheriff thinks you murdered Sadler."

She stopped weeping with a gulp. "I did n-not hurt Mr. Sadler."

"Why? Did you come home to scold Mr. Sadler, or did you come home because of Ruth?"

"Both. I … take care of my … family."

Now she couldn't leave for Soddy Daisy if the Union attacked.

Early Friday Morning
May 30th

Mary Beth listened for her father as she checked her appearance in the mirror. This morning she was going to the bank again, and such thoughts made her head ache. His condition had weakened in the last few days. Now she valued every moment in his presence.

"What is this?" Sergeant Glass shouted.

She detoured toward his room rather than her father's room. Maud cowered just inside the sergeant's door, and a breakfast tray, complete with eggs, sausage, and coffee sat on the table by his bed. Mary Beth groaned. She'd never promised the soldiers such service.

"I don't like sausage." Glass struck the tray, splattering the food on the hardwood floor. "Why can't you do what you are told?"

Heat exploded inside Mary Beth. "Just a moment, Maud. Sergeant, what do you think you are doing?"

"Your slave didn't follow my orders." The sergeant's eyes blazed.

She longed to choke him, but his chest looked large and hard. Doubtless, he could overcome her. "She's not supposed to follow *your* orders."

He stood with his legs spread, arms crossed. "Even if I don't get what I want?"

"None of us receive what we truly long for in life. War brings scarcity. Look at the food you wasted." She gestured to the floor.

He puffed out his chest. "I paid you good money—lots of it."

"Not enough to squander. You may leave. Now."

"You will hear more about this." He stomped out.

"That man a bein' nasty." Maud shook her head

Mary Beth crumpled into an armchair, her head spinning. She was angry enough to scold someone or break dishes. Neither would solve her problem. "Maud, come. I shall help you clean this up."

"I'll be a thankin' you, ma'am. I be a fearin' of him comin' ta blows."

Mary Beth used the napkin to pick up the splattered food. "The sergeant struck you while I wasn't here?'"

Maud's unusual silence and downward gaze told her story.

The cad—striking a woman. Such discourtesy must not happen—would not happen—in her house. If she'd known what he was like, she never would have agreed to let him stay. She'd speak to Dr. Bell as soon as she could. "How despicable. I promise I will not allow that in my home again."

"I'm mighty proud you be standin' up to him," Maud said.

She was learning determination.

Early Friday Morning
Chandler Home

After Sheriff Campbell's visit, yesterday, Anna had not left the house. Today, she huddled in her bedroom, terrified of being arrested. She pulled aside her heavy brocade draperies and peered out to the road. How embarrassing that her scheme to support Peter had gone amiss. Knowing Peter heard the conversation made her nauseated. She could never harm anyone, but proving her innocence would not be easy.

Once more she pondered what to do. The sheriff believed someone murdered Sadler, and Anna needed to find out who it was to clear her name. She couldn't think of anyone she could turn too. Ira Campbell, the sheriff's wife, was her best friend, but she could not confide in her. Peter had far too much on his mind, besides, her goal was to protect him. Mary Beth might be an ally, if not for the stress of her father's illness.

She glanced around the room, and her gaze landed on Sadler's diary, which she'd deposited on her bedside table. Perhaps perusing Sadler's words would give her insight into his motives for embezzling and reveal who might want him dead.

Chapter Twenty-Five

Mid-Morning
May 30th

Mary Beth was already at work in her father's office when Peter arrived. He allowed himself to gaze at her beauty a moment. This morning he wanted to consult with her, and that surprised him. As a child, she was giggly and fun, especially if she followed his directions for play. However, her thoughtful evaluation of Miss Fitch had impressed him, and he looked forward to her insights.

She looked up and met his gaze. "Good morning, Peter. Do you need me?"

Yes. *Need* was a better word than want to describe how he felt about her, perhaps in several ways. "There are several things we must do. Soon."

"I like that word, 'we.'" She put down her pencil. "Would you like me to choose which one we do first?"

"No." Some lighthearted fun would suit him right now, release the tension. Besides, he loved to tease her. "As for making decisions, I remember when you couldn't decide which dress for your doll to wear."

She rolled her eyes and smirked. "Will you ever forget that?"

"I finally had to pick one for you, and even then, you worried."

"The dress my doll wore set the mood for our adventure." She leaned back in her chair.

"Mood?" He guffawed. "We planned to chase a pretend pirate ship. How on earth would the doll's dress matter?"

"Men. You have no appreciation for color."

"Actually, that's not true." He'd inject a dose of honesty, hoping she would be pleased. "I find the blush on your cheeks quite attractive."

"Peter. Is that the reason you would pester me until I got mad? You liked to make my face red?"

"Partly, I suppose." He'd keep an eye on her face. Her response might tell him something. "But you're awfully pretty either way."

"Alright, at least you admitted your sin." She held out her hand for him to come in. "I loved the compliment. Now I want to know what's on your mind. I'm quite capable of making decisions now. I am no longer a girl."

He grinned. "I thought we could do a couple of interviews today, but I wanted to share something with you."

"Pull up a chair. I'm ready to listen."

He sat right beside her. "Sheriff Campbell visited Mother last night. She's a suspect in Sadler's death."

Mary Beth's mouth fell open.

"I don't believe she's guilty," Peter said. "She returned from Savannah to stop Mr. Sadler from interfering with my job. Grant told her Sadler was talking behind my back."

"Your mother is so gracious. I cannot see her standing up to anyone like that."

"She can." He chuckled as he recalled the time she scolded him for annoying his sister. "A mother bear will protect its young."

"I can understand *that* tendency."

"Now we must unravel this mess, not only to save the bank but to clear Mother's name."

Friday Afternoon
May 30th
Cleveland, Tennessee

Mary Beth was glad her work wasn't time sensitive since this trip and interview would take most of the day. Their train had just pulled into the Cleveland depot, and she accepted Peter's hand onto the platform. Bright sunshine and warm temperatures greeted them as the stepped outside.

Peter consulted a map he pulled from his coat pocket. "Mr. Grant's family came from here, and he was kind enough to draw me a map. We'll have to walk several blocks."

"Perfect. I'll enjoy the walk."

"Mr. Haskell reported he found this bill when he went through his safe last week. He believes the soldier who passed the bill was on furlough. His name was Sergeant Ben Fuller."

They turned down several side streets, and the houses grew smaller and more rustic. "From the looks of the neighborhood around here, the family won't have a butler. Should a lady come to the door, I think I should ask the questions," Mary Beth said.

Peter nodded. "On the other hand, if the soldier answers, I shall do all the talking. I understand the couple just had a new baby."

"In that case, I hope he's innocent."

"According to this map, that's the house."

A shack of rough lumber stood several feet from the road. The single brick step up to the ramshackle porch didn't look inviting. "I would hardly call that a house."

"Someone lives there. Let's go." He took her arm.

Mary Beth almost stumbled on the uneven ground, and a skinny brown dog raced toward them, barking. He bared his teeth, and she hung back.

"Boxer, come 'ere!" The dog slunk back to the porch. A slender lady with a small paunch came to the door. "Are you a looking for someone?"

Mary Beth moved closer. "Are you Mrs. Fuller?"

"I am. What's your business?"

"I'm Mary Beth Roper from Chattanooga, and this is Mr. Chandler from C&R Bank."

The lady stepped back. "We don't owe nothing to nobody."

"You misunderstand. We would like to talk to your husband."

"He's done gone."

The sight of the woman in such circumstances made Mary Beth want to cry. She exchanged a look with Peter. "Will he return soon?"

Mrs. Fuller sniffled. "Not if them Yankees shoot 'em down. An' me with a brand new young 'un."

"How old is your baby?" Mary Beth offered a genuine smile. She wanted to do something for this poor lady.

"Three weeks today." She gave a tentative smile. "He keeps me busy."

"May I see him?"

She nodded and inched to the edge of the porch, turning the baby to face them.

Mary Beth admired the baby's pretty round face, but his ragged shirt made her sad. "Oh, he's so beautiful. You must be so proud."

"I am." She looked down at him and smiled. "He's the spittin' image of his daddy."

"I understand your husband was in Chattanooga last week."

Mrs. Fuller frowned. "Is there some kinda trouble?"

"No, ma'am. Nothing like that. He saw a lawyer named Mr. Haskell and paid with one of the new paper dollars. We're checking to see how well the new currency is accepted. We wondered if you knew where he obtained that dollar."

"I feared you was asking for money, and we ain't got much of that." She chuckled. "I knowed he visited his pal at that there army hospital and got repaid for a loan. I fussed at Ben when he made that loan. I surely thought we'd never see that there cash again. But I'm willin' to admit when I'm wrong, and I was."

"When did your husband return to his regiment?"

"Yesterday. I miss 'im already."

"Thank you for your time, Mrs. Fuller. I wish you and your husband well."

Peter held her hand as they headed back to the road.

Mrs. Fuller said her husband visited the army hospital. Mary Beth wondered if the counterfeit bill came from there.

Peter hated the condition of the Fuller's home, but Mary Beth was gracious and tactful. He would have intimidated Mrs. Fuller. "Good work! I think I'll hire you."

She giggled. "What's the position? I've just accepted a job at a Chattanooga bank, and I'm going to have less time. You'd have to pay me a lot."

The word '*wife*' came to mind, but he worried about her reaction. "I'm going to hire you to handle difficult women. I'm no use with them."

"Difficult women? Mrs. Fuller wasn't difficult. She was poor. Besides, I doubt I would like a woman if she was truly cross."

"You're right, of course. How about if I pay you to visit Miss Fitch?"

"I was already going, but now you want to *pay* me?"

"Yes." He probed his mind to decide what he could offer. "How about payment with a dinner at my house tomorrow night? Mother adores you."

"You aren't going to give me any counterfeit money? I guess I'll have to make do with food."

"Mother has been wanting to pair us up again ever since Eddie died. I suspect she'll be thrilled."

"Hmm. That would give me a chance to question her about Mr. Sadler and his wife." She cocked an eyebrow. "That's a little mystery too."

He chuckled. She was amazing. He'd always liked her, but he respected her good judgment. "How splendid. We eat and investigate at the same time."

"Don't forget the courting, Peter."

Forget? That's all he thought about.

Friday Evening
May 30th
Roper Sitting Room

Mary Beth pulled her gaze from Reverend McCallie and glanced down at the makeshift bandage on her finger. While darning a sock, the needle had pricked her finger. Now a small pool of blood grew, and she tightened the piece of cloth to stem the bleeding. The seeping wound represented her life without Papa—the joy oozing out.

When she was a girl, Reverend McCallie's long face, and deep-set eyes frightened her, but he demonstrated kindness and concern. She was revising her opinion. "I assumed you came to see Papa."

"I want to know how you are. These are tough times for you."

"You're so terribly kind. My father is the one who is sick."

"The soul can suffer just like the body. In those moments, God aches with us."

She nodded, groping for words. His description fit her distress, but she did not sense God's presence. Besides, the pastor might be upset about her doubts. She hated herself for questioning, but she couldn't seem to quell her anxieties. "I am quite unhappy about Papa's condition. Losing him is my worst nightmare."

"I'm listening."

She breathed in to squelch the oncoming tears. "I'm too young ... to be an orphan."

"I remember losing my father," he said. "I escaped to my room and cried for hours."

His mannerisms gave her the impression he would listen. "If only God answered my prayers. I try so hard to trust him. Not only is Papa sick, but there are also problems at the bank. Now I'm working with Peter to unravel it all. I ... have some ... doubts and fears. It's all so upsetting. I wonder why God doesn't do something."

"Sometimes we can't see what God is doing because of our pain."

The thought jarred her. His wife commented God might have a higher purpose, and she'd mulled over that. Perhaps she underestimated Reverend McCallie and his wife. "Is that common? Aren't Christians supposed to be joyful?"

"Read Psalm eighty-eight. The author writes from the depths of despair. Having hope doesn't mean we can't grieve. Jesus Messiah came to embrace the broken-hearted. Matthew twelve says, 'a bruised reed shall he not break and smoking flax shall he not quench.'"

His words made tears well up in her eyes.

Reverend McCallie bowed his head. "Almighty God, I lift up this young girl in her time of heartache. Help her to see you have *already* tread these dark paths with her. Fill her with your peace. Thank you for our hope in Christ."

As the pastor left, she realized his visit was an answer to prayer.

Chapter Twenty-Six

Friday Night
May 30th

A sound pulled at Peter. He fought to thrust aside the heavy blanket of sleep as the noise came again and again. He hauled himself up in the bed, his ears attuned. Silence surrounded him, yet his pulse thundered.

Perhaps he dreamed. A shiver ran through his body as he placed his bare feet on the cold wooden floor. He pulled on his dressing gown and slippers and searched the house, checking every window, but he found nothing.

There, again—a sort of pinging sound. This time, he was certain. But where should he look? An empty house echoed at night. He waited, but once again, nothing gave him clues. He moved toward the stairs and slipped to his mother's window facing the woods. Gloom veiled the trees. Even the white lawn furniture appeared black. Did something move on the edge of the woods? Perhaps a wild animal roamed about the manicured garden. He could not be sure

When the morning sunshine chased away the shadows, Peter still wondered what had disturbed him in the night. He walked around outside the house before breakfast but found nothing out of place. Inside the house he made his rounds of each room, particularly gazing at the windows. He found nothing, which made him wonder if he'd been dreaming last night when he thought he heard noises.

He pushed aside his fears as he hurried to the bank.

Saturday Afternoon
May 31st

Anna settled at her secretary desk to check off her list. The evening must be perfect. She'd planned on Mary Beth's favorites. The housemaid would place fresh flowers around the house. Table linens were starched, and the sitting room rugs were clean. She was almost euphoric about Mary Beth's visit.

A knock sounded on the door, and Billy stepped inside. "Excuse me, ma'am. You have a message."

"Thanks." She snatched the message off Billy's tray and gave him a quick smile of thanks in case she'd been too curt. She didn't need to be distracted right now.

Madam,

I know what you did. Tell no one what you know.
Your son's life will be in danger unless you obey.

Anna shivered. Who was her anonymous correspondent? Surely this referred to her not-so-secret visit to the bank the night Sadler died. The entire city must have been awake and watching. Her befuddled mind refused to strategize. How long did she have before Mary Beth arrived? She glanced at the clock and froze. No time remained for calming herself.

A knock sounded again, and Billy announced, "Miss Roper is here."

Anna donned her public smile. "Dear, dear child. I was over-joyed when Peter requested we invite you for dinner. I worried you couldn't come, especially with your father so ill."

"Dr. Smith agreed to sit with Papa tonight. He believes I require more rest."

"He's entirely correct. What would we do without our town doctor? I often wonder how he manages to be town doctor and mayor."

"I've had help from Reverend Mrs. McCallie. She comes in the morning hours when I'm helping at the bank."

"You certainly deserve the respite."

Mary Beth turned pink. "I almost feel guilty when I'm away, especially if I enjoy myself."

"Nonsense, my dear. You must not allow such feelings. I'm sorry Mr. Field returned to Savannah. I know Peter wanted him to meet you."

"Peter promised he'd update me tonight on the meeting they had. They discussed his investment strategy." She looked down. "I might be his partner soon."

"You enjoy working at the bank?"

Mary Beth nodded. "When I'm not wishing I was at home with Papa."

Anna longed to mother this dear girl. Such unselfishness. Ruth now resisted Anna's affection, but she tried anyway. "What a wonderful daughter!"

"My father's the wonderful person."

Anna glanced at the clock. "Where is Peter? I thought he'd be here by now."

"His workload is daunting. I should be helping him."

"Mary Beth, you have my permission to forget about work tonight."

"While we wait, I wonder if I could see the Chandler library. I've heard of its beauty, but we were never allowed to play there as children."

"Of course. Follow me." Anna grabbed an oil lamp and held it aloft. She led Mary Beth down the hallway, pointing out portraits of the Chandler family. Opening the door, she waved her guest inside first.

Mary Beth gasped.

Anna took a moment to focus. Mahogany bookcases lined three walls, but half the volumes were scattered about the floor. Papers and balance sheets were flung all over the enormous carved desk that dominated the room, and the leather executive chair was overturned. The chaos looked as if a tornado had ripped through the room. She sucked in her breath. "How dreadful!"

"Could someone else have been here?"

She bit her lip. "Ruth comes in here at times, but she's never left it like this."

"What does Peter keep here?"

"He keeps track of family accounts and pays bills here." She touched a drawer in the desk. "This is where he stores property deeds and legal papers."

"So nothing in this room is confidential?"

"No, certainly not to Ruth. He does bring documents from the bank, but he always leaves them locked in his briefcase."

"When did you first see Ruth in here?"

Anna had to stop thinking about the warning to think clearly. "I feel sure it was about five months ago."

"Who cleans in here?"

"Billy does the floors. He used to hire maids from the city to dust, but since the war, he does that himself."

"Does Peter know Ruth comes in here?"

"I've never burdened him with her behavior. He thinks I spoil her, but only a mother understands her broken heart."

Mary Beth placed a hand on Anna's arm. "Thank you for telling me. You have been tense for a while."

Anna released a sigh. Things weren't going as she planned. Her goal was to make Peter realize Mary Beth's worth and nurture her like a mother. Instead, Mary Beth was taking charge. "Yes, I have."

"We'd best leave the room until Peter gets home."

The mess perturbed her, especially when she tried so hard to make the house perfect for Mary Beth's visit. "What will Peter say?"

"Oh, I think he'll be fine, Mrs. Chandler. I'll ring for Billy."

"Madam?" Billy stood in the doorway.

"I'm the one who rang, Billy." Mary Beth said. "Please lock this door."

This young girl might end up mothering her instead.

After Dinner
May 31st

Peter pushed past his mother and Mary Beth to gaze at the mess in the office—papers and books intermingled with his family records. His heart hung in his chest like a lump of lead. He questioned Billy and the maids without gaining a result. "Mother, I want to speak to Ruth right away."

His mother nodded. "I'll fetch her."

Mary Beth inched away. "You can find me in the sitting room when you finish."

He reached for her. "If you don't mind, please stay with me."

"Are you sure?"

"Yes." The last few days, he'd spent hours restructuring employee policy at the bank. Extra hours meant less sleep. Consequently, his temper might be short. "Ruth mentioned how much she likes you. I suspect a friendly ally will prove useful."

"I shall do whatever you need. Would you like help reorganizing?"

"We'll get that done later."

Ruth walked in the room and slunk back as if worried.

Peter put a hand on Ruth's shoulder. "Someone vandalized my office. Do you know anything about this?"

She met his gaze for a second. "No."

"Isn't this dreadful?" Mary Beth asked.

Ruth nodded and inched toward her. "Indeed! Did someone break in?"

"That's what we are trying to determine," Peter said. "We cannot find anything else in the house disturbed. Have you ever seen anyone come in here?"

"Billy."

"Mother reports that you come in here. Is that true?"

She shrugged, keeping her gaze on the floor. "Yes. Sometimes."

Maybe if he gave her permission, she'd say more. "That is fine. I've never minded you coming in to read or study."

She shook her head, but her gaze went to Mary Beth. "I read in my bedroom."

"Can you think of any reason for this?" Mary Beth asked.

"No." She folded her arms and looked toward the door. "May I go now?"

"Yes. If you think of something later, please tell me right away," Peter said. Once she left, he turned to Mary Beth. "What do you think?"

"She's not forthcoming. I've never seen her so subdued."

"I agree with you. Tomorrow I shall consult with Billy again. Details seldom get past him."

"Could this have anything to do with the bank?"

"I do keep bank documents here sometimes," Peter said.

Mary Beth wondered who might else might know.

Chapter Twenty-Seven

Monday Morning
June 2nd

Mary Beth accompanied Peter into the same printing office she'd visited while he was in Savannah. The same balding gentleman came toward them that waited on her.

Peter held out his hand. "I'm Mr. Chandler of C&R Bank."

The man smiled. "Oh, yes, I remember you."

"Miss Roper and I are calling on clients this week. As your partner in the business, we want to help you succeed. I would like to discuss your income and chat about how we might help your business. Miss Roper will be glad to take any extra money you intended to deposit."

"You came about calling cards. Did you find someone to engrave your signature?"

Mary Beth looked down while she thought. She tossed a coy look at Peter. "I'm still interested, but my name may change. I'm sure you understand."

The man chuckled and glanced at each of them. "Very sweet."

Another gentleman accompanied Mary Beth to the safe in the back, where he gathered money for a deposit. She watched as he handled each bill, and she almost sighed with relief when she saw no counterfeit money.

An hour later, she met Peter at the front door.

"Mr. Fox, I commend you for your excellent work. Your business looks quite good," Peter said.

Once she and Peter walked outside, he turned to her. "Did you see any of our bills?"

"No. About half of their money is in the new legal tender, but the other half is in gold."

Peter nodded. "That may give rise to problems in the future, but the business is in good shape for now. Who is next on our list?"

"Nelson General Store."

He chuckled. "Your favorite place to visit?"

Her face grew hot. "No."

"I can drop a hint about us," Peter said. "Maybe that will help."

When they arrived at the store, Mr. Nelson rushed to the door. "Mr. Chandler, sir. So good of you to drop by. We've prepared our quarterly interest payment already, so you can get it while you're here."

"Excellent," Peter said. "We're here to keep in touch and see what you need. I'd like to chat about your income, and Miss Roper will take any money you plan to deposit."

Mr. Nelson gave her a dark look, but he didn't object.

Mrs. Nelson took Mary Beth's arm and led her to the back room. Once she opened the safe, Mary Beth spotted a one-dollar bill bearing Peter's signature. "I'll take that bill, Mrs. Nelson. It can be part of your interest payment."

"Oh, I thought you only accepted gold."

Mary Beth nodded. "We do. Occasionally we make an exception so we can tell Confederate officials we've done that. Mr. Chandler insists on gold most of the time, and I have to follow instructions."

Mrs. Nelson leaned close and laughed, her stomach bouncing. "As long as we make them think they have control."

After they finished, Peter said, "You seemed more comfortable with Mrs. Nelson."

"I was." She held up her bag. "They had one of our forged bills. It was a one-dollar bill, so I included that in their quarterly payment."

"I approve of that way to confiscate." He laughed. "You can be clever on your feet, which is wonderful."

"Today we visited six businesses, and only found one bill. That's good news. Perhaps there's not much circulating."

Peter's face darkened. "No. It will be good news when we find the culprit and stop the bogus money."

**Tuesday Morning
June 3rd**

Mary Beth glanced about, hoping to find Bell's room empty. She had overlooked searching his room for clues. In fact, doing Sadler's job and mixing her father's medications took lots of her time. She'd allowed the investigation to dominate her time because Peter had less time to devote to the search.

Bell's door stood ajar, and she peeked inside, getting a glimpse of clothing hanging from open drawers.

She flinched as Bell turned toward her, his dark eyes bored into her. "Oh. Uh. Hello, Dr. Bell. I must speak to you about something."

"Indeed."

His round face did not look friendly, but she had burst into his room. "It's your assistant." She couldn't think fast enough. "He's giving me some problems, and I thought—"

"Craig. That boy ..."

"Boy?" That's the last word she would use to describe him. Nuisance or rude fit him better. The dumped breakfast flashed into her mind, but she scrambled for words. The doctor would need a clear, concise explanation, but her mind refused to supply that. "He's trouble."

"Can you be more specific? Now and then he needs a firm word, but nothing more."

"This morning he dumped his breakfast on the floor."

"You saw him do that?"

How frustrating. She was the witness so he couldn't deny what she saw. "He thumped his tray, making food spill on the floor."

"Do you mean he appeared upset? He does get angry from time to time."

Her problem might seem minor given his sick patients, but she could not tolerate Glass any longer. "I heard him yell at my housekeeper, and when I entered his room, he was quite angry."

"He may have accidently knocked the food on the floor. His parents pulled him from medical school and made him enroll in the military. He must wait until the war ends before he can complete his education. Of course, he tends to be angry. His goal was to work as a doctor rather than an assistant."

Mary Beth allowed Bell to lead her into the hall. "His behavior is disrespectful and—"

"But it makes sense if you understand his background." The doctor released her arm and walked down to the front door. "I have to return to the hospital. Be patient with Glass. He will loosen up in time."

She stood at the top of the stairs as Dr. Bell strode outside.

"This foolish behavior must end."

The doctor did not acknowledge her words. If only she could choke them both. As Bell closed the front door, she headed to his room. Time to investigate his belongings.

Bell's room was chaotic. His bedcovers lay in a knotted pile on one side of the bed. The floor under his bed had two boots, lying askew, as if he'd thrown them there in a hurry. An assortment of medical tools resided in the top drawer of his dresser. Also, he had clothes, socks, and the usual aprons worn by surgeons. His bedside table held several letters and a couple of faded miniatures, a comb, a razor, a pair of scissors. But she found no money. How odd. Maybe he kept cash on his person. He could be guilty, but she didn't think so. His easy manners and gentle way of speaking made her think he was harmless.

She pulled out the bottom dresser drawer, but a sound downstairs made her rush into the hall. Was he coming? She walked toward the stairs, and Dr. Bell appeared in the foyer. "Doctor, I thought you left."

He bustled toward the steps. "If you'll excuse me, I forgot a piece of equipment I need."

Mary Beth's heart pounded as he walked past her to his room. She hoped he didn't notice the drawer or else he might suspect her of tampering with his room.

Wednesday
June 4th
Office of C&R Bank

Peter had not expected Dr. Smith to drop by the bank. He held his breath, hoping the doctor brought clues to unravel this tangle.

The doctor handed his black bag to Mr. Riddle. "I won't need that unless your headache persists."

Every passing day could mean more bills in circulation—a terrible situation, which he must find a way to stop. "I have nothing that needs medical care, Doctor."

"A magistrate from Atlanta arrived yesterday, and I asked him a few questions. He didn't know of any Southern towns that made the effort to prosecute counterfeiters. He expects the problem to worsen before the war ends. Growing inflation will drive up the need for a medium of exchange."

"I expected as much." Peter sighed. "When the South falls, and I believe it will, those banks who loaned money to the Confederacy will go under because they have no assets."

"The Union now issues paper money—legal tender," Smith said. "They passed a law saying citizens cannot go to the bank and demand gold."

"If Tennessee passed such a bill, our bank would be safe while we hunt for the culprit," Peter tapped a newspaper sitting on his desk. "I keep up with the Confederate legislature. They appear to favor legal tender, and then they back off."

"Issuing Treasury notes amounts to the same thing, but they refuse to admit it."

Peter jotted himself a note about contacting state politicians. "I agree. I'm bothered when Confederate officials pay their debts by issuing more bonds. I pray the hostilities end before we end up with rampant insolvency. Banks that issue paper money not backed by gold will crash when the Union wins."

"Of course. The Union won't recognize the dollars printed by the Confederate government."

"Does the Chattanooga city council have a strategy for handling counterfeit?"

Smith shook his head. "No. While we are fighting a war, everything else, including counterfeiting, becomes a low priority."

He and Mary Beth must continue to search for the charlatan by themselves.

Wednesday
June 5th

Once again Mary Beth sat in the Sadler's sitting room with Miss Fitch. She looked slimmer than ever, even spare. Seemingly, the loss of her cousin subtracted what few reserves she had. "Hello, Miss. Roper. Thanks for visiting again."

"I wanted to see how you are doing and to see if I could help."

"Mrs. Sadler has been even more difficult since her son died. She didn't even attend the funeral. We feared she couldn't contain herself."

"I'm sorry for what you've been through," Mary Beth said. "Tell me how I might help. Do you need to see a lawyer or handle any details?"

"Please call me Sara."

"Very well, Sara." Mary Beth hoped she had accomplished trust.

"Mrs. Chandler agreed to help me with the lawyer, but thank you."

"Is there anything else I can do?"

"I'll think about it, but right now, no," Sara said.

Mary Beth rose to leave. "Take care of yourself the next few days, and I shall return to check on you."

Mary Beth took her leave. She was confident Sara would unburden—in time.

Chapter Twenty-Eight

June 5th

Peter stood before Mr. Roper's bed wondering how much time he had left. The skin on his face was haggard, and his breathing was raspy.

The knots in Peter's shoulders grew tighter. Mr. Roper might offer clues about Sadler if he felt strong enough, but he hated to ask. "How are you?"

"Good."

Unbelievable! He must be near death. "I'll let you rest."

"Stay, please."

Peter grasped his icy hand, hoping to infuse warmth. "Do you want an update?"

"Yes, everything. I may be able to help you."

Peter sank onto the bed and updated his partner.

"As Sadler aged, he became increasingly morose, and I was wary. He knew I watched him."

Peter leaned toward the bed. "Why?"

Roper paused. "He was secretive."

"Yes, I noticed that."

The man mumbled.

Peter sighed and got closer to his face. "Sir, please repeat that."

"Proverbs ... twenty-six ... twenty-four ..."

He spotted a Bible in a bookcase beside him and looked up the passage. "I shall read it aloud. *He that hateth dissembleth with his lips, and layeth up deceit within.*"

The man gave a slight nod. "Deceit is evil. People cover their sins."

"Yet, Mary Beth described how kind Sadler was to her." Peter closed the Bible and returned the book to the bookcase.

"Quite ... fond of children. His baby died young."

"That explains his attitude."

Roper gave a slight nod. "How's it going with Mary Beth?"

He chuckled, almost embarrassed. "We are doing well with our plan to court again."

"Excellent."

"I'm very fond of her." Peter paused, giving Mr. Roper time to process his statement.

"Take care of my girl." Mr. Roper spoke the words louder than he had the entire visit. Afterward, he closed his eyes.

"Sir, I shall keep my promise." *Even if she won't marry me.*

"Pray."

Peter nodded. "I do. I could not survive without prayer, sir."

Friday
June 6th

Peter looked up to see Maud step inside his office. She was panting, and her shawl hung at an awkward angle. "Mr. Chandler, we need Miss Roper. The doctor insists she return home now."

Mr. Riddle hovered behind her, "I sent her up the moment she arrived, sir. Can I assist in any way?"

Dreadful. Peter massaged the throbbing in his temples. Could this be the moment? He'd best accompany Mary Beth. None of her relatives lived in town, and he couldn't leave her alone. "Thank you, Mr. Riddle. Keep the bank running."

"I shall pray, sir." Mr. Riddle backed out

"Maud, I shall take you to Miss Roper."

"Oh, no, sir." She held up a hand. "That is, I be obeyin' orders. The good doctor be wantin' something from his medicines at his home. I must be sayin' my news and goin' there."

"Mary Beth." He dashed into Mr. Roper's office, where she labored over a spreadsheet.

"The doctor sent for you. We must leave now."

The color disappeared from her face, and the pen fell from her fingers. "Is he—?"

He rushed to her side as she rose, and she crumpled into his arms.

"I cannot do this." She covered her mouth as tears flowed.

He held her tight. "Yes, you can. The Lord promised never to abandon us."

"But Papa improved last week. He's not …"

"Come." He lifted her shawl and bonnet off the coat stand and eased her toward the door.

Peter remained tense all the way to Mary Beth's house. What news awaited them? Except for sniffling, Mary Beth maintained silence, gazing straight ahead.

The front door opened, and Mrs. McCallie appeared. He released Mary Beth's arm as the pastor's wife embraced her. "I am glad are here. The doctor wants you to wait for him in the sitting room."

"But is Papa—"

"Your father woke up with severe pain and shortness of breath. I called Doctor Smith, who is with him now. I'm going home to fetch Reverend McCallie."

Mary Beth nodded, her face white.

What could he do? He loved her, but all he could do was stay by her side.

Mary Beth sprang to her feet when Dr. Smith entered. Her gaze locked on his dark eyes. If only he would give her hope. But he pressed his lips together and wrinkled his brow, obviously worried.

Her heart begged for information while dreading what she would hear. "How is my father?"

The doctor licked his lips. "Come and sit."

"I do not ... think I can." Her voice trembled, and tears burned her eyes.

"My dear, I want you seated." He guided her to the sofa with gentle firmness. "Your father is alive, but you will need your strength for this vigil."

She perched on the edge of the cushion. "I am terrified."

Peter sat beside her, drawing her close.

Dr. Smith settled himself on the wing chair across from the sofa. "That's better."

Mary Beth put a hand to her throat. "The news ... is not good?"

"Your father woke with chest pain and began sinking into a coma. Mrs. McCallie contacted me immediately. When I arrived, his breathing was sporadic. I administered a stimulant. At first, I got a sluggish response, but he's coming around now."

She forced her mouth to say the words. "Is he out of danger?"

The loose skin on his face wobbled as he shook his head. "No. I shall stay overnight. He's quite frail. His body could rally, or this could be the end."

The very thing she dreaded—death.

Peter's embraced tightened.

All she wanted was Papa. She longed to throw herself on his bed and kiss his face. This could be the last time he responded to her. "May I see him?"

The doctor took a deep breath. "Mary Beth, he's too fragile."

So, she must wait and keep her sanity. Her pulse raced even faster.

Pictures of an open grave flashed into her mind, and heat sizzled up her spine. She glanced at Peter. "Do you have to go back to the bank?"

"No. Mr. Riddle does well in a crisis."

The doctor marched toward the sitting room door. "Very good, Mr. Chandler. I want you to remain here. And I prescribe a pot of hot tea with sugar and milk for both of you."

When Dr. Smith departed upstairs, she took a slow, deep breath, hoping to relax. Her heart slowed a little. "Let's discuss something unrelated."

"How about the bank?"

"Yes. Thank you, Peter. My mind needs something to unravel, and I'm going to order that tea." She stood and rang for Maud.

"Did you uncover anything new?"

"I cannot focus." She bit her lip as tears surfaced. "What will I do?"

"Stay right here with me, Mary Beth." His arms went around her. "And remember the Lord won't leave you, ever."

She let herself go in his arms and cried.

Maud entered, and Peter asked for tea with extra sugar.

Mary Beth shifted enough to look at Peter. "I'm drenching your coat all the time these days."

He offered his handkerchief. "I can replace it."

She blotted her face and sighed. Piece by piece her life was coming undone. "What shall I do?"

"Wait, for now."

Saturday
June 7th

Fatigue made Peter's eyelids heavy. The hall clock chimed three a.m. He wouldn't go to work anyway, since Saturdays brought in fewer customers. Mary Beth dozed on the sofa. Elsie sat in a chair nearby, her needle flitting in and out of gray fabric.

Footsteps echoed through the quiet house. Peter stood and tiptoed toward the hallway.

Reverend McCallie met him at the bottom of the stairs. His collar hung open, and his shirt was wrinkled. "Doc suggested you go home and sleep."

Peter released a pent-up breath. "What about Mary Beth?"

McCallie shook his head. "She's been sleeping since about eleven. I'll tell her the doctor ordered you home."

Peter's legs had the stamina of jelly. Could he walk home? Had he fulfilled his obligation to the lady he loved? He hated to leave.

Dr. Smith appeared at the top of the steps, his salt-and-pepper hair was mussed. "Peter. As your doctor, I prescribe sleep. I shall tend to things here."

"What of Mary Beth?" Peter's heart longed to stay in the sitting room with her.

"She's going to need you rested. Be off with you."

"I'm quite fond of her," Peter said as he trudged toward the front door.

"I know," Dr. Smith said. "You will need to stand by her."

Later that morning, Peter staggered out of bed and threw on his dressing gown. How long had he slept? He yanked open the curtains and winced as the light stung his eyes.

How was Mr. Roper? All night he'd dreamed of Mary Beth. She would be weeping, and he couldn't reach her. Thank goodness that part was a dream.

A knock sounded on the door. "Sir?"

"Come in."

Billy entered with a silver tray. "Miss Roper sent a note. Would you like lunch?"

Hopefully, the missive brought good news. He'd hate to have left Mary Beth to face the worst alone. Surely he could trust Dr. Smith. He had cared for Chattanooga residents for many years. "Yes. And please bring tea. What time is it?"

"Noon."

He groaned, wishing he could wake up and do something useful. Today he must decide what he could do to help her recover. He grabbed Mary Beth's note and read as Billy headed out his door. "Make the tea very strong."

Dearest Peter,

Dr. Smith told me you stayed until the wee hours of the morning. I appreciate your kindness and loyalty more that I can express. How embarrassing that I fell asleep so early. As you know, I'm not a night owl. Nevertheless, I wish I could have shown more commitment during our sad vigil.

The doctor now believes Papa had another heart attack. At present, he's very weak, and won't live much longer.

This morning, I spoke to Papa about Sadler. He told me he hired the man, and he always demonstrated complete devotion to our family. On the other hand, Sadler came to dislike your father, but only after the death of his wife, Elizabeth Sadler. Perhaps his response to her demise explains the dilemma we face.

Lovingly,
Mary Beth

Peter gazed at Mary Beth's words. He should be protecting her, but he didn't know how.

June 8, 1862
First Presbyterian Church

Bang! The earth shook with the rumbling of cannon fire, and Mary Beth froze in her pew. Such a sound should not occur when one sat in church. Never during a prayer. Peter grabbed her hand and squeezed. Would he also reach for his mother on the other side?

And what about Ruth? Was she the one sniffling at the end of the row? Other women openly cried.

Mary Beth had preferred staying at home this morning, especially after the shelling last night. Peter assured her Confederate forces in the city outnumbered Union troops who fired from the other side of the Tennessee River. Her father also wished her to go. After all, she longed for God's presence and comfort, and she reasoned the Almighty would be more apt to answer prayers if she obeyed.

Reverend McCallie continued his final prayer with his eyes closed. Several more volleys exploded with deafening noise.

God, keep us safe, please!

Crash! A huge volley landed outside the building, rattling the stained-glass windows. Women screamed. Bits of plaster and wood fell from the ceiling. Children cried.

"We must leave," a woman said, her voice had an edge of tears.

A deeper voice responded. "Sh-sh. The minister is still praying."

"That sounded close." The woman behind Mary Beth spoke aloud

A man's voice boomed. "Stay down."

"Sh-sh."

Trembling, Mary Beth opened her eyes. A number of families slipped out of the auditorium. Mrs. Chandler pulled away from Peter and headed out with Ruth beside her. Ladies wept while huddling on the floor, holding their children.

When the next crash came, several more men escorted their wives and children toward the door. A cannonball must have careened into the foundation. Another blast sounded nearby, and the building quivered. The windows rattled but did not break.

Muffled sobs filled the room.

As another cannon ball whizzed by, Mary Beth slid off the pew onto the floor. Her insides jostled around like jelly. She should pray, but only one word came to mind. *Help.*

Moments later, Peter eased down beside her and put his arm around her shoulders. "Almighty Father, protect us."

Another blast landed nearby, but the church remained intact. "Thank you, Father," Mary Beth said.

Peter held Mary Beth close as they inched onto the porch of the church. If only his mother had stayed in the service, so he could see her home as well. No ominous noises greeted him. Instead, birds twittered, a butterfly flitted past, and the sun blazed down from a cloudless sky. He released a pent-up breath. With Mary Beth trembling beside him, he descended the steps.

His job was clear. He must keep his loved ones safe. Mary Beth clung to him.

The road before them boasted a huge crater, and he kept a firm grasp on Mary Beth as they stepped past the damage. Whiffs of smoke drifted past, bearing the odor of fire.

Peter glanced at Mary Beth's pale face. "Are you okay?"

"The silence alarms me. What are the soldiers doing?"

"Maybe they retreated or perhaps they're out of ammunition." The scenario was unlikely, but he had to keep her calm.

"I hope so."

"Let's hurry home. We will be safer there."

"Unless they invade. What should we do?"

"I shall make some inquiries. We may need to leave."

"How can I? My father …"

He pulled her closer. "I'll make sure you're both out of danger."

"How?"

His jaw tightened. For weeks, he'd prayed hoping this invasion wouldn't come. He wasn't sure how he would keep the Ropers safe.

After Church
June 8th

Anna Chandler darted into the foyer as Peter entered his house. She carried a bonnet and a stack of clothing. "Peter, I'm so glad you are not injured. Ruth and I packed. You'd best gather some things also."

He grabbed her arms. "Mother, relax. We do not have to leave. The danger is gone."

"But the shooting—"

"Mama, it is over. The Union retreated. Calm down. We're safe."

She burst into tears, and he put his arms around her. If only she and Ruth had remained in Savannah. He shoved the thought away.

Dear Father, I cannot bear to lose my mother and sister. Please give me the wisdom to move them before another attack comes.

**Sunday Afternoon
June 8th**

Mary Beth hovered about her father's bed. Since she returned from church, he had not stirred. What would she do if an army invaded? Peter promised to get them to safety, but he never told her how. Elsie advised her to pack some clothes and necessities in case they had to leave. Her gaze moved toward the array of medications her father took. The thought of gathering those made her skin prickle.

Her father's Bible lay beside the bed. She thumbed through and gazed at various passages. "Papa, I'm going to read Psalm ninety-one. *He that dwelleth in the secret place of the Most High shall abide under the shadow of the Almighty. I will say of the Lord, He is my refuge and my fortress, my God, in him I will trust.*"

What about war? Did God protect dying men when soldiers raided? Or women or children? She knelt by the bed while her ears strained for sounds of shooting. *Father, forgive my doubts. Please protect us.*

A knock sounded on the door, and she stood. "Come in."

Maud held out a note. "Mr. Chandler sent this. I knew you'd want to read it right away since I feel sure he be givin' instructions. And my, do we need instructions. God help us."

Mary Beth grabbed the note and released a sigh.

Dearest Mary Beth,

After leaving your home, I met Mr. Henderson downtown. He reported the small band of artillery packed up and pulled away after the firing ended. Confederate troops pursued them, and he believes the threat is over for the immediate future. Because of the situation, scouts will be placed in key locations outside the city. They will report any further enemy activity and alert residents.

Lovingly, Peter

She clasped the letter to her chest as a chuckle rose. God had heard and answered.

Maybe God did listen. However, her father's health had not improved.

Chapter Twenty-Nine

Sunday Evening
June 8th

Mary Beth's knuckles turned white as she sat by her father's bed and clasped her hands in prayer. He lay on his side in the darkened room. The doctor told her he didn't have much time now, and she sent for Peter.

The answers she sought still eluded her, but she stayed close to God. Despite the turmoil and questions, she must hang onto her faith. She twisted her neck and shrugged to loosen tightness from her vigil. Her eyes burned, and fatigue made her limbs heavy. When the doctor came by, he said her father would not last until morning. A few moments later, he got an urgent call from a mother in labor. She could not face being alone.

Father, help me to remember your presence.

Silence. The raspy breathing had stopped. Her hand flew to her mouth. She inhaled to steady herself and leaned close to him. No, he wasn't breathing.

Wait. Did he move?

Yes, he took a gulp of air and another deeper one. She ran a shaky hand over her face.

"Papa?"

No response.

A tremor ran down her back. "I love you."

She reached into the pocket of her skirt and grabbed a handkerchief. The soppy wet cloth couldn't hold any more tears, but she wiped her face anyway.

A soft thud came from the hallway, and she turned. "Hello?"

Peter peered into the shadowy room.

Jumping up, she threw herself into his arms and allowed the tears to flow.

"I came as soon as I could convince Mother she was safe." His chin rested on her head.

Still sniffling, she pulled back to look at his face. "Thank you."

"Is he ...?" His eyes darted to the bed.

"His breathing stopped for a moment. Dr. Smith said such changes are typical."

"I see." He licked his lips. "I shall stay until ... the end."

"This vigil could last until tomorrow." The doctor said it wouldn't, but she didn't want to inconvenience Peter. "What about the bank?"

"Banking can wait."

A sob rose from her chest. A fresh tornado of tears swept over her.

He offered his dry handkerchief. She poured her tears into the tailored softness. When the tears subsided, she stepped back and glanced at the now sodden cloth. "I'm sorry. We'll have to launder it now."

"Never mind." He closed her hand over the fabric. "We can ask Maud to bring more."

Yes. She should have thought of such. Simple things escaped her these days. "Do you know how your father—?"

"No. We know very little. The train derailed and overturned. It was over in a moment."

The news took her breath.

He pulled her close. "The suddenness, the shock overwhelmed me. I was touring Europe before I came home to the bank. He insisted I go because he believed travel would open my mind, but I never saw him again."

"How sad."

"God's grace sustained us."

"Thank you, Peter. I need to hear you speak of our Father."

Peter nodded, tears filling his eyes.

"I am losing Papa a little at a time." He already knew, but saying the words made it easier. "At times, he would be very alert and talk. I treasure those moments. He shared his deepest thoughts. Dr. Smith said he would not live to see tomorrow."

Peter tightened his grip.

She put her head on his shoulder as sobs wrenched her body.

Monday Afternoon
June 9th

The pipe organ crooned out the strains of "Amazing Grace." The Roper family encircled Peter, but he searched for Mary Beth. He must support her today. Everyone filed into the reserved pews. He found himself beside his cousin, Julie, and behind Mary Beth. The organ music ended, and Reverend McCallie rose to the pulpit. "I shall read from the Gospel of John, chapter eleven. *Jesus said unto her, I am the resurrection, and the life: he that believeth ...*"

Peter had to focus on the pastor's words and overlook his cousin's melodramatic whimpers. As far as he knew, she'd never met Mr. Roper.

"*And whosoever liveth and believeth in me shall never die.* Those are the words of our Savior."

"Mr. Chandler, please come forward and lead us in prayer."

Peter rose and strode to the podium. He swallowed to moisten his mouth. "Almighty God, I praise you for your grace. Even in our grief, I praise you for the hope Christ grants us. Thank you that our dear friend, Mr. James Roper, is now in your presence. Comfort our hearts in his absence. May we stay in the shelter of your arms, not just today, but the rest of our lives. In the name of Jesus, I pray. Amen."

Peter stepped down, taking slow, deep breaths. There was a space on the front row by Mary Beth, and he headed straight for the spot. She moved her skirts to make room, and he sat beside her.

Reverend McCallie stood at the pulpit. "I shall speak to you today from First Corinthians fifteen, verse fifty-five. *Oh, death, where is thy sting? O grave, where is thy victory? The sting of death is sin, and the strength of sin is the law, but thanks be to God, who giveth us the victory through our Lord Jesus Christ."*

She eased toward him, and his heart ached. If only he could spare her this pain. Mary Beth convulsed with silent sobs, and Peter put his arm around her shoulders.

The pastor continued. "Today I have nothing but thanksgiving for the man who lies before us. His faith in Christ never faltered. During his final illness, I visited him, only to have him pray for me. He said, 'Reverend, you must guide this congregation through the war. I shall be safe. Let me pray for you.' Right now, he is in the presence of Jesus in glory. That is victory. And because Jesus rose from the dead, Mr. James. Roper will not stay in the grave. He will rise again. We will see him again. Praise God."

Mary Beth sniffled. Peter's gut twisted into a knot, and he squeezed her shoulders. Her tears would embarrass her. *Father, give her strength.*

After the Funeral

Mary Beth filled her lungs and released another sigh as the hearse stopped at her house. What would she do now? Peter jumped out and extended both hands. Grabbing her by the waist, he lifted her to the ground. Grateful for his attentiveness, she glanced at his face. He gave her a gentle smile and handed a tip to the driver. They ambled, arm in arm toward her house.

At the steps, Peter scooped her up in his arms and took her to the sitting room. Flowers, bouquets, and tussie-mussies filled the room—all of them beautiful, but they were a poor substitute. A fresh torrent of tears rushed down her face. The too-sweet smell nauseated her as Peter placed her on the sofa.

Mr. King appeared, twitched his nose in disdain, and marched from the room. What would she do now? She was alone, and nothing mattered.

"Faith ... is the assurance of things not seen, Peter." Her voice sounded weak, but that didn't matter. "I'm holding onto Christ."

**Wednesday
June 12th**

Swoosh, thwack. Peter raised his head and looked toward Mr. Roper's old office where Mary Beth worked. Worried about the bank situation, she insisted on coming to work at the office. He rushed inside the adjoining office to find her slumped over the desk still holding a pencil. A pile of ledgers lay in a heap on the floor.

Her father was buried days ago, and she'd hadn't slept since before his death. Peter's heart pounded as he gazed at her pale complexion. Was she—? No, she was breathing. He had promised Mr. Roper to look after her. Today she needed a guardian "Mary Beth."

"Hmm?"

He caressed her hair. "How long has it been since you slept?"

"I ... don't know." She sat up, rubbing her eyes. "It doesn't matter."

"Of course, it does. You cannot work without getting rest."

"I can. We must save the bank." She swayed.

"I don't think you should work today."

"I insist, Peter. We have to find—"

"Come, I shall take you home." He took her arm. Everything his father worked for would crash without her help. Their legacy would go away forever, but the loss didn't matter. Mary Beth mattered more, and he would not lose her.

"I don't want to go. No one is there."

"I shall take you to my home and my mother."

She slid her arm from his grasp. "There's no need. I'm a bit tired, that's all."

"I'm not listening." He pulled her from the chair and guided her to the door.

"Then we should get Mr. King." Mary Beth frowned. "I shall not budge unless we get him. He hates being alone."

Peter nodded. Today, nothing mattered but Mary Beth.

**Afternoon
June 12th**

The shadows lengthened as Peter paced in his sitting room. He squeezed his hands into fists as he waited for the doctor. He must keep his promise.

Mr. King curled in a cushion of the wingback chair and succumbed to sleep. If only life could be as simple. He whispered a prayer for Mary Beth, and a sigh rolled from his soul. He had breathed the exact words several times now, but surely God understood. Peter could almost feel Mary Beth's cheek next to his and the pressure of her hand in his. She had no idea how much this frightened him.

Heavy footsteps came down the hall. Peter sprang to his feet.

As the sitting room door opened, Peter spoke. "How is she?"

"Mary Beth is suffering from exhaustion. This is common in the midst of great loss," Dr. Smith said. "It's good you brought her here. She needs a mother's touch."

Why hadn't he paid more attention to her symptoms? He'd worked alongside her without realizing how tired she was. What kind of man was he? "But will she recover?"

A smile twitched the doctor's lips. "She needs good food, and I recommend companionship and love."

"I do love her."

"Keep telling her that."

"I intend to." If the bank failed, he'd find another profession. Somehow.

Chapter Thirty

Late Afternoon
June 12th

Mary Beth gazed at the lavender bed covers while yielding to a yawn. Nothing had ever looked more comfortable. She longed to slip into oblivion. Turning to Mrs. Chandler she said, "It is too pretty to use."

"I made the blankets myself as a gift to Ruth, but she changed her favorite color a year or so later. This is my guest room. You are welcome here."

Mary Beth ran a hand over her itchy eyes. "You are so kind."

"Nonsense." Mrs. Chandler smiled. "I have always thought of you as a daughter. You will find several nightgowns in the armoire. Help yourself."

Once Mrs. Chandler left, Mary Beth lay down, allowing her muscles to relax.But the moment she closed her eyes, images raced through her mind—her father's last breath, the open grave. She turned over, prayed, counted to a thousand, and hummed a tune. No sleep came.

At last, she rose and dressed. When she parted the curtain, warm sunshine filtered in. The garden below made her smile, so she slipped outside and eased into a wrought-iron chair beside the roses. She had happy memories here. As children, she and Peter had played here. Closing her eyes, she thought of the fun times.

A crunching sound, like a footstep, sounded at the edge of the woods. She looked up, and saw a young boy, staring over her head. He was about ten and had a thin, wiry frame.

"Hello. What's your name?" she said.

The boy shrank back into the woods. Perhaps he tended toward shyness, which she understood. Strangers had frightened her when she was that age.

Her gaze drifted to the roses alongside her. Two chickadees burst into song, and she took a deep breath. Maybe she could manage a nap outside—a place one didn't have to sleep.

She soon nodded off, but a noise drew her back.

Now the boy sat in the chair next to hers. He kept his eyes on the woods, but his winsome expression tugged at her. She kept her voice soft, "Hi, I'm Mary Beth. Will you be my friend?"

"Friend."

"Do you live nearby?" She leaned toward him, thinking he would make eye contact. Instead, he slid from the chair and waved as he slipped back into the forest.

"Mary Beth?" Peter came to where she sat. "I saw your door open, and I wondered where you were."

"Did you see him?" She waved in the direction the boy ran off, thinking he might catch a glimpse. "He just disappeared."

"No. Who was out here?"

"He was a young boy wearing ragged clothing, too shy to speak, but cute." She patted the chair beside her. "Sit. I tried to sleep but couldn't, so I came out here."

"Would you like to walk?"

"Yes, thank you."

"We might even find your new friend." Peter set a leisurely pace as they headed into the wooded area.. "We used to play here."

"Not this far out. Your mother always called us back."

"She's protective. Now she's extended the tendency to you. Billy has gone for clothes so we can stay over for a few days."

"Wonderful. I detest being alone. Before he left, Uncle asked me to live with them, but his wife stood behind him shaking her head the whole time he pleaded. He wanted me, but she didn't. I said no."

Peter draped an arm about her waist. "Never mind. You are welcome here."

"Look at that." She grabbed his arm and pulled. "Come on. It appears to be a pile of rocks."

He squinted. "I don't see—"

"It's just beyond those trees."

They walked a few yards and came upon a pile of smooth stones. Several lay apart from the others, forming the shape of a square.

She knelt and touched a rock. The cold surface reminded her of the past. "These look like mine."

"Yours?"

"I helped with Ruth when you went away to college." She looked up at him. "Papa and I collected rocks from the riverbed and devised a code to convey messages. I taught Ruth. It was our private game."

"Do these stones say anything?"

"They say, 'I miss you.'"

"Ruth left a message?"

She nodded. "I wonder if it could be for the boy I saw moments ago."

"That's possible."

She glanced around. "Who owns the property adjacent to yours?"

"We own seven acres, but several farms border ours. Mr. Fox, Mrs. Davenport, and Mr. Allen all connect to this property."

"The boy could be from one of those families."

**Dinner
June 12th**

Mary Beth struggled to breathe as Ruth's arms enveloped her at the open bedroom door.

"It's great to have you staying here." Ruth bounced up and down.

Mary Beth let her gaze roam over her young friend. "You look very nice."

"Do you like my dress? I wanted a scoop neck with lace."

"I saw the unfinished version in your mother's sewing room weeks ago. It's very pretty. Come in." She waved the girl inside. "I am almost ready for dinner."

"Peter said you will stay several days." She gave her another quick hug. "I am delighted. My brother is correct. You shouldn't stay alone. I still get teary-eyed thinking about my father's death, and it's been a while."

Mary Beth sighed as she gazed into the mirror. "I feel dreadful."

"Ah, I understand."

Mary Beth finished pinning up her hair. "The good news is we can spend time together."

"Yes. I have so many fun things to show you." Ruth's eyes shone.

"I saw the message."

"Message?"

Mary Beth hoped a straightforward approach would work. "Peter and I stumbled across the rocks in the woods."

"Oh, yes." Ruth placed a hand over her mouth. "I forgot about those."

"Was the message meant for me, or for someone else?"

"Someone else." A blush spread up Ruth's neck and face.

"You're turning pink. Is it somebody special?"

"He is the youngest son of Mr. Allen. John is his name. I haven't seen him for a while, though. He's a bit unusual."

"So you left a message saying you missed him?"

Ruth nodded. She kept her eyes on the floor near the door.

A knock sounded, and Mrs. Chandler stepped in. "There you are, Ruth. Cook said dinner is ready."

Ruth bolted past her mother into the hallway. "Come along, Mary Beth."

Mary Beth hoped she could reconcile this sweet family.

Peter's stomach growled as he inhaled the aroma of fried chicken and mashed potatoes. His mother and Ruth sat across from him, and he seated Mary Beth beside him. Fresh air had returned color to her cheeks.

"Let us give thanks." Peter turned to Mary Beth. "It's so good to have you here. You may not remember our tradition. We hold hands around the table. May I?"

She offered her hand.

Peter gazed at his sister. "Ruth, please take Mother's hand."

With a huff, she obeyed.

Peter prayed, "Father, we thank you for fellowship with those we love around the table, and for the provision of Jesus for our sins. Use this food to sustain us. Help us keep our eyes on you, even during trials. In Jesus' name, I pray, Amen."

Maud stepped in with a steaming bowl. "Miss Roper, let me be the first to welcome you, sitting among the Chandlers like you belong and, oh my, this is so much better than eating dinner alone. Mr. Chandler, I suppose there's no need for me to spy anymore?"

Mary Beth's mouth fell open. "Spy?"

"Maud." Billy's face wore a scowl.

"Did I forget—?"

"What is she talking about, Peter?" his mother said.

Mary Beth's face reddened. "I'm wondering too."

Peter tried to recall what he'd said.

"Well?" She glared at him. "Did she spy on me?"

When he did not answer, and Mary Beth ran out.

Moments Later
Chandler Sitting Room

Mary Beth blotted each tear. She hated how she looked when she cried. Peter sat across from her on his mother's velvet sofa. The last thing she wanted was a conversation with Peter, and she avoided his gaze. She knew he would want to talk, but the thought made her skin bristle.

"Mary Beth, I asked Maud to keep an eye on McDonald, not you," Peter said. "He came to my office with a prospectus which sounded fake."

"You didn't trust me enough to tell me?" She couldn't keep the sound of tears from her voice. This situation didn't make sense. Peter had always told her everything.

"No." Peter reached for her hand. "I did tell you. Remember?"

"But you asked Maud to spy on my family?" She glared at him. His face looked grim, which made her feel worse. Did she have to hurt this man? She wanted to lash out, even though the desire made no sense. After a lifetime together, she knew him. He would not mistreat her. "You are the honest one—almost too much so at times."

"It appears I have failed you more than I realized, and I'm quite sorry. Lieutenant McDonald upset Maud terribly. I gave her a reason to return to your service because you needed her, and I wanted someone to watch his movements. Will you forgive me?"

If only she could be alone and rest. Running away might be a great idea, but where would she go? Another crisis would overwhelm her. She needed quiet where she could think, and this conversation made her head ache. "I should, but I am very annoyed right now. I shall go outside and take the air. The outdoors seems to help."

Peter stood as she marched out.

Evening
June 12th
Behind the Chandler Home

Rest ...

Mary Beth inhaled the warm evening air. She willed her muscles to untangle and pushed aside all troubling thoughts.

A sound in the woods jerked her back to alertness, and she looked up. Ruth stood at the edge of the woods frowning.

"Are you looking for something?" Maybe she could learn something more about her friend.

"Yes. I thought I might find John, especially since you saw him."

She patted the chair beside her. "Sit down and tell me about him."

She scampered toward Mary Beth. "Sure. He's quite different. Did you notice he never looks at you?"

Mary Beth's heart beat faster. "I did. He does that to you too?"

"Always, but he's actually quite kind. He taught me all about wildlife in the woods."

"He must be smart."

"I don't know. I doubt he's ever been to school. The other kids around here call him odd. But he's different. That's all."

"What do you mean, different?"

"He stays to himself and hardly speaks. I told him about you, and that's probably why he felt comfortable sitting beside you," She said. "But I know he's angry with me."

"Why do you say that?"

"He was upset when I told him about our trip to Savannah." Ruth slumped. "But I had no choice. Peter and Mom insisted."

"Did you explain?"

She shook her head. "He didn't understand, and I haven't seen him since I got back. Three weeks!"

"Tell me what you do with him."

"We follow animals and watch them. He even gathers things for them to find. Sometimes he needs help with things, like writing his name."

"And you help him?"

"Yes. The Bible says to be kind to others, and he has no other friends."

"Did you ever tell Peter or your mother?"

"No. But I'd best go to bed, or Mother will scold me."

Mary Beth nodded, wondering what Mrs. Chandler would say about her. She stood and trudged to bed, realizing she'd hadn't slept in the garden.

**Early Morning
June 13th**

Mary Beth woke. Again. The sky was still dark, but she could not fall back asleep. She shifted her position, hoping that would help. Surely her muscles would relax soon. She had already tried her back and her right side. If only she could stop reliving her father's death in her dreams.

Warm milk often helped, so she slipped out of bed and tossed on her robe. On tiptoe, she eased down the steps, avoiding the creaky spots.

Thump!

What was that sound? She stopped and listened. Odd noises came from the library, so she headed there. Once inside the darkened room, the scraping sound came again—from the window behind the desk. She hurried over and pulled back the curtain. Someone ran from the house into the woods. John?

Her gaze fell on the window lock, which lacked a quarter turn to being unlocked. John or Ruth? She sank into Peter's desk chair,  listening, but no further sound came. Her limbs became limp as she drifted toward sleep. She got up and hurried back to her bed, realizing she'd never made her warm milk.

Chapter Thirty-One

The next morning, Mary Beth almost panicked as she opened her eyes. The lavender bedclothes didn't look familiar, and she didn't know where she was. Then memories returned. A dark casket and open grave blazed into her mind. This was the first time she had slept, even fitfully, and she was at the Chandler's home. How pleasant to forget her pain during sleep.

She moved to the dressing table and ran the brush through her hair over and over. The sensation of the bristles against her scalp pleased her, and nothing much did anymore. Even the sunlight streaming through the gap in the draperies annoyed her. She chose not to wear a bun today; the task was too tedious. Besides, Papa liked her hair down.

But he was dead.

She was an orphan.

The world was bleak and cold.

Lord, give me wisdom and perspective. I do not know which way to go.

Her gaze darted about until she saw a Bible on the bedside table. Yesterday Mrs. Chandler had marked a passage for her. With trembling fingers, Mary Beth opened at the bookmark. Mrs. Chandler had written *Jesus* by the underlined passage. *A bruised reed shall He not break, and a smoldering flax shall He not extinguish.*

Mary Beth placed a hand over her mouth as fresh tears, healing tears slid down her cheeks. This verse proclaimed the mercy of Jesus. Something she had never considered.

She did not understand how God worked, but she had asked for guidance. With a fortifying breath, she glanced at the clock by her bed. The Chandlers had allowed her to sleep later than usual, and Ruth would doubtless be awake. What better way to push aside the powerful emotions than by investigating John's activities?

Ignoring the heaviness in her chest, she dressed and hurried down to breakfast. Just as she reached the dining room door, Ruth came in, her drooping posture clearly showed she was upset. "Good morning, Ruth."

"I agree it's morning, but it's not good."

"Is something wrong?"

She let out a moan. "Mothers. Why must I have one?"

Pain seared Mary Beth's heart. If only she had one. Better yet, she wanted her father back. Living without a family was like carrying around an empty cup. However, she must keep her emotions out of the conversation, at least for now. *Lord, help me minister to Ruth.* "Do you want to talk?"

"Yes, but where?"

"The dining room?" Mary Beth looked in. "Is anyone in there?"

"No, I was the last to leave." She leaned against the wall. "Except you, I guess."

"Come get a cup of tea while I eat, and we shall talk." Mary Beth hoped the Lord would give her the proper words to open up a conversation.

"All right." Ruth shrugged. "I guess I can."

Mary Beth helped herself to tea and toast. Ruth fixed herself coffee.

"Try the bacon." Ruth forked a piece onto Mary Beth's plate. "It's pretty good."

She suppressed a chuckle at Ruth's forceful hospitality. This would not be the moment to teach manners. How should she start an easy chat?

"Well. Back to Mother. She wants me to show her a paper Auntie asked me to write in Savannah. The problem is, I never had a chance to write it. Nor do I have the material to do it."

"And your mother doesn't know this?" Mary Beth added up the consequences of the girl's choices as she chewed her toast.

"When she finds out, she'll yell at me."

What a different way of thinking. All her life, Mary Beth had tried to imagine how her mother might respond to various circumstances, and she'd dreamed of an affectionate relationship. She considered her next words. This sweet girl was unhappy for some reason. *Guide me, Lord.* "Let me understand what you're saying. You think your mother wants to hurt you?"

"No. I guess not. I didn't mean that."

"Then why not explain you did not do it. If you talk to her, she might try to help." She pushed aside her plate. This conversation had ruined her desire for food. All she wanted to do was heal a broken relationship.

"I'm afraid."

Mary Beth searched for an illustration to reach Ruth's heart. "Imagine yourself a mother with a tiny baby. You care for the baby as he grows. Would you want your child to fear you?"

"Never. All I wanted to do is help John."

"How wonderful. You mother would be so proud of you." She patted Ruth's hand. "Speaking of John, can he get inside the library?"

Ruth's head popped up. "Yes. I told him he could—"

"Mary Beth?" Peter stood at the door, briefcase in hand. "May I speak with you?"

She suppressed a groan, wishing Peter had waited a few minutes.

Peter jumped out of Ruth's way as she barreled out the door. "Did I interrupt something?"

Mary Beth let out a sigh. This family suffered a loss and were unable to heal the fractures. "Yes. Ruth and were catching up."

"I apologize. I'm about to leave for work. Should I wait for you?"

"Give me another hour or so." She stood and peeked into the hall.

"Good. I'm pleased. I shall work here for another hour. Please talk to Ruth."

Later That Afternoon

Pencil in hand, Peter completed a long calculation and compared his numbers with the prospectus he held in his hand. His figures agreed with material presented, and the client would pay in gold. Excellent so far.

"Peter?" Mary Beth appeared beside the desk, a determined set to her chin.

He offered a smile, but his mind sank back into the depths of the prospectus, which could be quite promising. He calculated profits based on cash investments of varying sizes. The income pleased him.

"I'm finished."

"Pardon me?" His mind continued adding and comparing potential income. Her words were fading. "What did you finish?"

Mary Beth shook him. "Peter!"

The prospectus faded. "What?"

"I completed my research on the accounting." She handed him a slip of paper. "Sadler embezzled two hundred nine dollars and seventy-two cents from January to May of this year. No other discrepancies appear."

The huge numbers explained the look on her face. He pushed away from the desk to give her his attention. "Have you edited all the books for this year?"

"Yes."

"All those tiny amounts added together make quite a large number. A friend who is serving as a lieutenant makes a hundred dollars a month. The amount stolen is twice his monthly salary."

"I shall continue into last year's books, if you like."

"Our financial statements balanced last year. I suppose he could have fixed all the ledgers so they would, but I don't want to waste your time. Nothing will change if we discover he took more."

"Nevertheless, I could keep looking for evidence. We have no other place to look—except the hospital. Dr. Bell knows I became skilled caring for Papa. He suggested I might help out there, and I agreed."

Peter massaged his neck. He must have misunderstood. His mind couldn't switch subjects as fast as Mary Beth. "Are you saying you plan to volunteer at Newsome Hospital?"

"I already did."

"What about the bank? Right now, you fill Sadler's job."

"Two days a week at the bank is enough to complete his work because I work much faster. I've been coming more to look for evidence, and I've found nothing. Now I shall spend several days each week at the hospital."

"Forgive me, but I'm quite alarmed. You just lost your father, and the doctor diagnosed you with exhaustion."

Mary Beth sniffled and wiped away a tear. "Yes, and if I dwell on him, all I do is cry. I might as well do something useful."

Peter walked around the desk to embrace her. Her father said to comfort first and then reason with her. He found this hard because he wanted to protect her. "I don't like this. I shall devise a way to check out the hospital."

"You'd best hurry. I start tomorrow."

Friday
June 13th

Mary Beth stood at the nurse's desk, peering into the nearest ward. The morning sun streamed through rows of windows along the upper part of the wall illuminating the cots. As far as she could see, bedridden patients lined both sides of the narrow room. She never imagined this many soldiers. Searching for clues might be harder than she expected.

The bespectacled lady at the desk looked Mary Beth up and down. "You must be Miss Roper."

"Yes. I am Mary Beth Roper.

"I'm the head nurse, Mrs. Decker. What a pleasure to have you helping here at Newsome Hospital."

Mary Beth could not wait to learn the floor plan and find hiding places. But now, she'd best gain this lady's confidence.

"Dr. Bell raved about how attentive you were to your father. He said you grew herbs and mixed medications too."

"He did?" She was surprised the doctor talked about her.

"Oh, indeed. We are pleased to have someone so experienced."

"Let me show you around." She stepped out from behind the desk. "The military converted a series of warehouses to make this hospital. Each room of the buildings forms a ward holding a hundred patients."

"One hundred?" This job was growing more difficult. She had to search for clues as well as nursing, but the number of patients seemed overwhelming.

"Patients come and leave constantly. Some have minor wounds. The ambulatory patients do the cleaning and laundry and help with cooking."

Mary Beth wanted to laugh at herself for jumping to conclusions about the amount of work. Things might turn out fine. "Quite useful."

"Each ward keeps records on its patients, but you will get to know long-term soldiers in the other wards. You will be required to see each man receives his diet and his prescribed medications. You will also provide encouragement and emotional support. Many of these men want to dictate family letters to the nurses. We encourage nurses to help."

Mary Beth motioned to a large door to her left. "Is this another ward?"

"No, that's the surgery. Those heavy doors muffle the sound of the procedures."

The huge cabinets would make a great hiding place. Mary Beth gestured to her right. "And these small rooms?"

"The desk contains our records on each patient, and you will find medications in the adjoining room. The next door is a private room provided for the hospital matron. Right now, however, I am staying with a nearby resident, and Major General Connelly uses the room."

Mary Beth pointed into the room she'd been inspecting. "What about the large entrance here?"

"That takes you into the first ward. Follow me."

Mary Beth accompanied Mrs. Decker as they strolled into the oblong room. A few patients sat beside their bed while others lay under sheets or light blankets. This room held no guilty secrets.

She had upset Peter with her decision to come and volunteer, so she hoped this decision produced information helpful to the bank.

Chapter Thirty-Two

Friday
June 13th

Sheriff Campbell entered Peter's library behind Billy. "Good evening, sir. I apologize for the lateness of the hour."

Peter's heart increased as he stood. He never expected the sheriff to call at his home, but perhaps he had information to relay. They must have answers soon, and he did not want any additional dead bodies. "You have not arrested my mother. Is she cleared?"

"I do not have evidence, or she would be in jail."

"Have you learned anything useful?"

"One of our citizens saw Mr. Sadler with a Lieutenant McDonald during work hours. Another person reports the two men were related. I have two questions for you. Were you aware these two men met?"

"No." Peter's legs wobbled. "I had no idea he left during the day, not that I watch my employees all day."

"None of that makes either man guilty."

"Of course not.".

"Can you confirm a relation between McDonald and Sadler?"

Peter's mind raced. If they were related, they might have conceived the counterfeiting between them. If that was true, he didn't want Mary Beth at the hospital, near the military compound. "No."

"I shall report when I learn more." Sheriff Campbell glared at him. "Do not engage in snooping about. That's my job."

Peter had to talk to Mary Beth.

June 13th

Mary Beth darted from the ward as sobs rose in her chest. She must get to the hallway before her storm descended. At the desk, she bumped into Mrs. Decker.

Taking Mary Beth's arm, she asked, "Miss Roper? Are you unwell?"

Tears cascaded down her face, and she could not answer.

"Come with me. I'd rather not unsettle the patients." She led her into the medication room.

"Lieutenant Johnson is ... dead." Sobs wracked her body again.

"Oh, dear." She patted Mary Beth's arm. "Did you watch?"

Mary Beth shook her head. Thank goodness she didn't see him die. "He asked me to write to his family. Once he finished dictating, I left his bedside for a moment. I noticed him arranging his hair, so I thought he must feel better. When I returned, he was gone."

Mrs. Decker nodded. "I have seen many arrange their hands and body prior to death."

"He was such a nice man."

"Once you recover, write your own note to the family. They will appreciate knowing their loved one died peacefully. Include a lock of his hair."

Mary Beth placed a hand over her trembling lips. "I-I cannot seem to stop."

"Never you mind. Death perturbs the best of us, regardless of age. I shall take you to Major General Connelly. A nicer man never existed, and he's about the age of your father."

Mary Beth had no desire to meet a dying officer, but she must obey for the moment.

Friday Evening
June 13th

Peter strode down the hallway toward the bedroom used by Mary Beth. Tonight, he intended to present a new plan of attack to solve the mystery. His mind kept returning to the soldier on the train depot—the one who'd almost punched him. Her idea of working at the hospital made him so uneasy.

His mother came alongside. "Mary Beth is at the hospital."

"I need to talk to her. When does she return?"

"She will be home about midnight, but she'll be safe. A soldier always escorts her."

Peter glared at the door. What would happen if someone caught her poking about?

Mary Beth entered the small room with Mrs. Decker, hoping she could think of a way to slip away and start searching. She glanced about the simple furnishings and decided this room wouldn't be a good place to conceal anything.

The officer, who had a streak of gray in his dark hair, sat up reading.

"General, let me introduce our newest nurse, Miss Roper. She has your medication and will bring your dinner."

"Welcome, Miss Roper."

His calm, regal bearing struck her. She handed him a cup filled with medicine. "This is your last dose today."

He gulped the liquid, making a face as he swallowed. "I have ordered the doctors to improve the taste of their nasty concoctions, but they have not followed orders. I suppose I should court martial them."

"We hope the medicine, however unpleasant, will do its job." Mrs. Decker said.

"Miss. Roper, you seem quite sad."

She glanced at the head nurse for guidance. Mrs. Decker nodded her encouragement.

"I must humbly admit my first patient here ... died."

"A soft-hearted nurse then?"

"No. Wounded describes me better." She tried not to think about the tears gathering in her eyes. "My father died recently making me an orphan."

"I remember the agony." He groaned. "Even though my father died years ago, I miss him still."

"My father owned a bank and taught me bookkeeping. He saturated my life with love. But ... that's gone now."

"Did your father know Christ as his Savior?"

Mary Beth suddenly became worried. Something about this man made her want to talk, though she seldom opened up to strangers. "Yes, he did."

"His warmth isn't gone."

She blinked, still amazed at how much her tongue unleashed. "Excuse me?"

"Your father's warmth migrated. He still loves you."

"I am the nurse." She looked at the floor and rubbed at a tiny spot with her toe. "My job entails encouraging you, General."

"And you are."

Mary Beth shook her head.

"How old are you? Twenty?"

He almost guessed, so she might as well tell him. "I turned twenty-one a week before Papa's first heart attack."

"I thought so. You and my Lizzie could be twins." He sighed. "I have worried I would not live to see her again. She's far too busy to visit. Every spare moment, she dances and flirts with every officer in Richmond."

Mary Beth's heart constricted. In light of her father's death, his information made her sad. "I am sorry."

"But you expend yourself for others—like Christ. Your choice makes me happy."

"I am not unselfish. It's just … I must occupy my hands." And find clues to save the bank.

"Perhaps you could read the Psalms to me at dinner?"

"I shall, if I can." She turned to Mrs. Decker. "May I?"

"Yes. We supply Bibles to the nurses."

"But what of the other patients in the ward?"

"We have enough staff today. At the moment, I want you here."

This was not what she came here for. If she couldn't search for clues, she should, at least, help someone. Now she had to follow orders. She would read to this officer until he fell asleep.

Monday
June 16th

Mary Beth looked left and right. Since she saw no one, she tiptoed into the operating room and closed the door behind her. Waist-high wooden cabinets lined the left wall. The large oblong table in the middle of the room contained dark stains, probably blood. Queasiness rose as she imagined the source. A large cupboard with drawers occupied the far wall alongside a small metal table with wheels.

She hurried toward the cupboard on the back wall, trying to work fast and quietly. On top sat a mortar and pestle, stethoscope, a jar of cotton, a bottle of laudanum, cloth folded into a cone, and a tin labeled '*chloroform*'. An eight-inch-high can labeled '*ether*' occupied a spot on the floor by the cabinet. A rubber tube came out the top beneath a metal thumbscrew. The first drawer held a collection of syringes, scalpels, scissors, and curved needles in various sizes. Bits of carved wood held what appeared to be material for sutures, but no place to hide counterfeit bills. The second held numerous clamps and tweezers, and what appeared to be face masks. The third drawer had a selection of dressings and leather tourniquets, which she moved around in case someone stored bills beneath them.

She stopped to listen for medical staff. When she heard nothing, she rehearsed her prepared speech. *I thought I might need supplies from here, so I wanted to familiarize myself with the contents of the room.*

Mary Beth hurried to the cabinets on the wall. Her stomach swirled as she saw knives and blades in various sizes and shapes. The last cabinet she opened held several microscopes and portable leather containers.

A stack of tin basins sat in the corner beside the closed door. Someone had covered one container with a stained towel. When she pulled back the fabric, a hand lay in the bottom, drenched in blood. She almost lost her lunch.

A footstep in the hall made her heart pound. At least, she knew nothing in this room proved useful to the bank.

If only she could slip out unnoticed.

Evening Tuesday
June 17th

Peter perched on the edge of the sofa in the sitting room, his gaze glued to Mary Beth's sagging features. She looked more exhausted than ever. He must convince her to resign her job at the hospital. "I am quite concerned about you."

She rubbed her eyes. "The job is intense, but I know I need to be there. When I return from work, I am exhausted enough to sleep."

"I came up with a better idea. I shall give some money to the hospital, and I will ask for a tour."

"Peter, you are kind. However, I doubt they would leave you alone so you could search. Give me another day or so. If I have not found clues, I will ask to take you on a tour."

"Perhaps I can go tomorrow. I'll consult with Mr. Riddle on appointments I can move." He drew himself up. "Sheriff Campbell reported on Mr. Sadler."

"Did he learn anything?"

"He found people who saw Sadler with McDonald—during the day. In addition, someone reported the two men are related."

"That makes me angry. Neither man was honest."

He placed his hand on hers. "I'm sure Mr. Sadler was fond of you."

"And McDonald?"

"I'm not sure what he wants, but I know he's dishonest. Have you learned *anything* at the hospital?"

"Not yet, but I am looking. I distributed water to four wards before I left."

"Did you find places where equipment or bills might be stored?"

"Yes, but I must sneak away to search."

A groan escaped his lips. He promised her father to protect her. "I am not comfortable with this at all."

"I had a perfect excuse ready when I examined the surgery today, but I crept in and out undetected. Their cotton resembles what I found on the bank stairs."

"How much can you do to cotton?"

She shrugged. "I don't know, but I am tired. I shall go back tomorrow and keep looking."

Peter shook his head. Tomorrow he'd clear his schedule and visit the hospital.

Chapter Thirty-Three

Wednesday
June 18th

Newsome Hospital came into view at the end of the road, and she turned to the brawny soldier beside her. If only she could recall his name. "I appreciate the escort, sir. You may return to your duties."

The soldier frowned. "But, madam, I promised the matron I'd see you inside."

"But I have to … use the privy."

His face reddened. "I'll be on my way, then."

Once his husky form disappeared in the barracks, she bustled toward the heavy oak door at the end of the building. There just ahead, as Mrs. Decker described, stood the unoccupied portion of the building.

Her heart sped up as she looked left then right to make sure no one observed her. The tarnished doorknob turned, but the door didn't open. She groaned as she shoved harder. Her early arrival would waste time if she couldn't get in.

Finally, she threw all her weight against the heavy wood surface and stumbled as the door flew open. Whew! As she regained her balance, she imagined trying to explain her filthy dress to Mrs. Decker.

Sunshine filtered through dusty windows on both sides of the huge room. A pile of timber in various sizes was stacked along the far wall. To her right, a mound of red bricks sat next to numerous barrels. She meandered farther into the room, leaning over to peer into the containers. One contained nails, the next had larger nails. Maybe railroad spikes?

"Miss Roper?"

She startled and looked behind her.

Major General Connelly stood there, supported by crutches. "I'm sorry, ma'am. I didn't mean to frighten you."

"I was searching for, uh, something." If only she could recall her excuse.

"Did Mrs. Decker send you on an errand?"

She shook her head, wishing she could evaporate. "No."

He chuckled. "You're quite pale. I believe I've truly upset you."

"I need to know what's here—" She clamped her mouth shut. Connelly did not need to know her real reason.

"Then let's explore. We have to walk this direction anyhow." He hobbled toward her. "I could not sleep, so I sat beside the river and watched the sunrise. Magnificent."

Willing her facial muscles to loosen, she managed a smile. "It is lovely, walking along the riverbank with Lookout Mountain rising on the other side of the river. But Mrs. Decker will scold you for being out of your room."

"I am trying to build up my strength. I take walks when the weather's pleasant, but I have never ventured this far."

If only she could hunt alone, but she might be safer with the General along. "You mustn't overdo. I hate to think how the doctors would scold you."

"It doesn't matter. I'll never return to the fighting, but I must to gain enough strength to return home."

"I'm sure your wife would like you safe from battle."

"Yes, and my daughter will despise it, but let's not discuss that."

"I'm sorry."

"Oh, it's nothing. Every other parent has regrets. Let's go." He waved her deeper into the room.

Mary Beth inched along to match his slow, limping gait.

He pointed to a wooden shelf. "Those are woodworking tools. A bow saw, block plane, smoother plane, and jack plane. And here's a selection of small nails used for molding and a number of hammers."

She motioned to the next shelves, where bottles sat encrusted with dust. "What are those?"

He put down a crutch and pried one open. "These are finishes. Every carpenter concocts his own formula to seal the wood. Some use oils, others resins."

"Maybe this is where they make coffins."

"If they make coffins, they are fancy ones. Most don't have molding. It is possible they make splints and crutches here. A carpenter must have used this building. See the workbench?" He sank onto a nearby stool. "Sorry. I have to rest often."

"You should return to bed."

"I shall, very soon. The main entrance is just beyond that door."

"How did you learn all this?

"My father enjoyed making furniture when he was not on assignment. I still have some of his pieces. He did fine work."

As an older man, Connelly knew so much. He might have some grasp of the problems occurring during the war. "Do you know anything about counterfeiters?"

"The South has far too many. In fact, I doubt much of what's circulating is authentic."

That would include the bills with Peter's signature. She must find answers soon

Late Wednesday Evening
June 18th

As Peter stepped outside the bank, he noticed aching in his neck and back. He and Mr. Riddle had taken inventory of the safe contents. Between that, another visit from Mr. Shaw, and several disgruntled customers, he had never visited the hospital as he had intended.

Now he must hurry home and set aside money for Billy to pay bills before turning in. He locked the door and trotted down the darkened street.

As reached the outskirts of the city, footsteps sounded behind him, and Peter glanced back.

"You sl-sl-slimy banker." McDonald reeled and staggered toward him. "You and your mother ruined everything."

The officer reeked of alcohol. Peter cringed and sped up.

"Slow down, Pete. I'm talking to you!" McDonald growled, his voice sounding angrier.

"I wish you goodnight, sir."

"Where are ya goin', banker?"

Peter looked again. Moonlight illuminated McDonald's scowling face as he pulled out a revolver. At least, he knew Mary Beth was safe with his mother.

Peter jogged toward a wooded area and ducked behind a clump of trees.

"Hey, come back here and face me like a man."

Peter flattened himself on the ground. A shot rang out, and then another. His chest tightened as the third, fourth, and fifth bullets whizzed past. Only one would be left. But several manufacturers made guns with twelve bullets. *Lord, not that kind, please.*

He crawled toward home by the back way, edging along so he made no sound. Branches scraped his hands and knees as he crept through the underbrush. The clothes he wore would be damaged beyond repair, but his life mattered more than his suit.

After crawling through the scrappy pine needles, he stopped to catch his breath. The cry of a coyote made his blood freeze. He gazed about until he spotted two glowing orange eyeballs. Would the animal end his life or would the gun?

"Chandler? Chandler?" McDonald's voice echoed through the trees, and fire sizzled up Peter's spine. He resumed creeping but increased the speed.

When his hand landed on a sharp pine cone, Peter gritted his teeth rather than make a sound. At least McDonald was drunk, so his marksmanship would not be accurate. A silent prayer flashed through his mind.

He inched along on his knees into the deepest part of the forest. Once he got on Chandler property, he stood and listened.

No footsteps.

He hurried home to his gun.

Peter placed the candelabrum on his desk and sank into his chair, rubbing his eyes. He had checked the locks on each door and window, even though he risked waking the family. A loaded rifle sat on a nearby chair—just in case. Maybe McDonald didn't know where he lived. His muscles screamed after the expedition through the woods, but he set to work.

His favorite pen, the one Mr. Field had given him, was missing. Odd. Before retiring last night, he'd spotted the modern quill on the blotter and secured it in the desk drawer.

Perhaps the pen had slipped from his fingers. He adjusted the candles to spread light on the floor and got down on his hands and knees to search. Nothing. Closing his eyes, he pictured himself by the desk. Without a doubt, he had used the pen yesterday. Then why wasn't it here now? Maybe the contents had shifted when he closed the drawer. He pulled out the drawer all the way. A bit of paper fluttered to the floor. The document must have been stuck. He picked up the paper and read a fragment of a letter he'd written to his father while at college.

Someone had cut off Peter's signature.

Ruth meets John in my office.

Did Ruth get the signature? If so, what did she do with it? Did she know the counterfeiters intended to bring down the bank?

He barreled toward the door as the floor clock in the hall chimed midnight. The tolling made him stop. Everyone was asleep. In the morning, he would report McDonald then question his sister. Maybe the pieces would fit together somehow.

Thursday Morning
June 19th

Briefcase in hand, Peter was ready to leave for work, but Maud stood at in the doorway of his office, wringing her hands. He was already late leaving home. Before he could visit Mr. Allen, he had to locate one particularly elusive file.

"I bein' sorry ... But I must be talkin' to you. You might be angry, but Billy said I must be doin' it. I have to." A tear ran down her face.

"Yes. What can I do for you?" He pulled out a chair for her and leaned against the desk ready to listen. He never imagined having to encourage Maud to talk.

"That there box—from the bank ..."

"Yes?"

"I forgot. It be here 'n ..."

"Are you referring to the crate with Mr. Sadler's possessions?"

She nodded. "Things from Sadler's desk you be askin' me to return. With Mr. Roper's death and all, I were busy with Mary Beth. But today I be findin' it, and I done forgot what it was. So, I be lookin'. Just a moment, you know. And the miniature paintin' be givin' me quite a turn. My heart still be poundin', 'cause it's the other man."

Peter rubbed his head, trying to figure out what she was saying. "I don't recall a painting."

"You be rememberin' the first time we talked. I be seein' the lieutenant and another man in the graveyard."

"Yes, the day you said you announced your marriage."

"Yes, sir."

"And you say the man with McDonald was in a painting. I don't recall a picture anywhere in Mr. Sadler's things."

"Oh, yes, sir." She hopped to her feet. "I can show you, if you like. Between them sheets of paper."

"Please do."

She scurried from the room, her skirt swishing.

Had Peter missed something when he searched Sadler's desk?

Footsteps sounded in the hallway, and she appeared at the door again, panting. She held up a small oval picture. "Here."

Peter marched toward her and accepted the picture, careful to touch only the edges. He gazed at a young couple. "This must be a miniature painting of Sadler and his wife."

"That man be the one I saw with the lieutenant. I am sure as I can be. I would know him anywhere. Just seeing his face makes my hands clammy."

"This is Mr. Sadler. Didn't you ever meet Mr. Sadler?"

"Oh no, sir." Her eyes widened. "I never be havin' business at the bank. I knowed he hated colored folk, and I be stayin' clear of people like that. Your family and Miss Roper's family were different. But that's the man I saw with McDonald."

"I believe you." Peter nodded. "You've nothing to fear from him. Please see the crate gets to Mrs. Sadler."

Chapter Thirty-Four

Thursday Morning
June 19th
Henderson's Office

Peter stepped aside as the clerk brushed past him leaving Henderson's office. His jaw tensed. He didn't look forward to this interview. The magistrate might scold him for withholding information. "Thank you for agreeing to see me, sir."

"Welcome. Please, take a seat and tell me how I can help."

Peter licked his lips as he sat on an overstuffed chair. "Several matters have come to my attention."

"You came to the proper place. I shall do all in my power to serve you. Your illustrious father was quite a favorite of mine."

"I'm surprised."

"Ah, the joys of chatting with a constituent versus coercing my staff to work. How rare to find a man who displays true virtue these days."

Peter's news would certainly dampen his enthusiasm. "I hesitated to report a suspected crime, since you already have so much to manage."

"Crime? Never hesitate to bring such odious matters to me."

"The suspect is in the military, so I was not sure what to do." Peter opened his briefcase and pulled out the file McDonald had given him. "This is a fraudulent prospectus for purchasing Confederate bonds and a fake prospectus for fake blockade runners. I received both from Lieutenant McDonald, who is stationed here with the medical unit."

Mr. Henderson donned his glasses before thumbing through both files. "I assume you are completely certain of your facts?"

"Yes, sir. Officials at the Savannah dockyards had never heard of the firm. Nor did Confederate Treasury officials have records of these so-called high-yield bonds."

"I shall take appropriate measures. Anything else?"

"Yes. Last night the same Lieutenant McDonald fired at me as I walked home."

The magistrate scowled. "My boy, what kept you from reporting this right away?"

"It was quite late, and I wasn't hurt."

Henderson dipped his pen in his inkwell. "I'll need details— time, place, the number of shots fired, witnesses. Hold nothing back. I'll start an investigation at once without delay, there-by extinguishing the danger for our city. As a banker, you're going to need protection."

Peter related the information.

"Be assured, I shall handle this promptly. You've been seen about with Miss Roper. We hope to hear wedding bells soon?" Henderson winked.

"Thank you, sir. I appreciate your time." Peter balled up his fists and headed outside. When he reached the street again, he scanned the engagements on his calendar. Anything to get his mind off Mr. Henderson's teasing.

Morning
June 19th

Long shadows still hovered over the ward as Mary Beth hurried down the rows of cots with a cup of medicine for Sergeant Harris. Most still slept, so the room was silent and still. She stopped at Harris's cot.

"Sergeant Harris? Sir?" She shook his shoulder. No response. He was too still. Not again. She walked closer to see his face. The gray eyes stared at nothing. His mouth lay open, as if he were about to speak. His skin was still warm, but he had no pulse. Tears smoldered in her eyes. Last night, he had joked with her. Now his life belonged to the past.

Rubbery legs carried her to the nurses' station. "Mrs. Decker, Sergeant Harris—"

"Yes? What about him?"

Mary Beth sank into the chair by the desk. "He's gone."

"Miss Roper, you look as if you might faint. Stay where you are." Mrs. Decker handed her a damp cloth and bustled out.

Mary Beth stared at the ornate clock on the wall hoping to conquer the nausea. The filigreed hands inched around the face, a jerk for each tick. Would she ever get used to death? The other nurses managed to keep working. Why couldn't she?

Mrs. Decker popped back in the room carrying a breakfast tray. "Miss Roper, this belongs to the General. Take it to him. Quickly now. It must not get cold."

Taking a deep breath, she headed toward the officer's room. Her stomach still cramped, but she was less wobbly. Once again, Mrs. Decker would see to her patients. How embarrassing.

General Connelly sat in bed humming and flipping through his Bible.

In light of so much death, the snappy tune grated on Mary Beth's nerves. She placed his food on his table and prepared to leave.

"You are quite pale, Miss Roper. What's wrong?"

"No." The general was recovering, and his thoughts should center on renewing his health. "I refuse to discuss the hazards of nursing."

He held up his Bible. "I've been reading the Psalms. What a prescription for the mind."

The Psalm her pastor recommended leaped into her thoughts. They'd never discussed the poem together. "I've been reading there also."

He handed her his Bible. "Read to me."

> Her fingers turned right to Psalm eighty-eight. The words pictured the misery in her soul. She read: *O Lord God of my salvation, I have cried day and night before thee: Let my prayer come before thee; incline thine ear unto my cry; For my soul is full of troubles, and my life draweth nigh unto the grave. I am counted with them that go down into the pit, I am as a man that hath no strength, Free among the dead, like the slain that lie in the grave, whom thou rememberest no more; and they are cut off from thy hand.*

She returned the Bible, trying not to meet his gaze.

He spoke softly. "Is this how you feel?"

Mary Beth nodded. Death followed her around. If she weren't here to rescue the bank, she'd leave for good.

"Pull up that chair, little lady."

Easing toward the door, she shook her head. "You should be eating."

"I'm not hungry." He reached into the top drawer and pulled out a handkerchief. "Here, you need this."

The tone of his voice sounded like her father, and she accepted the handkerchief, pressing the cloth over her mouth.

"Those verses are in the Bible for a reason. God knew how much pain a sinful world would give us. We need to grieve."

How very true! She gave in to her fatigue and allowed herself to sit. "Life without Papa is so bleak, empty. I came here to work, and I witness more suffering and death."

"Miss Roper, you're still grieving your father, so it's probably premature for you to be working here."

Maybe she should have listened to Peter, but she had to come. Who else could investigate the hospital? She couldn't tell the general why she volunteered.

"Allow yourself to cry, to grieve. There's no shame there. Remember Jesus wept."

"If I stayed home, I'd cry all the time. At least here, I might help someone. Assuming I quit swooning at the presence of death." And maybe she would solve the bank mystery.

"God values our dreams for good things. Do you remember the story of Daniel?"

What was he doing now? Trying to distract her? "Yes."

"Think about his life. Strangers snatched him from his home while he was in his teens. In a foreign land, he had to work for a government which oppressed his people. We have no record of a wife or children."

Mary Beth nodded. "So you suspect he had no offspring?"

"Exactly. He longed for his people to be back in the Promised Land in a proper relationship with God. And he knew they would return after the seventy years of captivity."

"I never thought of those facts. Did he ever go back?"

"No. God knew he would never see the thing he longed for the most."

"How sad. Unkind people ripped away his dreams."

"But God gave him visions of the future." He turned several pages and handed the Bible to her. "Read that passage. An angel spoke to him."

"Now I am come to make thee understand what shall befall thy people in the latter days: for yet the vision [is] for [many] days. What does this mean?" Mary Beth asked.

"God knew Daniel's fondest dream would come true after his death. So he sent visions to this holy man, so he'd know that what he wanted would happen. God let him see the plan for restoring Israel. That is what he longed for."

"Amazing." She stared at the words. "God cared about his dreams that much?"

"His character was excellent, and his longings were pure, just like yours. God also desires you to see life from an eternal perspective, like Daniel did."

Finding the counterfeiter was good, so her motive was pure too. In addition, she hoped to help someone. "An eternal perspective? How can that help me now?"

"You'll mourn, but life does not end there. He will also lavish his love on you, and I think he already has."

"What do you mean?"

"In the short time we've known each other, I feel like I have gained a daughter."

What a surprise, but warmth shone from his brown eyes. "You're so kind."

"I'm telling you the truth, Miss Roper, not seeking to be kind. You say your family's in banking. Bankers rely on gold. It keeps its value. Seek for the true gold and pursue God. He never changes. Besides only God can meet your deepest needs. I know. I've seen him fill lives with love."

She shrugged, and glanced away, not wanting to meet his eyes. "I've doubted a lot since Papa's illness. I suppose … I thought I wasn't good enough, and that's why … God didn't answer."

He creased his brow. "God doesn't work that way, not during heartache. Jesus came to lavish his grace on you."

Afternoon
June 19th

Mary Beth sighed, relaxing as she caressed the smooth gold necklace her mother once owned. She sat on the hill outside Newsome Hospital during her lunch break to process her thoughts. Down below, the Tennessee River meandered past. To her left, sheer cliffs of Lookout Mountain rose from the riverbed. What incredible beauty.

General Connelly talked about seeing life from eternity—like Daniel. The prophet lost everything he valued in life. Yet he never forsook his faith. God blessed him by giving him a peek into the future. He knew firsthand he would rejoice in eternity. General Connelly also said she should pursue God the way you'd pursue gold.

She folded her arms. Her sorrow had made her question God's goodness and love. Even as a young child, she'd understood the Savior's sacrifice. She trusted Jesus to forgive her sins, and she knew heaven was her home. Maybe she never expected anything to go wrong, but the Bible didn't teach faith would take away sorrows.

Was she blessed? Yes, despite her sorrows. She had lost her mother, but God had blessed her with Elsie. No one could have given a better mix of kindness and discipline. Her father was a good man and had often reminded her he leaned on the Savior. Reverend Mc-Callie offered both guidance and support, although her own anger and fear had kept her from accepting his help.

Peter flashed into her mind. His kindness and love served as an anchor too. Her uncle and aunt couldn't offer her a home, but Peter had brought her to his home to rest. She should reflect more on his kindness, especially after she had rejected him for Eddie.

And General Connelly came along right when she needed someone. His warmth enveloped her right away. God was there, but she hadn't seen his hand at work.

Mary Beth slid onto shaky knees. *Dear God, forgive me for not seeing your grace. I'm not really an orphan. My heavenly father has been there all along. Guide me now. Guide Peter too. Help us to find all the fake money before we lose our bank.*

Chapter Thirty-Four

Late Afternoon
June 19th

Standing on a hill overlooking the Allen land, Peter compared the improvements promised with the plot he saw before him. Heat sizzled through his body. The client had promised to clear the field to the left of the house for additional cash crops, but the area had scrubby pine trees and knee-deep weeds. Allen had pledged to plant a large vegetable garden behind his home and sell the produce in the city to pay off his loan. Instead, a pile of rotting wood sat beside a muddy ditch. Additional farm equipment purchased would be housed in a new barn. Peter found neither.

Peter folded the paper and descended the hill. As he stomped toward the house, Reverend McCallie's sermon on Ephesians flashed into his mind: *Be angry and sin not.* If only he could avoid sin today. He should have visited the Allen farm more before now, especially in light of the large loan Allen requested.

Whack, crack.

Peter hurried toward the sound of wood being chopped.

Allen stood by the house, holding an ax and a freshly cut piece of wood. "Afternoon, Mr. Chandler. What brings you here?"

"I wanted to see the improvements you planned with last year's loan."

"I am working on those."

"But now you insist on a bigger loan when you did not finish the improvements from last year."

"The cost of materials is going up. I need more money."

"You *need* it? I'm not loaning you anymore."

The bushes behind Mr. Allen rustled, and Peter squinted, thinking he saw someone dressed in blue.

Allen shook his fist. "We'll see who owns the bank this time next year. I have bills with your signature, enough to bring down your bank."

Gunshots rang out, and Mr. Allen ducked.

Another shot. A Confederate soldier ran up and whispered, "Get down, Chandler. I spotted Union scouts."

This man knew his name. Just this morning, Mr. Henderson said something about protection. He must have reported McDonald's assault and asked for a military escort.

In the distance, a Union soldier crouched behind a large stump, his gun pointed toward Peter. Two Confederate soldiers crept along in the grass to his left.

"Sir, I suggest you find cover," another Confederate soldier said. He nodded toward the woods. "There's several Union soldiers out here."

Peter crept away. When the third shot came, pain seared through Peter's left thigh, and blood gushed from his leg. He sank to the ground as the world went dark.

Later That Day

Someone elevated Peter's shoulders and held a cup to his lips. Where was he? He had no time to lie in bed. The bank needed him, but a sharp pain radiated up his leg. His muscles were flaccid and weak.

"I want you to drink this. Doctor's orders."

Cold water touched his lips, and he drank. "More? May I have more?"

Feeling the cup at his lips again, he drank. He tried opening his eyes, but the world was fuzzy. For some reason, his eyes refused to focus. "Where am I?"

"I'm Sergeant Baker, and this is Newsome Hospital."

"I am not military." He was so sleepy, yet his leg burned like fire. How did he get in a hospital? "I was visiting Mr. Allen's farm."

"Yes. Private Fry was assigned to protect you. He encountered Union soldiers on Allen's land. They exchanged gunfire, and several Confederates went down. You got caught in the crossfire."

Peter managed to get his eyes opened. A dark-haired man, wearing a white uniform, stood over him. "Is Mr. Allen here too?"

"I can't discuss that." Baker lowered his voice. "But you aren't in the army. If you can keep a secret, I'll tell you. Another civilian got bruised, but he refused treatment."

Peter needed to go back to work, but his body was limp. "Why can't I wake up?"

"The medics gave you pain medication. You'd be quite uncomfortable otherwise."

The news made sense, and Peter allowed himself to succumb to sleep again.

A cool cloth bathed his forehead. "Peter?"

Mary Beth? He tried to open his eyes, but he was too tired.

"Are you thirsty?"

He nodded.

She raised his shoulders again and placed a cup to his lips.

Peter's lips were thick and dry, but the water was wonderful.

"Yes, young man," a gravelly voice said. "You should drink. We want you to stay alive."

**Late Afternoon
June 19th**

All afternoon, Mary Beth had listened for Peter while she tended other patients. She was thankful his injuries were minor, and she prayed he'd recover without complications.

She poured water over her hands and grabbed a bar of soap. As she scrubbed her hands, her eyes roamed to the clock. Her shift would end at midnight, and the ward was quiet. Now she could slip back in to check on him.

The moment she stepped into the ward, her gaze went to his bed. He lay on his side, dozing. His cheeks now had more color, and his breathing was even. "Peter?"

He opened his eyes.

"How do you feel?"

"Much better, thank you." He smiled. "Mother came."

"Yes, I sent her a note. Can you tell me what happened?"

"I went to see Mr. Allen's farm because he kept demanding another large loan. I wanted proof he had done what he promised last year."

"Yes. Dad had me send him several letters asking for his quarterly report and interest payment. He never replied."

"Mr. Allen showed up the moment I arrived." He shifted his weight and winced. "Allen threatened to flood the city with fake money if I refused to give him money."

"Mr. Allen? Peter, he's not nearly clever enough for such a scheme, nor does he have the money to pay for the engraving."

Peter nodded. "I agree, but not many people knew about the counterfeit money, so he must be guilty."

"This doesn't make sense. Where did he get the signature?"

"I didn't ask. Before I had a chance, I saw a Union soldier and got shot."

"I'm pretty sure Mr. Allen favors the North," Mary Beth said. "Maybe he used bank money to help the scouts."

"That would explain what happened. Henderson sent Private Fry to protect me, and the Union soldiers at Allen's home fired at them."

Peter still appeared groggy from medication, and she thought he ought to sleep. "I'm free tomorrow. Perhaps I could interview him."

"No. We will ask the sheriff to arrest him. I do not want you trying to deal with him alone."

A number of questions regarding the counterfeiting problem still needed answers. They could wait until Peter felt better. "Can I do something for you?"

"Do you have a Bible?"

"I could find one. Shall I read to you?"

He smiled and nodded. "Psalm twenty-three."

Mary Beth found a Bible and read the Psalm he selected. Afterward, she turned to Psalm 100. Ever since talking to Connelly, her mind echoed with those praises.

Peter's features relaxed and his eyes closed, appearing to fall asleep. She stood to slip away, but he reached up and grabbed her hand.

"Thank you," He said, squeezing her fingers.

"I thought you were asleep."

"No, you read another Psalm."

"Yes, it was Psalm one hundred. I have learned a few things about God's eternal plan during the time I've worked here. Even though my heart still aches for my father, I know God can fill the void. I must pursue God the same way you pursue gold for the bank."

"I am glad to hear that."

"I unsettled you with my doubts and fears, but now my soul is at peace. I can cry and still praise God. He gives me hope."

"You have no idea how happy that makes me." He sat up enough to drop a kiss on her hand. "I love you, Mary Beth. And I—"

"Nurse." Dr. Sims rushed into the room. "I need you right away."

"Peter—"

"Now."

She hurried from the room without a backward glance.

June 19th

The clock read five till twelve, and Mary Beth got off at midnight. She planned to take Peter back to the Chandlers, so she went to the front desk to arrange transportation.

Mrs. Decker was sitting there with the night nurse. "Here are the names of the deceased. Wait. I have one more. Peter Allen Chandler died. His funeral is tomorrow at the local cemetery."

Mary Beth froze. This could not be. She had chatted with him earlier, and he was fine. "Excuse me. That's my friend. Remember, you promised to arrange a carriage for me to take him home."

"I am very sorry." The night nurse patted her hand. "His wounds were extensive."

"No." She was so hot. She could not lose someone else. "A bullet grazed his leg. He was to leave with me."

"Come, I shall show you his body." Mrs. Decker led her into one of the wards.

Mary Beth followed. She had never let him know how much she appreciated him, ever. But her feelings went further than appreciation. She loved him.

Mrs. Decker pulled back the sheet revealing the man's face.

Trembling, Mary Beth looked down at the man. He was too still, stiff. Something distorted his features. His face was not that long, nor his mouth that wide. She stepped back. "That is not Peter."

"No. That's my cousin from Soddy Daisy."

Mary Beth turned to find Peter standing behind her, a crutch under one arm. She grabbed him, and he swayed, just barely staying on his feet. "Peter! My love. I was terrified you were dead."

"I'm injured, but I shall be fine. What's the confusion?"

Mary Beth pointed to the bed. "They called him Peter Allen Chandler."

"No. That's Peter Frederick Chandler. Remember you found his initials at the bank? Our names are close, so he chose to be called Freddie or P.F. Chandler."

344

Mrs. Decker groaned. "I detest mistakes of that nature. Let me get to the desk and correct our records."

12:45 a.m.
June 20th
Traveling to the Chandler Home

Mary Beth and a medical assistant settled Peter in the carriage and draped a light blanket over his legs. She was exhausted and embarrassed she had admitted she loved Peter right in front of the head nurse. She should say something to explain, but words would not materialize.

"Did you mean what you said in the hospital?" Peter touched her arm.

"Oh, that." She laughed awkwardly. "I thought I was losing someone else I love. Yes. I love you."

"Oh, sweet lady. You have made my task a bit easier."

"Task?"

"You see, I intended to—that is, once I professed love for you, I meant to ask—" He took a deep breath. "Mary Beth—I meant to ask for your hand."

She blinked. "You did?"

"Yes. A true gentleman would never speak of love without a proposal of marriage."

"You could now."

"Now?"

"Yes. Please do."

He leaned toward her. "Dearest Mary Beth, I would be honored to have you share my life. Will you accept my hand in marriage?"

"Yes, Peter! Yes!" She could not say the words fast enough. He was alive, moving, and talking. What a wonder. Her chest might explode with the joy.

He put his arm around her. "Mary Beth, I love you."

"And I love you." She didn't know if she was going to laugh or cry.

Peter's lips touched hers, first gently and then with warmth. He pulled away and whispered, "What a place to propose."

"Yes, it is, but—"

"What?"

"I imagined you on your knees."

"I wish I could." He pointed toward his left leg. "But I need a crutch."

Laughter bubbled up.

"What was funny?"

"I pictured you trying to kneel and falling. You are not like Lieutenant McDonald. He would have found a way."

"McDonald?"

She leaned closer. "I'd rather have you. The lieutenant uses women. I despise false-hearted gallantry."

He sighed. "I worried he bewitched you."

"He did, at first." She took his hand. "But we work well together. I worried Angela Phipps captivated you."

"Mrs. Phipps?" Peter's mouth fell open

"You were kind to hire her," Mary Beth said. "And she is pretty."

He frowned. "And much older too. I have never loved anyone but you."

11:30 a.m.
June 20th

Mary Beth's gaze roamed the graveyard as she stood by Peter within a cluster of family members at Citizen's Cemetery. She was here for Peter's cousin, but she couldn't stop thinking of Papa. Wiping a tear, she eyed her father's still-fresh grave.

"Come," Peter said. "The service is over. But you appear teary-eyed."

She had missed the entire service. At least, no one knew her mind wandered. She took Peter's arm and headed toward the road.

"Miss Roper?"

The voice sounded familiar. She turned to see Mrs. Decker coming toward her.

"Hello," Mrs. Decker said. "I'd forgotten you might be here. My uncle and aunt are buried here and I wanted to visit their graves."

Mary Beth nodded and hoped she did not appear a soggy mess.

"I thought I would mention you had a shawl and bonnet in the hospital storeroom. The staff surgeon plans to clean out the room, so you had best come soon, or your things might be given away."

"Oh, I did not hear that. Thanks."

She turned back to Peter. "She's a nurse from the hospital. I left some things in the storeroom downstairs."

"Let's go there now and fetch them."

"Are you sure you feel up to walking?"

"I do. Let's go."

She looked down, not wanting him to see the pain in her eyes.

"I'm sure the service brought back memories of your father's funeral. Is that why you were crying."

She nodded but didn't elaborate. She hated to cry in public. "Let's get my shawl before the hospital staff gives it away."

Chapter Thirty-Five

Noon
June 20th

A musty smell greeted Mary Beth when stepped into the storage room. Peter hobbled in behind her. "Do be careful. They have piled up a lot more crates since the last time I came here, and I have to walk through them because my shawl is on the back wall."

"I shall stay here."

Mary Beth stepped past several boxes then stumbled.

Peter limped over and grabbed her elbow. "Are you okay?"

"I'm fine."

He knelt and shoved a few containers out of the way. "Now, moving about should make it easier."

"Thanks. Are you okay?"

"Yes. Give me a moment." When Peter put his hand on the top crate to heft himself up, the lid gave way. "Someone opened this one, but I'll put the top back."

"Do you need help?"

"No. Something is keep it ajar. I shall take off the lid." He gasped, "Here they are. Stacks of counterfeit bills—from C&R Bank!"

She hurried toward him, peering in at bills of all denominations. "They all have your signature. What should we do? Take them with us?"

"Sh-h. Do you hear that? Someone's arguing. I think they are coming here. Get out of sight."

She huddled by the clothes rack, cringing as Peter limped toward her.

Footsteps thundered down the hall.

"You did not hear me, Dr. Bell. I want the bills. My man told me the delivery came, and Chandler knows I have 'em. Give me the boxes now so I can make good on my threat."

"How many times must I say no? I am only moving them because I received notice the staff will clean this afternoon. Besides, I might not need them since Chandler succumbed. The court might grant me the bank since I'm a relative."

"What! Liar! You owe me money. My son managed to get the signature, and you promised me half."

"I never said half. You're mistaken."

A sickening thud sounded outside—bone smacking bone. "I'm getting what's due me." The door opened, and Mr. Allen marched in, a huge knot growing beside his left eye.

"I don't need you anymore." Bell yanked him backward and shoved cotton over his mouth and nose. Allen's eyes rolled back in his head, and his body went limp. Bell jerked his neck, making a cracking sound. Allen collapsed on the floor, blood running from his nose. The doctor slammed and locked the door. "Fool. You could never outsmart me."

Mary Beth's heart pounded. They were in danger. She crept closer to Peter. If only the doctor would leave without looking to his left.

Peter pulled her to his side, but he lost his balance. He swayed and grabbed a box, but his cane fell to the ground with a clatter

Bell twirled around, eyes blazing. "Mr. Chandler, I thought you were dead. Miss Roper, what's in your hand?"

Mary Beth opened her mouth, but words wouldn't come. She wanted to strangle the man and run away at the same time.

He moved toward them. "Both of you saw the bills? Now I'll have to contrive an accident like I did for Mr. Sadler. He was determined to stop me."

"Fred Bell. What are you doing here?" Peter said.

"You know him?" Mary Beth asked.

"He's Mother's half-brother," Peter said. "He wanted to go into business with my father. So it's you. You're the one who wanted the bank."

Bell frowned. "No. You got it wrong. I couldn't care less. But my father, George Bell, did want the bank. And you are going to die—soon."

"Fred Bell was not Mother's half-brother, really. Fred was her stepfather's son."

"You do remember. Do you also remember my father wanted a share in the bank? Andrew Chandler would not allow such."

"Your father could not be trusted."

"Enough. You'll not slander my father. I shall have what I'm due—after you're dead. But because I'm kind, you will feel nothing. Many doctors don't use anesthesia for anyone except officers. I do, especially for those facing death."

Metal on wood pummeled the door unnerving Mary Beth. General Connelly shouted, "Open the door, Dr. Bell. We are armed and will enter forcibly."

"Just a moment." Bell rolled his eyes. "I am gathering supplies."

"Then open the door."

He stepped toward Mary Beth.

Peter limped in front of her.

"Break it down," Connelly commanded.

With a loud crash, the frame of the door splintered. Dr. Bell shoved Peter away, knocking him off his feet. As Peter fell backward, the doctor reached for Mary Beth. Throwing an arm around her waist, he put a scalpel to her throat.

The cold blade dug into the soft tissue, and her pulse pounded. Was this death? Did she discover God's grace and Peter's love only moments from entering heaven?

To her left, Peter groaned and struggled to his feet.

With a bang, the door gave way, and three officers ran into the room with rifles ready. General Connelly shuffled in behind them. "Bell, what is the meaning of this? A man dead? And you have Miss Roper. You think you can get by with this because you are a doctor?"

Bell squeezed her waist harder as he stepped back. "I'll kill her if you come any closer."

The contents of her stomach rose. She was going to die.

Connelly lifted his rifle, aimed, and fired.

The bang echoed through the room, and smoke filled the air. She fell forward as the doctor's hands released her. The blade clattered to the floor, and darkness enveloped her.

"Miss Roper?"

"Mary Beth?"

When she opened her eyes, the room was spinning. Peter's face hovered over hers, while Mrs. Decker swabbed her face with a damp cloth. She tried to sit up, but nausea gripped her.

"Lie still." Mrs. Decker pushed her back down onto the wooden floor. "You fainted, and I think you'd better rest."

Peter nodded and caressed her cheek. "You're safe now. Bell's dead."

"Correct." Connelly gazed down at her and beaming. "The danger is over. I was not about to let someone hurt my friend."

Two soldiers lifted the doctor's body. They placed him onto a stretcher and placed a sheet over him.

Her head swam. "But General, how did you know—?"

"My friends and I were out walking. I hoped to do some target practice," General Connelly said. "I saw you enter with a man—"

"He's my fiancé, Mr. Chandler."

"I didn't know that, and I convinced my friends to follow you. I look out for people I care about."

"You saved my life, and I'm grateful," Mary Beth said. "But, I am still not sure how you knew I was in trouble."

The officer shrugged. "Why would a girl who owns a regional bank work in a military hospital? And why would she search for things? Once you asked about counterfeiting, I knew you had a mission here. I determined to help you."

"I am so glad," Peter said.

"I prayed for guidance." The General nodded. "I knew I did the right thing when I heard Bell arguing loudly."

"Dr. Bell was evil." Peter squeezed her hand. "I'm glad the General was here."

"I knew Bell wouldn't value your life," Connelly said. "The doc didn't know I am a superb marksman, or he would not have defied me."

Mary Beth glanced up at Peter's face. "I'm so grateful."

"I'm glad to meet your fiancé, Miss Roper."

"Peter Chandler, this is General Connelly. He talked me through my grief."

Peter leaned toward him and extended a hand. "General, how can I thank you?"

The soldier grabbed it and shook. "You take care of this lovely lady. She's quite a gem."

"Yes, sir. That's exactly what her father asked me to do."

Mary Beth wiped a tear. "The General is almost like a second father."

"I'm honored to stand in his place, ma'am."

Mary Beth closed her eyes and tried to think. So much had happened. "Peter, why do you think Allen came here today?"

"Mr. Allen said he needed the bills to make good on his threat to me," Peter said. "He probably came here for the money as soon as he could."

"I am so glad the Lord provides," Mary Beth said. At last, she and Peter were finding answers.

A Few Minutes Later

Peter was worried about his fiancée. She was now sitting in a chair in the storage room. A nurse stood beside her blotting Mary Beth's face with a damp cloth. "Let the doctor look at you. I would prefer to have you checked out before you leave."

Mrs. Decker walked in with a cup in her hand. "I want you to swallow this all in one gulp."

Mary Beth took one sniff. "That smells horrid. What is it?"

"Whisky and a few other things," Mrs. Decker said. "You will feel more like yourself."

"I do not want this. Nor do I need that wet rag. I'm fine." She handed the cup back and pushed away the other nurse.

"I need to speak with Ruth to clear up a few details," Peter said. "Then I'll come back for you."

"I'm going with you," Mary Beth stood. "If I need to see a doctor, I shall call Dr. Smith. He's cared for me as long as I can recall."

Peter glanced at the head nurse. She frowned but offered no help.

"I promise I shall call Dr. Smith as soon as we get home."

"Let's summon him to meet us there," Peter suggested.

"This afternoon." Mary Beth. "I'm a nurse now. I know I'll be fine."

"Very well." He hoped this was the right decision.

Chapter Thirty-Six

Noon
June 20th
Chandler Sitting Room

Anna kept her eyes downcast after the doctor arrived. He had known her long enough to know if she was hiding something. She was not going to tell him the reason she was feeling poorly, but she would divulge the symptoms. "I appreciate you coming so promptly, Doctor."

"I am here to help you, Mrs. Chandler," Dr. Smith said. "You seem restless. Why not sit down and tell me the problem?"

"Indigestion. My stomach is often … uneasy, even after meals."

"Any nausea? Maybe a burning sensation?" The doctor pulled his brows together

She tugged at the brocade curtains, nodding. "Yes, a burning sensation. That's a good description."

"Hmm. When did your stomach begin to give you problems?"

"Let me see." She began to feel sick when the sheriff told her she might be arrested for murder, but she was not going to say that. "I tried to ignore the discomfort, but the pain persists. The problem began three of four days ago."

"Can you pinpoint a particular event triggering this difficulty?"

"Hmm." She pictured the sheriff in this room. "I shall think about that."

"It sounds as if you're worried. I can give you a preparation to ease the discomfort a bit, but it's best if you deal with the problem directly."

"So many things have gone wrong lately. Peter was shot, and his cousin died." She would not mention the rest, like being accused of murder or the anonymous note threatening Peter.

"Perhaps a visit from your pastor might also help." Dr. Smith reached for his bag.

"What a good idea." She nodded. "Thank you for your guidance."

"I am leaving this elixir." He handed it to her. "Read the instructions and follow them exactly. I shall check in on you soon."

How easy for him to point out anxiety, yet how hard for her to overcome the emotional upset. She sank onto the sofa as the doctor left.

"Heavenly Father, what a mess I made trying to be helpful. I need forgiveness and wisdom. Years ago, I could lean on Andrew, but he was a mortal man. In desperation, I throw my burdens on you. All of them, even Ruthie."

Blotting away tears, she picked up her Bible to read. A quiet peace crept into her heart as her soul absorbed the words.

The sitting room door opened, and Ruth entered. Ruth froze as her gaze met Anna's. "Oh, excuse me. I didn't mean to bother you."

Anna stood and went toward her. During the long nights, she often thought about her daughter and the heartache she endured after her father died. Anna's grief had prevented her from guiding Ruthie through the loss. "Please, come in, honey."

Ruth hung back as if worried about staying.

"I owe you an apology." Anna took a deep breath. "After your father's sudden death, I often failed to be sensitive to your grief. Instead, I overreacted to what you may have done out of the grief. Please forgive me. I never intended to hurt you."

Ruth burst into tears. Anna rushed across the room and pulled her daughter into a hug.

"Mums, remember when Papa left on his last trip … I begged to go with him."

Anna nodded. "I'd forgotten you wanted to go."

"I have often wished I had gone so I could be with Papa in heaven." Sobs burst forth afresh.

"Ruthie, I am so glad you did not." Tears burned Anna's eyes as she squeezed her daughter closer. "I love you, honey."

Anna held her daughter close while she sang a favorite lullaby. She could feel Ruth relax in her arms.

"I love you, Mummy." A smile graced her face. "I haven't been very obedient at times. I'm sorry. I am glad I'll get to see Papa in heaven."

1:15 p.m.
June 20th
Chandler Sitting Room

Leaning on his crutch, Peter gritted his teeth as he held the sitting room door open for Mary Beth. She did not need to know the extent of his pain, especially after her experience with Dr. Bell. He admired her determination. Without it, they might not have answers to their mystery.

Anna sprang from the sofa where she sat with Ruth. "I wondered where you were. Mary Beth, your face is pasty white. Are you ill? Dr. Smith was here earlier. Shall I have Billy fetch him?"

"Oh no." Mary Beth chose the wing chair. "Peter sent for him to come later this afternoon."

"Let's get you some tea, my dear." Anna rushed to the bell. "Are you okay, Peter? You must be in pain. Let me—"

"I am truly fine, Mother." He eased into an overstuffed chair, propping his leg on an ottoman. His injury was minor, and he did not want her worrying. "Billy is bringing my pain medication and tea. I think we could all use some. Ruthie, have you been crying?"

Anna smiled and patted Ruth's knee. "We had a talk this afternoon, and we are both feeling better. I apologized for not being more sensitive after her father died."

"Oh, then we interrupted you," Peter said.

Anna grabbed a pillow. "No, please stay, Here, this will elevate your leg."

Peter wondered if his impatience kept his sister from cooperating with him. "Ruthie. I haven't been very patient with you either. I'm sorry."

"I forgive you, Petey."

Her pet name for him brought a chuckle. "Right now it's time to talk—"

A knock sounded, and Billy rolled in a tray with tea, coffee, and muffins. "Maud made the tea strong, as you requested," he said.

"Excellent," Peter said.

Billy bowed. "I observed the sheriff coming toward the house."

Anna gasped, "The sheriff? I have *no* desire to entertain him. Did you invite him, Peter?"

"I did, Mother. Put extra sugar in Mary Beth's tea. Doctor's orders."

"What's all this about doctor's orders?" Anna asked. "Did something happen?"

"We will explain, Mother," Peter said.

Maud knocked and entered. "Sheriff Campbell is here."

Anna offered the newcomer a nod as she continued to pass around tea.

"Welcome, Sheriff," Peter said. "Would you like tea?"

"No tea. And I prefer to stand," Sheriff Campbell said. "Mr. Chandler, I believe you have something to discuss."

"I do," Peter said. "It's important we are all here, so we can each share our part of the story. Mother, tell everyone about your *cousin,* Fred Bell."

"You want to hear the story?"

"Yes, Mother." Peter sat back.

"Well, Bell was not my cousin. Fred Bell's father, George Bell, married my mother after my father died. Fred was about my age. He always called me Cousin Ann. He never relented when I told him my name was Anna or that we weren't cousins.

"Tell us how George Bell felt about the bank, Mother," Peter said.

She sucked in air. "George Bell wanted to be Andrew's partner when we started the bank in 1839. Andrew refused since George could not be trusted. George Bell was good at carpentry, and he made several desks we purchased when the bank opened. Bell was never happy with the amount we paid, even though Andrew paid him generously."

Peter continued, "In 1862, Fred Bell, George's son, came to Chattanooga, hoping to get part of the bank his father coveted."

"I saw Fred at the church dinner," Anna said. "I was interrupted before I could speak, but I wondered what he was doing here."

"It's now making sense." Mary Beth put down her tea cup. "He decided to make counterfeit money because he knew it could cause the bank to fail if too many people demanded we exchange the bills for gold."

"Precisely," Peter said, "But in order to counterfeit money, Fred Bell needed a signature."

Peter turned to his sister. "Ruthie, are you comfortable talking to all of us?"

She nodded and smiled.

Peter continued. "Tell us about your friend, Ruth. How old is he?"

"John is nine, and I like him even though he's different, really different. He does not have many friends either."

"I have met him too," Mary Beth said. "He seldom speaks."

Peter noted Mary Beth's improved color and energy. Nothing could hold back his lady.

"Yes. He doesn't talk." Ruth smiled. "But he loves animals. He showed me how to walk through the forest without making any noise."

Anna spoke up. "I wish you had told me about him. We could've invited him to dinner."

"Oh, being in a crowd might scare him. He's pretty shy," Ruth explained. "His oldest sister takes care of him because his mother died. Maybe we can invite them both."

"Mother, invite them to dinner," Peter said. "Once he gets to know us, we can all be his friend. How long ago did you meet him?"

Ruth shrugged. "I don't know. A few months. We have had such fun together."

"Is he why you didn't want to go to Savannah?" Anna asked.

"Yes. He did not understand why I had to leave, and he cried," Ruth said with a frown.

"Did John come in Peter's office?" Mary Beth asked.

"Yes. He admired you, Peter. John made a noise when he wanted to meet me, and I opened the office window. I think he made the mess in your office. When he gets confused, he becomes angry. I try to help him understand so he will not be uncomfortable."

Peter thought it was time to protect his sister. "You've been very good for him, Ruthie. Why not go outside and see if you can find him?"

She got to her feet and hugged Peter as she left.

Anna frowned "I don't understand all this."

"I do," Peter said. "Remember, Mary Beth, when Dr. Bell and Mr. Allen were arguing? Mr. Allen said his son had obtained the signature. John's father, Mr. Allen, told his son about me and instructed him to obtain my signature. That's why John suddenly appeared on our land. Their land borders ours so he did not have to go far. Ruth made friends with him and let him into my office."

"How do you know John got the signature from your office?" Mary Beth asked.

"I found a letter with my signature torn off. John's not quite normal, so I doubt he understood what he was doing. In his mind, he was doing as his father asked."

Mary Beth's complexion lit up. "I understand. The signature for the engraving."

"Yes." Peter held up a counterfeit bill. "Each of these bills has my signature on it, but I never authorized such. We knew someone forged my name, and we tried to discover who the forger was. My signature was torn from a letter I sent to father. I think that's the one the engravers used for the bills."

"Wouldn't his loan documents have it?" Mary Beth chimed in.

"No," Peter said. "When he took out his loan, Mr. Roper signed his contract, but Allen knew about Mr. Roper's illness. Since I ran the bank, he had to get mine to prepare the counterfeit bills."

"Mr. Allen." The sheriff headed for the door. "I'll arrest him right away before he spreads any more of those bogus bills."

"Sorry, sir," Peter said. "I thought the hospital had informed you about his murder. I have more to tell you."

The sheriff stopped. "I guess I should stay for the rest."

Peter nodded. "There's more. Mary Beth, please tell about finding the counterfeit bills."

"As a banker's daughter, I didn't plan to accept this new legal tender when shopping. However, inflation came along, and I did accept some. Later, I found the first counterfeit bill and showed it to Peter."

"That was right before my trip to Savannah," Peter said.

"Yes," Mary Beth confirmed. "I was worried what might happen in his absence. Two medical soldiers boarded with me, and they paid with a roll of the new bills. Fred Bell was one of the men, but I had no idea about his relation to Mrs. Chandler. Bell, however, must have known about my association with the bank."

"From that time, Mary Beth and I worked together to gather clues on who might try to counterfeit money," Peter said.

"When Mrs. McCallie could stay with Papa, I audited bank records," Mary Beth said. "I discovered Sadler was embezzling small amounts of money by decreasing deposits, but I had no evidence he participated in the counterfeit scheme."

"I can tell you what happened next," Anna said. "Matthew Grant said Sadler was trying to undermine Peter's authority at the bank. I came home from Savannah early to confront him. His wife was my best friend, and I thought he might listen to me."

Campbell's face turned red. "You told me he was alive when you left."

"He was." She glared at the sheriff.

"I also have a report McDonald entered just after you left," Campbell said. "I have not located him yet, but I want him for questioning."

Peter groaned. "The entire city must have been there. We are going to change the locks."

"I'm not finished." Peter's mother clapped her hands. "Mr. Sadler was a meticulous person who wrote down everything, probably a habit from years of keeping accounts. He kept a diary, and he requested the diary be given to our family in the event of his death. Miss Fitch gave it to me, and I read it."

Peter moaned. "Mother, why didn't you tell us?"

"Here's why." She pulled a slip of paper from her pocket. "Someone threatened me."

Campbell stomped over and snatched the note. "It's a crime to make threats. You should have reported this."

"And have my son murdered?" She shook her head. "No."

"Then tell us what you know, Mother," Peter said. "Please."

"Sadler recorded what he learned of a counterfeiting scheme from a Lieutenant McDonald. I didn't know it was our bank. How horrible. McDonald and Sadler were distant cousins. McDonald wanted to participate, but the mastermind would not allow him. McDonald asked Sadler for help, but Sadler didn't want the bank to fail. He pretended interest in order to stop it. We now know the mastermind was Fred Bell."

"Bell poured chloroform onto cotton and made Sadler unconscious, then broke his neck," Mary Beth said. She shuddered. "As a doctor, he could make it appear to be an accident, except that Bell dropped the cotton. It was underneath papers Sadler had dropped. Bell must not have seen it after the murder."

"You should have called me to the crime scene." Campbell's face grew darker. "Especially in a murder."

"We weren't sure anyone murdered Sadler," Mary Beth said. "I suggested the possibility, but Dr. Smith believed he fell. The cotton gave us our only clue."

"The cotton convinced Mary Beth," Peter said, grinning. "My intended is clever. I was not persuaded, or I would have called the sheriff."

"What?" Anna's mouth fell open. "When were you going to tell me the two of you are engaged?"

"Mother, a lot has happened since I proposed last night," Peter said. He kept his tone gentle.

"You said you slept so late, you almost missed the funeral," his mother said.

"I still don't understand Uncle Sadler. If he wanted to save the bank, why did he embezzle money?" Mary Beth asked

"You called him Uncle Sadler?" Anna said. "I heard Peter mention that title at the funeral."

"Uncle was my affectionate name for him," Mary Beth explained. "He was not my uncle."

"I know that. Sadler's diary had the answer," Anna spoke up. "He felt the bank owed him for all those years of service. He disputed with Andrew about his pay just before the train accident. I had forgotten until I read what Sadler wrote."

Sheriff Campbell spoke up, "I must arrest this Dr. Bell."

Peter shook his head. "It's too late for him too."

Campbell groaned. "He's dead too? You should have sent for me."

"We were in the storage room at Newsome Hospital," Peter said. "The only person you might arrest is McDonald, and I reported him to Henderson since he's the liaison to the military."

"And he's guilty of what?" Campbell asked.

"He forged fake prospectuses for government bonds and blockade runners. And a few days ago, he shot at me."

Anna gasped. "He did what?".

"Lieutenant McDonald was supposed to be one of Dr. Bell's assistants," Peter said. He scratched his head. "I'm not sure what his duties were beside stalking Mary Beth. I believe he wrote the anonymous note you have."

Anna turned to the sheriff. "Arrest McDonald now."

Mary Beth groaned. "The lieutenant showed up daily to tell me my boarders would not eat dinner. Then he begged me to take the air with him. He was annoying."

Campbell headed toward the sitting room door. "Lieutenant McDonald committed a crime in Chattanooga, and he belongs in my jail."

"Why did Mr. Allen and Dr. Bell arrive when we went to get my shawl?" Mary Beth asked.

"Someone told them the staff would clean the room this afternoon. Bell didn't want his money found," Peter explained.

"But I still do not know why the doctor ordered Mary Beth to have tea with lots of sugar," Anna said. "As her future mother-in-law, I want to know."

"Actually, he didn't, but he would have, if he was there. Events unfolded so fast." Mary Beth rubbed the spot on her neck. "Bell held a knife to my throat, and a soldier shot him. I hope it didn't leave a mark. For a moment, I was really afraid."

Anna covered her face and groaned. "I could have lost you both."

"But you didn't, and now Mary Beth will be your daughter-in-law," Peter said.

**Monday Afternoon
June 23rd**

Mary Beth accompanied Peter onto the porch of the Roper home. Maud and Billy had been rearranging furniture, but they were gone. Glass had moved, and Mary Beth had returned Dr. Bells belongings.

"You are sure you want us to live here after the wedding?" Peter ran his finger along her cheek. "If you chose my house, Ruthie could see you more often."

"I am sure. I would feel like I was usurping your mother if I moved into her home. Besides, all the memories of my father are here."

Peter drew her close. "You will be here alone for a week."

She shrugged "I am not entirely alone. Cook and Elsie are with me. If I get lonely, Ruth offered to stay a few days. Besides, I want to alter Mother's dress for the wedding. You are not supposed to see my gown until I wear it next week."

"How will I survive?"

"I shall be in my father's office, which adjoins yours."

He shook his head. "I have gotten used to you being near all the time."

"You've forgotten. I was gone to the hospital a lot." She shook a finger in his face. "But I thought I might keep a running audit of our accounts so we could catch problems early."

"Great. I *will* get to see you daily."

"No, that's after the wedding. Until then, you could come by in the evenings, and we'll take the air."

He gave a mock sigh. "I suppose I shall have to suffer through."

"Yes." She put her hands on her hips. "An entire week will be dreadful."

"But afterward—"

**Monday Evening
June 30th
The Chandler Home**

Peter gazed at his soon-to-be bride sitting next to him at the dining table. His mother had hosted a meal in their honor on the eve of the wedding. Mary Beth's beauty outshined everyone. Tiny curls surrounded her face and cascaded from her upswept hair. He leaned close. "You look lovely. I'm impressed with the new hair style."

She beamed at him. "Your sister suggested this and sketched it out for Elsie."

"Ruthie?"

"She's so talented, and she's truly bloomed in the last week."

He glanced toward the end of the table where Ruth sat with nine-year-old John Allen and his oldest sister, Beverly. Ruth pointed to items on the table and enunciated words. John nodded each time but never repeated after her.

"I agree. She managed to convince John to come tonight."

"John hugged me and called me 'friend.'"

"What a compliment. I can't get him to say a word." Peter raised an eyebrow. "Do I have competition?"

"No," she said. "I prefer my groom to be taller."

"Oh, I almost forgot." He reached into his pocket and extracted a small box. "I bought this just for you."

Mary Beth flipped the box open and oohed as she fingered the beautiful gold locket. "How lovely."

"Remember how we're supposed to pursue gold? I pursued you because you're worth more gold than I'll ever own, and I'm going to pursue God because he gives good gifts. I thought you might wear this on your mother's chain."

She giggled. "You won't believe what I have for you."

"What?"

She sighed. "It's heavy, so I'll just tell you about it. In his safe, Papa had a two hundred seventy-five-ounce bar of gold he purchased in Paris. As I give it to you, I promise to keep pursuing my relationship with God and with you."

"What are those two love birds talking about?" someone asked.

Mary Beth gazed into her full-length mirror. She wore her mother's wedding gown and veil. The scooped neck of white lace gathered into an empire waist with a slender pleated skirt, very typical of European dresses in the early eighteen hundreds. She'd attached her mother's veil to a simple bonnet, allowing the lace to flow about her shoulders. Today was the day she had dreamed of, and she would be happy despite the circumstances. Her father was not here to share her joy, but she was certain he knew.

Maud and Elsie had assembled a striking floral arrangement for this room where she and Peter would stay. They had also decked the sitting room with flowers for the reception afterward.

Elsie came to the doorway. "You be awfully lovely, girl. I be a hopin' I don't drown ya with my tears."

"I don't think I could marry without you." Elsie had acted as her mother, and her heart swelled as she thought of all Elsie taught her. She turned away from the mirror to embrace her former nurse. "Is the carriage here?"

"Yes, ma'am." Elsie moved out of her embrace. "Maud be bringin' the roses for ya to carry."

"Then I guess I should go."

Maud met her at the foot of the stairs with an armful of white roses. Maud and Elise helped her inside and then accompanied her as the carriage made its way to First Presbyterian Church.

General Connelly stood waiting when the carriage stopped. He helped her down to the street and then up the steps into the small white church. The morning sun blazed through the stained-glass windows as Mary Beth stood in at the entrance to the sanctuary. Friends and family occupied every seat, and a few stood along the walls. Jane and Ida, who served as her bridesmaids, proceeded her down the aisle, wearing elegant pink frocks.

Peter, handsome in a navy suit with a white rose on the lapel, awaited her at the altar by Reverend McCallie. How proud she was to marry such a godly man.

Elsie adjusted her skirts before she walked down the aisle. She teared up. "You be lookin' just like your mama. I be lovin' you."

"And I love you, Elsie." The word *love* meant so much more than ever. All her life she had used that word, but how much more her heart swelled now with love than ever before. A lifetime of memories and caring came too. Such moments were too precious and would stay with her forever.

Major General Connelly escorted her down the aisle as the organ played Felix Mendelssohn's "Wedding March."

The music ended, and Reverend McCallie began. "We are here to join this man and woman in holy matrimony. Who gives this woman to be married to this man?"

General Connelly spoke up. "On behalf of her father, I do." He blotted a tear as he stepped away.

Reverend McCallie said, "Peter requested you face each other when you said your vows. Please do that now and join hands."

Jane came forward for the roses, and Mary Beth faced Peter. Gazing into his eyes, she saw the love she'd always wanted. Now she could accept what she had all along, a man who was trustworthy, wise, and kind.

At last, the pastor pronounced them husband and wife. Peter pulled her toward him, and she melted into his kiss as tears flowed. Her name was now Mrs. Peter Chandler, and she would learn to be an excellent wife for her exceptional husband.

About the Author

Cynthia loves younger women and enjoys using new technology to encourage them. She grew up in Chattanooga, TN, where she attended the Erlanger School of Nursing. After she married Ray Simmons, she homeschooled their five children through high school, including her youngest son who has severe disabilities.

Unafraid of tough topics, Cynthia writes The Big Question column for *Leading Hearts Magazine*. In addition, she and her husband host apologetics' discussions with college students over tea.

An avid reader and writer, she served as past president of Christian Authors Guild, teaches writing workshops, and directs the *Atlanta Christian Writers Conference*.

"Cyndi" adores history and longs to peruse every archive she comes across while traveling. When speaking and teaching, she includes lively vignettes from history and laughs about how she loves women from the past.

She hosts and produces Heart of the Matter Radio and does quarterly interviews for Clash of the Titles. Cynthia also cofounded Homeschool Answers, which presents one-day seminars for homeschool mothers. She loves to hear from her readers, so visit her website and leave a message. www.clsimmons.com.

Appendix

Questions for Thought and Discussion

1. Mary Beth dreaded the death of her father. Have you ever struggled with grief after losing someone near you? If so, share what you learned.

2. Read 1 Thessalonians 4:13 and Psalm eighty-eight. Based on these verses, describe grief. How does it feel?

3. Read Genesis 2:16-17. Discuss the reason for death and the impact the loss has on our lives.

4. Peter didn't trust Mary Beth after she treated him poorly. Review the story of Joseph in Genesis 42-45 and discuss the role of forgiveness and trust.

5. Mary Beth's world crumbled around her, and she worried about her future. Read Romans 8:18–22. Why does God allow suffering in the world?

6. Mary Beth had to watch her spending because inflation made her finances tight. Read 1 Corinthians 4:2. Discuss ways to manage your money.

7. Peter and Mary Beth chose to pursue God after their adventures. Read Philippians 3:10-11. Name some ways you can pursue God also.

8. Read 1 Corinthians 3:18. Describe how pursuing God will change you.

Author's Notes

Reverend Thomas McCallie and his wife, the former Ellen Jarnagin, lived on the spot that is now First-Centenary United Methodist Church. He served as pastor of First Presbyterian Church and as a civic leader as Chattanooga grew. Ellen was an active person, always keeping her home open to visiting pastors or anyone needy. She often cared for wounded soldiers during the war. The couple had sixteen children, and eight lived to become adults. Today a major street bears the McCallie name as does a boy's school, which two of their sons founded.

Dr. Milo Smith moved to Chattanooga in 1838 with his sister. He loved Chattanooga, and residents demonstrated their fondness for him by naming their offspring after him. During the war years, he lived on Cameron Hill with his wife, Caroline. He worked for the Confederate military in the city, served as mayor during the war, and cared for Chattanooga citizens as well. A brilliant man, he had many interests and helped found First Presbyterian Church. Dr. Smith was known for his generosity and never requested payment for his services.

"The General" was a steam engine built in 1855. The locomotive made the trek between Chattanooga and Atlanta. In 1862, spies attempted to cripple transportation in the South by destroying bridges and rail lines. James Andrews led a group of spies who stole "The General" at Big Shanty, Georgia (now Kennesaw), on April 12, 1862. The men, who had dressed as civilians, took the train toward Chattanooga, destroying rail lines and telegraph lines along the way. Officials captured the men when they ran out of fuel and housed in them in the Chattanooga jail. "The General" now resides Kennesaw, Georgia.

Glossary

Bill—paper used in place of gold; the same as legal tender

Blockade runner—a ship that attempts to get around those blocking the harbor

Invest—extending a loan with interest to support or expand a business

Gold standard—using gold or silver as payment for debts

Legal tender—paper money used in place of gold

Prospectus—a business proposal requesting a loan

Specie—gold used for exchange, and sometimes silver

Tender—to pay for goods or services

Made in the USA
Charleston, SC
25 February 2017